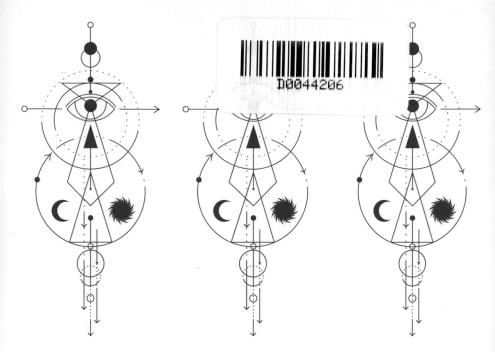

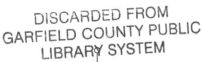

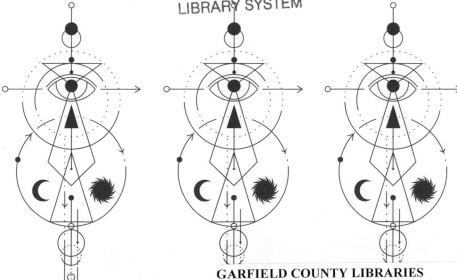

A GOLDEN FURY

A GOLDEN FURY

SAMANTHA COHOE

WEDNESDAY BOOKS
NEW YORK

First published in the United States by Wednesday Books, an imprint of St. Martin's Publishing Group

A GOLDEN FURY. Copyright © 2020 by Samantha Cohoe. All rights reserved. Printed in the United States of America. For information, address St. Martin's Publishing Group, 120 Broadway, New York, NY 10271.

www.wednesdaybooks.com

Library of Congress Cataloging-in-Publication Data

Names: Cohoe, Samantha, author.
Title: A golden fury / Samantha Cohoe.
Description: First edition. | New York : Wednesday Books, 2020.
Identifiers: LCCN 2020024224 | ISBN 9781250220400
   (hardcover) | ISBN 9781250220417 (ebook)
Subjects: CYAC: Alchemy—Fiction. | Ambition—Fiction. |
   Blessing and cursing—Fiction. | Great Britain—History—1789–
   1820—Fiction. | France—History—1789–1815—Fiction.
Classification: LCC PZ7.1.C64255 Go 2020 | DDC [Fic]—dc23
LC record available at https://lccn.loc.gov/2020024224

Our books may be purchased in bulk for promotional, educational, or business use. Please contact your local bookseller or the Macmillan Corporate and Premium Sales Department at 1-800-221-7945, extension 5442, or by email at MacmillanSpecialMarkets@macmillan.com.

First Edition: 2020

10 9 8 7 6 5 4 3 2 1

For Caleb. We bet big on each other, and we won.

NORMANDY, FRANCE

1792

My mother was screaming at the Comte. Again.

I slammed the front doors behind me and walked down the carriageway, under the dappled shade of the poplars that lined it. A hundred paces away, I still heard her, though at least I could no longer hear the Comte's frantic endearments and low, rapid pleading. He should know by now that wasn't the way. Perhaps I should tell him. Adrien was the first of my mother's patrons I had ever liked, and I did not want to leave Normandy just as spring was breaking. Just as we were beginning to make progress.

Though perhaps we were not. Mother would not be screaming at the Comte if the work were going well. She would not take the time. Alchemy was a demanding science, even if some scoffed and called it charlatanry or magic. It required total concentration. If the work were going well, the Comte would scarcely exist to her, nor would I, now that she would not let me be of use. The composition must have broken again. This was about when it had, last round. I could not be certain, since she had taken away my key to the laboratory. She could hardly have devised a worse insult than that if she had tried, and lately she did seem to be trying. The laboratory was mine as much as it was hers. If she did succeed in producing the White Elixir—which turned all metals into silver—then it was only because of my help. She had found Jābir's text languishing in a Spanish monastery, but it had been I who translated it when her Arabic wasn't nearly up to the job. I had labored for months over the calcinary furnace to make the philosophic mercury the text took as its starting point. I had the scars on my hands and arms to prove it. And now that success might be close, she wished to shut me out and deny my part, and claim it for herself alone.

But if she was acting ill and cross, it meant she had failed. A low, smug hum of satisfaction warmed me. I didn't want the work to fail, but I didn't want her to succeed without me, either.

A distant smashing sound rang out from the chateau. My mother shattering something against the wall, no doubt.

I sighed and shifted my letter box to the crook of my other arm.

I knew what this meant. Another move. Another man. The Comte had lasted longer than the rest. Over two years, long enough that I had begun to hope I would not have to do it all again. I hated the uncertainty of those first weeks, before I knew what was expected of me, whether Mother's new patron had a temper and what might set it off, whether he liked children to speak or be silent. Though I was no longer a child, and that might bring its own problems. A chill passed over me, despite the warm afternoon sunshine. God only knew what the next one would be like. My mother had already run through so many of them. And with the recent changes in France, there were fewer rich men than ever looking to give patronage to an expensive alchemist, even one as beautiful and famous as Marguerite Hope.

I veered off the carriageway, into the soft spring grass, dotted here and there with the first of the lavender anemones. I sat by the stream, under the plum tree.

There was no screaming here, no pleading, no signs that my life was about to change for the worse. I inhaled the soft, sweet scent of plum blossoms and opened my letter box. If this was to be my last spring in Normandy, I wanted to remember it like this. Springtime in Normandy was soft and sweet, sun shining brightly and so many things blossoming that the very air was perfumed with promise. Everything was coming extravagantly to life, bursting out of the dead ground and bare trees with so much energy other impossible things seemed likely, too. I had always been hopeful in Normandy when it was spring. Especially last spring, when Will was still here. When we sat under this very tree, drank both bottles of champagne he had stolen from the cellars, and spun tales of everything we could achieve.

I took out his last letter, dated two months ago.

Dear Bee,

This is my address now—as you see I've left Prussia. It turns out that everything they say about the Prussians is quite true. I've never met a more unbending man than my patron *there. One day past the appointed date and he tried to throw me in prison for breach of contract! He thinks alchemy can be held to the same strict schedule as his serfs.*

Laws against false alchemists were very harsh in Germany, as Will knew full well when he sought patronage there. I had begged him to go somewhere else, though he had few enough choices. He was my mother's apprentice, with no achievements of his own to make his reputation. His training had been cut abruptly short when Mother found us together under this plum tree, watching the sunrise with clasped hands and two empty bottles of champagne. She'd seen to it that Will was gone by noon. It was no use telling her that all we'd done was talk through the night, or that the one kiss we'd shared had been our first, and had gone no further. He had behaved with perfect respect for me, but she wouldn't believe it. My mother had imagined a whole path laid before my feet in that moment, and scorched it from the earth with Greek fire.

I turned to the next page.

I blame myself, of course, Bee, for not heeding your advice. I can picture your face now, wondering what I expected. It would almost be worth all the trouble I've caused myself if I could come to you and see your expression. You must be the only woman in the world who is never lovelier than when you've been proven right.

The keen thrill of pleasure those words had brought me when I first read them had faded now, and left me feeling uncertain. Should I write back knowingly, teasing him for his recklessness? I had tried this, and was sure I sounded like a scold no matter what he said about my loveliness when proven right. I took out my latest draft, which struck a more sincere tone. I read the lines over, saying how I worried for him, how I missed him. I crumpled it in my hand halfway through. Too much emotion. It didn't do to show such dependence on a man. My mother had shown me that. I didn't wish to emulate her in everything, but I would be a fool to deny her skill at winning masculine devotion. I tried again.

Dear Will,

I am sitting under the plum tree where we had our last picnic. I know how you feel about nostalgia, but I hope you will forgive me this one instance. I fear this will be our last spring in Normandy—perhaps even in France. Many of my mother's friends have left already, and though you may well condemn them as reactionaries, the fact remains that there are very few good Republicans with the ready cash to pay for our pursuits.

I sighed again and crumpled the page. Somehow I could never seem to write to him about the Revolution without a touch of irony creeping in. I didn't want that. Will had put his hopes for a better world in the new order, and even though I was less hopeful than he, I loved him for it. At least he wanted a better world. Most alchemists simply wanted better metals.

I tried to imagine he was here. It wouldn't be difficult then. He was so good at setting me at ease. His admiration was as intoxicating as wine, but unlike wine it sharpened my wits instead of dulling them. I was never cleverer than when Will was there to laugh with me.

My chest constricted at the memory of Will's laugh. I didn't know anyone who laughed like him. The Parisian aristocrats I had known all had so much consciousness of the sound they made when they did it. The Comte wasn't like them, but he was a serious man and laughed rarely. My mother didn't laugh at all.

But Will. He laughed like it came from the loud, bursting core of him. Like he couldn't have kept it in if he wanted to, and why would he want to? And when he was done laughing, he would look at me like no one else ever had. Like he saw only me, not as an accessory to my mother, but as myself. And not as an odd girl whose sharp edges would need to be softened. Will liked the edges. The sharper they cut, the more they delighted him.

"Thea!"

I threw my letters into the letter box and snapped it shut. I looked around for somewhere to hide the box, and noticed too late that one of my crumpled drafts had blown toward the stream. My mother appeared on the hill above me, the late afternoon sun lighting up her golden hair like an unearned halo. She walked down the hill with measured steps and stopped a few yards above me, I assumed because she wished to enjoy the experience of being taller than me again for a few moments. Her eye moved to the crumpled paper. I ran to it and stuffed it into my pocket before she could take it, though my haste in hiding the failed letter told her all I didn't wish her to know.

"Oh dear," said my mother. "I do hope you haven't been wasting your afternoon trying to find the right words to say to that boy."

My mother was tolerant of my letter writing these days, perhaps because she was confident I would never see Will again. She had smiled when she heard of Will's contract in Prussia. *He won't find it so easy to charm his way past the Prussian alchemy laws. In Germany, one must deliver results, not pretty smiles, or end in prison.*

"I wouldn't have an afternoon to waste if you would let me into the laboratory," I said.

"Don't be pitiful, Thea," said my mother. "Surely you can think of something worthwhile to do when I don't happen to need your assistance."

I clenched my teeth so tight that my jaw ached. Shutting me out of the laboratory, *our* laboratory, was the greatest injustice she had ever committed against me. Worse than all the moving about, worse than sending Will away, worse than any insult she could think to level at me. Before she had done that, I believed we were together in alchemy at least, even if nothing else. That she had raised and trained me not simply to be of use to her, but to be her partner. Her equal, one day. Throwing me out of the laboratory just when we might achieve what we had worked for told me that Will was right. She would never let me claim credit for my part of the work. She would never accept me as an alchemist in my own right.

And yet she described it as though she had simply let me off my chores. As if I were no more necessary than a servant. There was no point in arguing with her, but even so I could not let it stand.

"I am not your assistant," I said.

"Oh?" she asked. "Do you have news, then? Have you found a patron on your own merits? Do you intend to strike out on your own?"

"Perhaps I will," I said, my face growing hot. "Perhaps I will stay here when you are finally finished tormenting the poor Comte."

My mother had a perfect, deceptively sweet beauty: golden blond and blue-eyed with a round, doll-like face. It made the venom that sometimes twisted her expression hard to quite believe in. Many men simply didn't. They preferred to ignore the evidence of their minds for the evidence of their senses. I, of course, knew her better than they did. I tensed, preparing.

But instead of lashing out, my mother turned aside, a hand to her chest. A tremor passed over her; she bowed her head against it.

Mother had been strangely unwell for weeks. At first I responded to her illness as she had taught me to, with distaste and disapproval, as though falling sick were an ill-considered pastime of those with insufficient moral fortitude. But if she noticed how unpleasant it was to receive so little sympathy when unwell, she did not show it. She had locked herself away in the laboratory every day until late at night, ignoring my silence as much as she ignored the Comte's pleas that she rest. I had not thought much of it until this moment. Any pain great enough to turn her from chastising me for thinking I could do alchemy without her must be serious indeed.

"Mother?" I asked.

"You will go where I tell you." Her voice was low and breathless, almost a gasp. "For now, that is to dinner. Wear the green taffeta."

"The robe à la française?" I asked, perplexed. I hadn't worn that dress since before the Estates General met. Its style was the hallmark of the ancien régime: wide pan-niered hips, structured bodice, and elaborate flounces. "But it's out of fashion."

"So is our guest," said my mother.

She went up the hill again, then turned back to me at the top.

"Thea," she said, all the sharpness gone from her voice. "I know you do not believe it any longer, but everything I do is for you."

It was the sort of thing she always said. Before this year, I had always believed it, more or less. At least, everything she did was for the both of us. She had considered me an extension of herself, so that doing things for me was no different than doing them for herself. Why else take so much care to train me, to see to it that I had the tutors I needed to learn every language necessary—more even than she knew? To take me with her in all her travels to seek out manuscripts? She was an impatient teacher at times, but a good one. A thorough one. And in turn I was a good student. The best.

Until we were close to our goal. Then, suddenly, I was a rival. And my mother did not tolerate rivals.

"You are right, Mother," I said. "I don't believe that any longer."

2

It was an ongoing project of mine to learn when I could give in to my mother without loathing myself, and when to fight the battle that came of defying her. I decided this was one of the former cases, and put on the green taffeta gown.

My mother was dressed lavishly as well, though not in the old-fashioned style she had instructed me to wear. She sat on the gold-gilt sofa in airy blue silk, sipping a glass of Madeira and smiling radiantly at our out-of-fashion guest. He stood as I entered and bowed low. My mother introduced him as the Marquis Phillipe du Blevy. His powdered wig, silk breeches, and waistcoat were courtly, ostentatious, and opulent. Much like my own gown. Together we made a perfect picture of unrepentant French aristocracy. An inaccurate picture, since I was in fact an expatriate English girl, neither French nor an aristocrat.

"Your daughter?" he exclaimed, when my mother introduced me. "Ma chère, can it be so? You are not old enough!"

My mother smiled. Unlike many French ladies, she never lied about her age, though no one would ever believe she was well past thirty were it not for the irrefutable evidence of my existence. A nearly adult daughter put even the youngest mother near middle age. Her perfect, girlish skin was carefully maintained by alchemical cosmetics of her own making—a testament to her skill, which she valued more than her youth. My mother had sold these cosmetics to the Queen herself, when the Queen was still free to make her own purchases.

We were called to dinner before the Comte arrived. It must have been on my mother's instructions. The servants would certainly not have thought to begin dinner without their master on their own. It confirmed my suspicion that the Marquis was here at my mother's invitation, as a possible new patron.

We clustered around one end of the long table, yards and yards of bone-white linen extending down before us. It was odd to sit so few at a table so obviously designed for many. I had eaten here only a handful of times since we came. Usually we ate in the morning room, at a reasonably sized table. I eyed the Marquis du Blevy with dislike while he occupied himself with charming my mother. Comte Adrien's general good character and relatively liberal sentiments about the poor sometimes made it difficult to accept Will's revolutionary opinions about the aristocracy. The Marquis, on the other hand, was exactly as dandified and pretentious as any Jacobin caricature. He was not as old as his elaborate powdered wig made him look at first. Older than the Comte, yes, but perhaps still in his forties. He was not nearly as attractive as my mother's usual patrons—a testament, perhaps, to the reduced pool of options. Nor was he a frequent patron of alchemists, so far as I knew. But my mother had turned more than one rich man with no natural interest in alchemy into a fervent supporter of herself. Judging from the way the Marquis looked at her, she would have no trouble doing the same with him.

I finished my consommé and considered pleading in-disposition. I did not like watching my mother groom Adrien's replacement in his own dining room. But before I could excuse myself, the Comte arrived.

Neither the Marquis nor my mother seemed discom-fited at his appearance. The Comte, though he was the only one among us not dressed for a day at the court of Versailles, did not appear surprised to see the Marquis. He sat, unfolded his napkin in his lap, and addressed him.

"So, you are going to England," he said.

The Marquis looked up abruptly and glanced nervously at the servants in the doorway.

"You needn't look so anxious," said Adrien. "It isn't ille-gal to cross the channel."

"Not yet," said the Marquis, leaning forward over the fine bone china. "But you know as well as I do it will be soon enough."

The Comte took a sip of his wine, his gaze steady.

"Ah, don't look at me that way, Adrien," said the Mar-quis. "There's nothing we can do here, you know that. But in England, there are many like us speaking to men of influence. Planning. Gathering strength."

My vague dislike of the Marquis sharpened.

"That is just what the National Convention says the émigrés do," I said. "Plan and influence the enemies of France. They call that treason."

And it had always seemed a rather hysterical accusation to me, until the Marquis had so calmly confessed to it. My mother shot me a freezing glare, which I ignored. The Marquis looked at me in surprise.

"True treason is to strip the king of his power to rule!" he exclaimed.

"But how would the English help the king?" I couldn't help myself. I had to provoke him. "Louis supports the National Convention."

The Marquis stared at me, his mouth agape and his face reddening.

"*King* Louis is a prisoner in all but name! What choice does he have but to wear a tricolor cockade and say whatever the rabble wish him to?"

The rabble. A vile way to talk about his own people, who were starving and desperate. Talking to enough aristocrats like this Marquis could make me a revolutionary more than Will ever had.

"So you would stir up the English to do—what—invade? Your own country?"

"Est-que c'est vrai?" asked the Marquis, turning to my mother in astonishment. "Is your daughter a Jacobin?"

"Certainly not, Phillipe," said my mother. Her own color rose as well, and a bead of sweat quivered on her forehead like a tiny, molten jewel. Her eyes were strangely glassy. "This is not her talking at all, but a worthless boy I employed as my apprentice for a time, before I realized he was a snake and a liar. He filled her head with this non-sense, and I have not yet shaken it out."

Adrien cleared his throat, cutting me off before I could retort.

"I have thought of leaving, naturally," he said. "Marguerite and I have discussed it. But she refuses to return to England."

"Ah, but you are a British citizen, are you not?" said the Marquis, turning to my mother. "And your daughter?"

"We are," said my mother.

"Then why?"

"England had its chance with me," she said, lifting her chin. Her eyes cleared with the defiance, and she looked more like herself. "I will not give it another."

The servants brought the fish course, sole in sizzling beurre blanc. My mother must have ordered the dinner to suit the Marquis's tastes. So much butter gave the Comte indigestion. I looked at her to confirm my suspicion, and found her looking into the corner with an expression of fear that made me glance there as well. There was nothing there.

"But Marguerite, ma chère," said the Marquis. "Surely it is better to swallow one's pride and return home to England than to die here in France?"

"Die?" I asked with disdain. "Who is going to kill us? The National Convention does not care what we do."

"Oh, but they will," said the Marquis. "Once Britain declares war, they will care a great deal about British subjects within French borders. Especially such a skilled one as your mother." I wanted to scoff again; indeed, I opened my mouth to do so. But as I did I caught the Comte's eye, and saw he was not scoffing. His taut, worried look stilled my tongue, as his fears about the violence of the Jacobins had often stilled my enthusiasm for them.

The Marquis went on. "And think, Marguerite, once we are at war, the revolutionaries will come for you, force you to make armor and weapons for them. You hate such work."

My mother had made her reputation with alchemical armor for the French king before the National Convention had taken away any of his responsibilities. It didn't seem such a terrible thing to me to make more of the same for him now. But I had never minded that quotidian work, however much more thrilling it was to pursue alchemy's highest prize—the Philosopher's Stone. Mother, on the other hand, had only ever seen metallurgic contracts as a means to an end. When unending life and limitless wealth beckoned, who could blame her?

"Perhaps, but the English would do the same, the moment I set foot on their shores," said my mother. The Marquis opened his mouth to argue, but my mother cut him off. "No, my dear Phillipe, I will not go."

And with that proclamation, my theory of her purpose for the Marquis collapsed. She could not be grooming him to be her next patron if she refused to go to England with him. Unless she simply planned to make him convince her, and feel he had won a great victory. I looked at her and wondered.

"But you are quite correct, of course, of the dangers. I understand that."

"Think of your daughter, ma chère, if you will not think of yourself!"

My mother glanced to the corner again, then turned her icy blue eyes on me. They were unnaturally bright, her color still high.

"My daughter . . ." she said in a low voice.

I drew back, startled. There was a strange intensity and a calculation in her gaze I did not recognize. My mother did not look at me this way, as though she were assessing my talents, my worth. She always looked at me as though she knew everything in me, and had always known it, and had no need to seek anything further.

"I should not like to part with her," said my mother, again in a low voice that was unlike her own.

"Then you must both come!" The Marquis glanced at Adrien. "Er—rather—you must all come! I have let a place in London with plenty of room—"

The Comte's jaw tightened. He looked at my mother with anger I did not understand.

"It is kind of you, most kind," said my mother. "I shall think on it. Not for myself, but as you say, I must think of my daughter."

"Your daughter has a father in England," said Adrien with forced calm. "And a mother who could go there tomorrow. There is no need for her to go unchaperoned with a man she does not know at all."

I straightened in my chair. The edge in Adrien's voice told me that this was not the first time this topic had been broached. I glanced at my mother, who was carefully ignoring the Comte's gaze, and I understood. The Marquis wasn't for her at all. She intended to send *me* away with him.

For all that she had turned on me and shut me out, I

never imagined this. We had never been parted. She had never allowed it, nor had I wished it.

"I am not going to England!" I exclaimed.

"Thea has a father in England she does not know, and who does not know she exists," said my mother, as though I had not spoken. "He is no use to us."

"What do you mean, he does not know she exists?" the Comte demanded. "You swore to me you would write to him of her! I saw you seal the envelope!"

"I sealed it, but did not send it," said my mother. "I had no need to, once Phillipe sent word of his plans."

Adrien slammed his fist onto the table, sending the glasses and silver rattling. The Marquis seized his wine with both hands to keep it steady, his eyes wide with shock.

"Marguerite!" Adrien thundered. "Thea is not going to England with this man!"

I stared at him. I had never heard him raise his voice to my mother, or give her an order. He was finished now. Mother might not be leaving France, but she would certainly be leaving him. These were lines no man could cross and keep any part of my mother's affections. Still, I was grateful.

"No," I agreed fervently. "I am not."

The Marquis pushed back his chair from the table, lips quivering with outrage. But instead of placating him, my mother leaned past him toward me, ignoring him completely. Venom sharpened her glassy-eyed stare.

"You will go where I tell you," she hissed. "With whom I tell you to go! Do you think you know better than I what is best for you? I protect you! But for me, you would have thrown your virtue away on that libertine—"

"I would not!" I exclaimed, my face aflame. "And Will is not a libertine, he is an alchemist!"

"You foolish child, you think you know more than I of men?"

"Not of men," I said. "But of Will, yes! You only hated him because he defended me from you!"

"Defended you?" My mother stood. Her cheeks were scarlet with rage, her eyes wild. "He turned you against me with flattery, and you were too stupid to see it! No alchemist who knew anything would say you were ready for your own laboratory!"

"And that was why you really threw him out, wasn't it?" I exclaimed, rising from my own chair as well. "Because he dared to suggest I did not need you, that I might even be better than you!"

"That was when I knew he was a liar!" Her eyes were strangely dark, pupils flaring, and her arms shook as she gripped the table. The Marquis stared at her, aghast, and so did I. She never lost control like this, not before a guest. "No one would say something so absurd without a sinister purpose! He thought to seduce you and steal my secrets through you!"

My breath caught. I shook my head, my mouth twitching and twisting around a denial.

"You thought he wanted you for yourself, I know it," snarled my mother. "But I saw you together. You were as clumsy as a giraffe and as blunt as a bull! You have no charm for men—it is why I have no fear of sending you with the Marquis!"

"Marguerite!" exclaimed the Comte. "You are being cruel!"

"I will take my leave now, Marguerite," said the Marquis stiffly. "I will not stay where I am so clearly not wanted. But if you should ever find yourself in need of assistance—"

My mother blinked at him, chest heaving, as if she had forgotten he was there. And somehow she had, surely, or she would never have spoken this way in front of him when she still wished to win a favor. After a long, dead moment, she held out her hand, which the Marquis bent over hastily.

I sat down again, rooted to my chair. I did not look at the Marquis as he left. My eyes and throat burned. Adrien was right. She was being cruel, and needlessly so, when it didn't even suit her ends. When the Marquis was gone, she turned, trembling, back to me.

"See what you've done, Thea!" she exclaimed. "Can you never control your tongue?"

"*My* tongue?"

"If you had not argued politics with him—"

"You were the one screaming how stupid and charmless I am!"

"Who will take you now?"

"No one!" I cried. "Because I am not leaving! Do you think I do not know why you wish to send me away? But I will not let you, not when we are near to making the White Elixir! I will not be erased from our achievement!"

My mother gripped the table, bending over it. She was damp and trembling. She shook her head. She *was* ill, there was no other explanation for it all. The Comte saw it and stepped toward her in alarm.

"No, Thea," she said. "You are wrong, entirely wrong. I do not want to send you away at all. It is only for your sake . . . for your safety . . ."

"I am not afraid of the National Convention." I forced the words through my closing throat. I swallowed. I would not cry.

My mother shook her head. "The Revolution is not the only danger," she said in a trembling voice.

"What then?" I asked.

She glanced into the corner again and looked away quickly. Again I looked where she looked. Again, nothing.

"Tell me, Mother." My voice broke. I wanted an explanation more than I could bear to admit. I needed a reason, a good enough one to excuse her for banishing me.

But she did not answer, and so I turned my head away and left.

The Comte called after me, but I could bear to talk to him even less than I could bear to talk to my mother. Whatever my mother had left to say might make me angrier. Adrien's sympathy would surely make me cry.

3

I lay on my bed in my shift, under the open window, breathing in the twilight scent of apple blossoms and swallowing angry sobs. I had cast off my green dress and left it and its ridiculous panniers where they lay. The warm spring air had turned cold with the sunset, and the fire burned down in the hearth, giving off little warmth. The hairs on my arms stood on end from the chill, but I didn't feel it. My mind and heart were raging hot.

I could not stand it. I could not believe it. But I could not deny it.

My mother wanted to send me away.

It was worse than I had thought, worse even than Will had thought. She did not simply want to keep me subordinate to her, or keep me from sharing credit once we made the White Elixir, the substance that turned all metal into silver, the last step before the Philosopher's Stone. Will thought she wanted to keep me for herself, to refuse to let me come into my own. But no. She did not want me at all.

Will . . .

It wasn't true, what she had said, that he was only using me to get to her secrets. It couldn't be true. She said she'd watched us together, but she hadn't seen everything. She hadn't seen him open himself to me, tell me about his parents' rejection of him, his hopes for a more equal world. She hadn't seen the way he'd looked at me before he kissed me. Still, her voice rang in my head.

You were as clumsy as a giraffe, and blunt as a bull!

I knotted my fists in the delicate white lace of my coverlet and felt it tear.

I threw myself off the bed, went to my dressing table, and opened my letter box. I lit a lamp and pulled all the letters out, searching frantically for the one that would disprove my mother best.

I found it, dated eight months ago, when Will was just settling into his contract in Prussia. I quickly scanned the first paragraphs, detailing the work and setting, and came to what I was looking for.

I miss you, Bee, and I worry for you. Do you remember when we talked of Rousseau, and the dim view he takes of marriage? I was inclined to agree with him, if you'll recall, and you were not. But being so easily parted from you has given me another, more practical view of the matter. Your mother could not have claimed you and sent me away if we were bound by marriage. I could

*have severed the chains of motherhood
she binds you with by chains of my own. I
wish there were a way to free you from her
without binding you to anything else, Bee.
You deserve to be free, truly free. But even
more than that, I wish I didn't have to leave
you there with her. I can well imagine how
she is treating you, now that you have dared
to have your own desires and goals. Don't
believe the things she says about you. You
are more brilliant, more beautiful, and more
full of life than she ever was or ever will be.*

I read it again, and then again, searching against my will for any signs the letter was a lie. I saw none. We had no hopes of seeing each other again soon. What did he have to gain from writing to me at all, except the continuation of our friendship? Surely he could not think I would send him secrets through the mail. Still, my heart seized at the thought. I scanned the letters for hints, questions, anything that might suggest he was probing for alchemical information.

But no. There was nothing like that. I let out a sigh of relief and read the letter once more, this time letting myself believe it.

Don't believe the things she says about you.

He had known this would happen, or something like it. And he was right. I breathed steadier. The tightness in my chest loosened. I took out my pen and yet another fresh sheet of paper, and started again.

Evening wore into night as I filled page after page with

words I knew I would not send. I detailed all the cruel things she had done and said, just as he had worried she would. I poured out all the pain of the last year, of her growing hostility and his absence. I allowed myself to feel the messy, undignified self-pity I could not afford to show in front of her and refused to show to anyone else. It was a relief, but only at first. Like scratching an itch, only to find it came back worse a few moments later. This was not the sort of thing that could be made better by weeping over it. I needed some kind of plan. Some way to make my mother let me back into the work again. A way to prove myself to her, beyond any possibility of denial. But nothing came to me, and I lost myself again in recrimination.

It was late when I stood, spent, and began to drop each page of my letter into the fireplace.

And then my mother screamed. Not as she had earlier, in anger. This was a scream of terror. I stopped in alarm.

Silence followed. She had suffered nightmares in the last few weeks—part of her illness, perhaps?—and woken screaming more than once. I turned back to the fire, nothing more than embers in my marble hearth, and pushed the remaining pages into the glowing ashes where they caught and burned away quickly.

Then she screamed again, and this time she didn't stop. It was her, and yet it wasn't. It was a shrill, hysterical sound of agony I could not imagine her making. I threw on my dressing gown and ran barefoot through the halls, nearly slipping on the spiraling stone stairway. The screams had stopped when I arrived outside her room. The Comte was there already, pounding on her door and pleading for her to let him in. There was no response. He held a candle in one hand, and I could see from the disarray of his night clothes that he had jumped from his bed with as much haste as I had. His eyes caught mine in panic. I motioned him quiet, and put my ear against the door.

At first I heard nothing, and then a creaking sound of the bed sinking under a weight.

"Mother?" I called. "What's happened? Why were you screaming?"

"It was a sudden pain," came my mother's voice. "But I am well enough now. Go back to sleep."

"Marguerite, please," the Comte objected. "You are unwell, chérie, you have been unwell for weeks. Let me call a doctor. I cannot bear you to suffer so."

"I am not suffering at all, except from your girlish whimpering, Adrien."

That sounded enough like her usual self to set me more at ease. The Comte's shoulders loosened as well, and he began murmuring endearments to her in a low voice. I backed away. They had fought, no doubt, after I left them at dinner, and now he wished to make amends. Well. I would let him try.

I went back to my room and sat on the bed again, beside the still-open window. It was cold now, and the apple blossoms had closed up, withdrawing their scent. I reached to close it and caught a whiff of something else, something alchemical. Not the usual burnt-sulfur smell of an alchemist's furnace, but sharp and energizing, and somehow rather pleasant. I did not recognize it, though it surely came from the laboratory. But I did know this: it wasn't the smell of a failed, broken composition.

I dressed hastily, ignoring the elaborate green for a

serviceable gray round dress, and went back down the stairs and out the back door of the house. I crossed the garden, and the new spring grass felt soft and wet under my slippers. I walked toward the cottage beside the woods. A bright half-moon hung over it.

A small, steady plume of yellow smoke rose from the chimney. I stared at it for a moment. The laboratory's fire had been burning yellow for over a week now. At first it had been only a slight tinge of gold, but now the smoke had a deep mustard color, and the new scent came with it. Undoubtedly, it meant progress after all. Progress my mother had made without me.

A rush of anger prodded me forward. I peered into the soot-fogged window and saw the fire burning a sparkling silver, a crucible pushed into the ashes. On the broad table in the center of the cottage were the remains of several glass crucibles, with their ruined contents sorted into small piles. There was a hint of red behind a fat, open book. I changed angles and squinted as hard as I could, but made out nothing else.

I rattled the handle of the door angrily, looking around for something to beat it down. Then, to my utter shock, the door opened.

Impossible. She would never be so careless as to leave the laboratory unlocked. Every alchemist kept their work protected, and Marguerite Hope was the most accomplished alchemist in France. While we were still in Paris, we had suffered countless attacks by thieves, especially after her great success with the King's armory contract. True, we were hidden in the country now, but she had told me often enough that we could be found by a determined seeker.

It was unthinkable that she would leave the laboratory unlocked—especially if she was truly as close to making the White Elixir as I had begun to suspect.

I caught sight of the exploded crucibles on the table again, and my heart stopped. There, behind the book, was a glass dish full of a distinctly red substance.

I picked my way across the cottage, stepping carefully over broken glass and other discarded implements. Mother had left the place in shocking disarray. Broken glass was a common hazard of an alchemist's work, since sealed crucibles had to be heated, and frequent explosions were the inevitable result. But my mother was orderly, and never left her work such a mess. Though she usually had me to do the tidying.

I lifted the bowl into the firelight. It was just as Jābir had described the transmuting agent, a fine powder of a deep red, like ground rubies. Next to it, a page had been copied from the book in my mother's hand. There was a picture of a winged man, the sun under one foot and the moon under another, holding scepters of snakes in each hand. I remembered this page. His eyes were disturbingly wide, and his tongue lolled out of his mouth. The back of the page was thick with Mother's cramped writing, in code. At the top of both sides was an inscription in Latin. CAVE MALEDICTIONEM ALCHEMISTAE. Beware the Alchemist's Curse.

The Alchemist's Curse. No one knew quite what it was, though Brother Basil, a fifteenth-century alchemist-friar, had written a sermon of that name warning that it would befall unworthy adepts. I touched the image again, and a shiver of apprehension went through me.

Behind me, the fire began to crackle. On an instinct, I folded the paper and slipped it into the pocket of my dress. There were red sparks in the flames. I picked up the tongs and moved the egg-shaped vase buried in the ashes, so I could see the inside. The liquid inside was a pure, dense white. My breath caught. The White Elixir. The last step before the Philosopher's Stone.

All my life I had dreamed of it. Some children were raised on stories of saints and filled with the hope of heaven. I was raised on the stories of alchemists and filled with the hope of the Philosopher's Stone. The Stone could turn any base metal into gold, cure any ill, and ward off old age, perhaps forever. My mother had made a name for herself with her skills, and that was no small thing, but no practitioner of alchemy could ever be satisfied with anything less than its ultimate prize.

No illness, no want, no death. The Philosopher's Stone gave everything humankind wanted but did not believe we could have in this life. With such a reward, it was not hard to see how so many great minds had wrecked themselves in its pursuit. But though these legendary outcomes transfixed me as much as any other adept, the lesser consequences were just as alluring. If we achieved this, we would become more than just women, even successful ones. There would be no more depending on patrons. No one would dare exclude us from any academy or salon. No one could deny our value. We would have respect. And not just from other alchemists—from the men who thought even male alchemists were fools and frauds. As much as I had longed for it, I had never really believed we would come this close.

My reverie was interrupted by another crackle, and another shower of red sparks. Then, as I watched in amazement, the edges of the White Elixir began to glow gold, then turn red. My pulse raced as my mind struggled to accept that it was happening, it was truly happening. This was the final step Jābir had described in making the Philosopher's Stone.

"We did it," I whispered.

"*I* did it," said my mother.

I turned, my hands tightening on the tongs. Absorbed in the wonder in front of me, I hadn't heard her come in. I straightened, anger stiffening my spine, and prepared myself for another battle.

"You could never have done it without me, whatever you want to pretend now," I said.

"*I* could never have done it without *you*?" Her voice was already shrill. Her eyes were bloodshot and unfocused, and her beautiful face shone with sweat. "And what would you be without me, you ungrateful girl? You did not make yourself an alchemist!"

"Ungrateful?" I wanted to stay calm, to be different than she was, but my voice was rising against my will. "And what should I be grateful for? Should I be grateful that I worked like a slave for this, only to be cast out just before the end result? Should I be grateful to you for shutting me off from everything and everyone, for making your work my whole life, and then taking even that from me?"

"Yes!" Her hands were shaking. "You should kneel at my feet and thank me! I made you different, I made you strong! And now you want to be like every other girl?

With no training, nothing to do but marry the first man who'll have you?"

I shook my head. That wasn't what I wanted at all.

"I have kept you safe and strong. And if I should—if I—"

She broke off into a scream. She bent double, clutching her head.

"Mother—" I started toward her, but she held out her hand to stop me and looked up with wild eyes.

"Get out, Thea." Her voice was strange, strangled and rough. I had never seen her like this before.

"You need a doctor—"

"Do as I say!" she screamed.

I didn't move. She was crumpling, arms wrapped around her legs now.

"Get out, get out, get out," she muttered, shaking her lowered head in a frenzy, her golden hair falling into her face.

I looked toward the glass ovum in the fire, where the White Elixir was entirely red now. Mother needed a doctor, clearly, but there it was—the Philosopher's Stone—impossibly, indescribably precious. I couldn't leave now. I turned back to my mother, and she lifted her head. I backed up at the look in her eyes, and held the tongs in front of me in both hands.

"Mother?" My voice shook.

A sound came out of her mouth—a growl. It wasn't a human sound, not even an animal one. I looked into her eyes, but I didn't see her there. Then she sprang.

I swiped at her with the tongs, knocking her aside. The tongs were hot from the fire, and her clothes sizzled where

I had hit them. But she was up again in an instant, then on me, stronger than she ever had been. I grappled with her as she seized me by the throat, wrapping her fingers around it, closing off the air. I clawed at her wild face, drawing blood she didn't seem to feel. I couldn't move her. Her breath was hot on my face, smelling, inexplicably, of sulfur. She was strong, too strong. How was she so strong?

And then she was lifted off me. I rolled, gasping, toward the tongs. I heard her shrieking before I saw her, across the table from the Comte, hands bared like claws. She leapt across it, but the Comte dodged her and ran toward me.

"Go, Thea!" he cried. "She has gone mad!"

Comte Adrien du Porre had a habit of stating the obvious.

"We have to restrain her!" The words were painful coming out, and I seized my throat.

She attacked the Comte again, throwing him easily to the ground. He was a strong man, but she tossed him like a child and leapt atop him. He threw her off, toward the hearth. She sprang back into a crouch. Before she attacked again, she reached behind her into the fire. She seized the glass ovum containing the substance, her fingers sizzling from the heat, and hurled it across the room.

I screamed then, though little sound came out of my swollen throat. I knew what would happen before it did. The Stone wasn't hardened yet. It was vulnerable. The glass shattered, and the Stone became a red smear dripping down the brick wall. I wanted to run to it, though I knew there was no hope. But Mother was upon Adrien again, and I swung the tongs at her with all my strength. She dropped onto the Comte, insensible.

Adrien pushed her off of him, but gently. He rolled her onto her back and felt her throat for a pulse. His fingers seemed to find what he hoped for, and he looked up at me with relief and reproach.

"Mon dieu, Thea, you could have killed her."

"She could have killed you," I retorted. But guilt gnawed at me, not so much for the blow itself—that had been necessary—but for how easy it had been to do. I had not even hesitated.

"We shall have to restrain her," murmured Adrien. "We cannot know if the fit will have passed when she awakes."

I stared down at her, my heart still thrashing in my chest like a caged thing. Whatever had just happened, the Comte was taking a more positive view of it than I. It had not occurred to me that this was a mere "fit" that might pass.

"What—?" I didn't know what to ask. "She tried to kill me. What madness is that? Have you ever heard of such a thing?"

"Men and women suffering madness can become violent, certainly," said Adrien.

"But she was so strong," I said. "Stronger than you. How could a disease of the mind have done that?"

"The mind has power over the body that no one fully understands. Put those down, Thea."

I stared down at the heavy tongs in front of me, then lowered them.

"She made the Stone," I said, looking back at the wall where the ovum had smashed. "It was in the last stage."

The Comte looked at me sharply.

"The last stage? The Philosopher's Stone? Are you certain?" He frowned. "She did not say so. Surely she would have told me."

"She was keeping it secret from both of us. It is why she barred me from the laboratory."

"Perhaps—perhaps she was waiting until she was sure. Perhaps she did not want to disappoint us—"

His eyes briefly met mine, then flicked away. We both knew that, whatever her reason, it wasn't that.

"It could have cured her! If only she hadn't destroyed it!" I went to the wall and touched the remains of the Stone with one finger. It was still warm. Tears of frustration pricked at my eyes. The Philosopher's Stone. The dream of every alchemist. Whole lifetimes of work, centuries of unfulfilled hopes, had nearly been realized in front of my eyes. But beneath the frustration, there was a spark of excitement. She had done it. At the very least, that meant that it could be done. My hand went to the pocket of my gown. She had done it, and I had her notes.

"You don't know that, Thea," Adrien said. "Even if it was the Stone—which I rather doubt—no one really knows what it does. Who can say what is myth and what is fact?"

I shook my head in irritation. The Comte was given to making pronouncements he had not earned the right to make. He had not labored over the texts, pieced together the fragments, or spent untold hours over the fires in the laboratory. The Comte was a patron, not an adept. All he truly knew about the practice of alchemy was how much it cost.

"Call the doctor," I said. "But if he can't help her, then I can, once I've made the Stone."

I started to hunt around the laboratory. If she had left any of the White Elixir, I could do it in a matter of weeks. If not, it would be months—months of Mother's madness. But there was none left that I could find. At least there was a good deal of the transmuting agent left. That itself took months to prepare, and it was essential to the last stages of the White Elixir. I tilted the red transmuting agent into a vial, corked it, and slipped it into my pocket with the notes. The Comte watched me, a mournful look on his handsome, beak-nosed face.

"I *can* do it," I said. "You needn't look so worried."

"No, Thea," said the Comte. "You cannot stay here. It is time for you to go."

I looked up at the Comte in alarm. "Not you, too!" I exclaimed. "I'm not going anywhere with the Marquis. I can't leave at all, not so close to achieving this! And Mother can't travel this way."

"Your mother will stay here. And you will not go with the Marquis. But you must go, your mother was right about that much. I wish she had broached the matter with you differently, but . . ." He sighed. "I have procured you a passport to leave France—"

"I will not go! If I leave now I might not be able to come back! I have a British name—"

"Precisely, Thea, you are a British subject. The National Convention grows more warlike by the day. You don't know how dangerous the situation has become. Even I—" He paused, then shook his head. "You must go while you still can. If Britain declares war, you could be arrested."

I stared at my mother, limp on the ground with her mouth open. If the Comte was so certain I was in danger here, perhaps it really was why she had wanted to send me away, not simply to be rid of me. A welt blossomed on her forehead where I had hit her. My stomach cramped with guilt.

"You'll go to Oxford," said the Comte. "To your father."

I knew very little about my father. Only that he and my mother had made their first forays into alchemy together when they were very young in England, and that now he was a respectable fellow at Oxford. This was quite a bit more than he knew about me. My mother had never even told him of my existence. She did not wish to share me with him.

"Won't that come as rather a shock to him?"

"He will recover. He could hardly refuse to take you in under the circumstances." This was very little reassurance, and my face must have shown it. The Comte's voice changed. "Any man would be proud to have you as his daughter, Thea. If he has half your wit, he will see that."

The Comte looked at me with strangely bright eyes, and it occurred to me that he might cry. Mother often complained of Adrien's excessive displays of feeling. Though, to be truthful, the occasion did seem to call for some emotion. Still, I looked away.

"Thank you," I said quietly.

Even if my father turned out not to have half my wit, he was an alchemist. He would have a laboratory. I could work as well there as here, and with no danger of the National Convention interrupting, either to arrest me as a British spy or to make me work on their weapons. I would make the Stone. Then, I could bring it back to heal my mother. I looked down at her limp form. I would succeed in all we had ever dreamed of doing, and then save her from herself. She couldn't deny that I was a worthy alchemist in my own right, then. Not when I had succeeded without her and given her sanity back to her in the process. Everything would change between us. It would have to.

Just imagining it was as satisfying to me as anything I had ever done.

In any case, I could do my mother no good here.

England had always loomed in the background of my life. I'd been born there. My father was there. I would never have admitted it to my mother, but I did want to meet him.

And he wasn't the only one I wished to see in England.

I helped the Comte carry my mother back to her room, and then took to mine.

I went to my morning table and took out yet another sheet of paper. Finally, I knew what to write to him.

Dear Will,

My mother has gone mad. I am coming to England now, because of the war. I will stay with my father. He does not know I was ever born. I miss you. Perhaps we will see each other soon.

And perhaps we would.

I watched the Oxfordshire countryside roll by from the window of my coach. Thus far, I was not at all impressed with the English spring. I had left Normandy at its best, the air sweet with apple blossoms and bright with fresh grass and sunshine. Here, the sun hid resolutely behind low-lying clouds, and all you could smell of spring was the musk of recent rain. Everything from the gray sky to the damp taffeta strings of my bonnet promised disappointment.

I had left France only two weeks ago. When my mother woke, and remained as mad and violent as the night of her attack, what was left of my hesitation vanished. Little as Adrien and the doctor could do for her, I could do even less. She was violent and malevolent as a demon, and the sight of her made me wild myself, as though I could not possibly get far enough away from her. Her animal screaming echoed in every corner of the chateau. I packed in haste and did as the Comte had arranged. And though the English would believe I ran from the dangers of the Revolution and war, in truth it was my mother and her madness I fled.

My stomach twisted when I thought of it, and I could not stop myself from thinking of it, no matter how I tried. Fear had taken root inside me, and guilt with it. I knew that the fear was as much for myself as for my mother, perhaps more. The doctor had said these things ran in families, especially in females. *She overexcited herself,* he said, *with her dreams and her experiments. And if one has a family tendency to such imbalances . . .*

I'd dismissed him at the time. He spoke as if total madness were a natural result of a woman pursuing rigorous scientific endeavors, as if he had seen it many times before. He hadn't. My mother's change was utterly strange, utterly uncanny. This was no common madness, not something for him to sigh over as if she could have prevented it only by listening to him. And yet, something had caused it. And I could not deny that madness might be a family trait, as I knew nothing at all of my mother's family. The more I pushed my fear down, the more it grew. I could think of nothing worse than to become what my mother was now.

The spires of Oxford came into view, pulling me from my anxious reverie. Domes, peaks, and turrets cut through the mist, like the oldest castles in France intermixed with its most beautiful gothic churches. Yet these were not churches, but houses of learning, of science. For all my mother's fame as an alchemist, she had never been welcomed into the universities and academies of France. And where my mother could not go, I could not, either. I touched the window and stared at the town with rising excitement. That was where my father lived, amid those cathedrals to science. He had made a place for himself there. A place for his work.

I drew my mother's letter to my father from my satchel, not for the first time. It was the letter the Comte had insisted that my mother write before her illness, the one she had written and never sent. I had been on the point of opening it more than once on my journey, and most likely would have if I had some way of sealing it again before giving it to my father. I am not a person who lightly invades the confidence of others. But these confidences in particular—confidences from my unpredictable mother, about me, to my mysterious father—these I struggled to respect. This letter would be the first knowledge my father ever received of me. Unfortunately, I had no choice but to let my mother make the introduction.

In the town, the streets were dark with recent rain and crowded with tall stone buildings, the halls of the colleges mixed with the humbler brick dwellings of the townspeople. In the center of town, the carriage rolled to a stop next to a towering wooden gate built into the medieval stone walls. The gate was adorned with flowers and crests at the top and triangular patterns lower down. The coach driver opened my door.

"Oriel College, miss," he said, and went to the back to unload my trunk.

I stepped out of the carriage, pulling my shawl more tightly around my shoulders. The walls of the college rose up above me. They were several stories high, made of stone,

and topped with pointed facades on the side and a crenel-
lated parapet at the top. It looked like, and perhaps was, a
medieval fortress. I could imagine archers aiming down
from the battlements. Together with the tall, dark gates, it
all sent a clear message of exclusion. I squared my shoulders and knocked on the door.

An elderly man opened the gate. He stooped, and I saw
he had huge, bushy brows that obscured the eyes beneath
them. He peered at me, my obvious girlhood, slightly foreign clothing and trunk, with a mild, quizzical glance.

"I am looking for Professor Vellacott. He is a fellow
here, I believe."

"Vellacott?" repeated the porter. "Yes, he is that, miss.
Might I ask what your business is with him?"

His eyes went from my trunk to my green bonnet. The
Comte had bought it for me not long ago. It was the latest
in Parisian fashion, and the porter clearly found it out of
the ordinary. I tried not to imagine what conjecture he
might be making.

"I am—" But I could not say I was his daughter, when
as yet the professor did not know he had one. "The daughter of a friend of his, a very old friend. I've had a very long
journey, sir, and I really must see him. It is important. I
have a letter—"

I pulled it from the pocket of my gown, a robe à la polonaise, and it occurred to me to wonder whether this, too,
might not be a common fashion in England. The porter
had glanced askance at my rather thin chemise, which the
robe did not fully cover in front.

"He's in the dining hall now, at high table," said the
porter. "But I'll ask him—what's your name?"

"Thea—Theosebeia Hope."

"Theabee—?"

"Thee-ah-see-bya. Miss Hope."

With his bushy eyebrows raised, the porter reluctantly invited me into the gate house. He pulled in my trunk, and I stood beside the fire. It was a pleasantly warm, wood-paneled room, and while I waited I looked around at the various seals and coats of arms that hung on the wall. They all signified some king or earl or the like, some rich and powerful man who had cast his beneficence here.

The porter returned not much later, not with my father, but with a slight young man with untidy dark hair and terrible posture.

"Master Dominic, this is Miss Thee—Miss Hope."

Dominic inclined his head and didn't meet my eyes.

"Miss Hope," he said. He had a low, raspy voice that I liked. It seemed older than he was.

"Are you a student of Professor Vellacott's?" I asked doubtfully.

"Something like," said the boy. "Is he expecting you?"

"No," I said, and a nervous laugh escaped me. Dominic looked at my trunk, confused. He did not know what to make of me any more than the porter did.

"I have a letter of introduction," I said. "I think—I think he will want to know I'm here."

It was the best explanation I could manage under the circumstances. Dominic's eyes flicked to my face, and then away again.

"I'll take you to the dining hall." There were traces of an erased lower-class accent in his speech. He dropped his *h*'s and his *l*'s were nearly *w*'s. "It's just across the quad. We can try to get his attention from the back."

Dominic went out abruptly, without another word. I followed, too nervous to mind his poor manners. The walls opened onto a grassy square lined with carved stone buildings. We crossed to one that glowed from the inside. The door was ajar, and high-spirited masculine voices rang out into the chilly evening, along with the smell of roasted meat and hot butter. I followed Dominic through the stone door into a small hallway. To our left were two archways, looking in on a handsome, crowded dining room. The ceiling soared up into wooden beams arching crosswise across the length of the hall. Three long rows of gleaming wooden tables were filled with young men, eating and laughing and belonging there. A few of them caught sight of me and stared. I ignored them and looked to the front of the hall at the head table, slightly elevated above the rest. Ten older men sat there, talking with a little more dignity than their students, but no less contentment. I scanned the table, quickly ruling out the oldest of the fellows, until my eyes rested on a dark-haired, carefully dressed man in his midthirties. He was sipping wine and looking at home.

"Professor Vellacott is there, third from the left," murmured Dominic, confirming what I instinctively knew. I stared at him, hungry to take in every detail I could. He was tall, or else very long-waisted, judging from his seated height relative to the other fellows. He looked young— younger than I had pictured him, though not quite as young as my mother. His curly dark hair was elegantly cut, as were his clothes. He held himself rather carefully as well. Straight-backed. His smile to his dining companion was restrained. He looked out across the hall, and his eyes caught mine. He set down his wine glass, and the smile vanished.

Perhaps it was the strange presence of a woman inside the college that made him frown. Perhaps it was that I was drawing the attention of his students and causing a disturbance. Or perhaps he recognized what I did, looking at him. My face was a younger, feminine copy of his own. In any case he did frown, very deeply, and then cast a look of distinct disapproval at Dominic.

"Are you going to go speak to him?" I asked Dominic, who still hovered by the archway.

"I'm not meant to be here," he said. "No more than you are. I hoped he'd come speak to us—ah, here—"

The professor—my father—was coming toward us, still frowning. He stepped past us, out of the archway so that he was no longer visible from the hall.

"Is something wrong at the laboratory?" he asked Dominic, his eyes gliding over me with discomfort.

"No, sir, I only came to tell you the substance is ready, but this young woman was asking for you at the gate. Miss Hope."

Vellacott turned to me, and if he had seemed stiff before he had gone rigid now. He stared at me for a long moment, his dark eyes wide with shock.

"Miss—Miss Hope—?"

"Theosebeia Hope," I said, and sank into a shallow curtsy. "I believe you knew my mother, Marguerite Hope. Do you remember her?"

"I—" Professor Vellacott recovered himself enough to lower his eyes. "I did. Certainly I do. She—is she here?"

He looked alarmed at the idea.

"No, sir," I reassured him quickly. "She is in France. But I had to leave her there. I find myself in need of a place to stay."

"And she sent you here?" Vellacott's frown deepened. "I can't imagine why. I suppose—"

He looked at me again, disquiet behind his disapproval.

"Dominic, see Miss Hope to the inn." He bowed to me. "Miss Hope. We may speak—" He hesitated long enough to betray his distress at the prospect. "Later."

He went back into the warm glow of the dining hall, and Dominic went quickly to the door. I followed him across the quad, forcing down the unruly feelings that tightened my throat and chest. I was grateful, now, that Dominic seemed so determined to look only at the ground. Perhaps he wouldn't notice my trembling hands and twisting mouth.

Back at the gatehouse, Dominic lifted my trunk more easily than I expected, and the porter opened the gate to let us out. He said goodbye politely, and with evident relief.

The great door shut behind us with a clang. I had been inside half an hour, at most, and the whole time everyone who saw me had been wishing me out.

Except Dominic. He shot me a keen glance that might have been sympathy, then looked back at the cobbled ground.

"Professor's got a room rented at the Tackley Inn." He nodded up the road. "Not far."

We set off toward it, and I let the brisk air and exercise loosen my tight chest and steady my shaking hands.

"Why does he stay at an inn?" I had hoped my father

was better established than a rented room would suggest, though of all my hopes to be disappointed today, this looked likely to be the least. "Doesn't he have a house?"

"No house. Fellows usually live in the college if they aren't married. But the professor gave his rooms to a visitor of his."

I eyed Dominic, easy to do when there seemed so little danger of him looking up. Other than the poor posture, there wasn't much to distinguish him from all the young men we'd just left behind. I remembered what he'd said when we were there.

"Why aren't you supposed to be in the college dining hall?" I asked. "Aren't you a student?"

"No," said Dominic. "I'm not enrolled. Can't be."

"Why not?"

"Costs money, for one thing," he said. "And I'm a Catholic."

"Are you?" This was just interesting enough to distract me from my own painful feelings. "I didn't think there were many of those left in England. Are you Irish?"

I supposed that might explain the squashed accent. I had assumed he was hiding a London slum argot, but perhaps it was in fact an Irish brogue.

"No," said Dominic shortly. "English Catholic. Church of England didn't stamp us all out."

"It's harder to do than you'd think, isn't it?" I mused. "You can still find the occasional Protestant in France as well."

"Is that where you're from?" He said it with a glimmer of interest, the first he had shown in me.

"I suppose it is." I laughed, and Dominic glanced at

me for another fleeting moment. He did have very nice eyes, when one managed to get a glimpse of them. Warm brown and very serious. "Though in France, I always said I was from England. I was born here, but all I remember is France."

"You don't have an accent," said Dominic.

"I learned English from my mother," I said. "French, too."

Thinking of her was as painful as thinking of my father. I frowned.

For a moment I thought Dominic might say more. He looked as though he wanted to, but instead he turned left onto a wider and busier street. The buildings were fronted with shops here, and in a few yards Dominic stopped in front of a bookseller's. We passed through an archway into a very narrow, covered alley. I followed Dominic up two flights of stone stairs and watched him set down the trunk and try the door at the top.

"It's locked," he said, and frowned. "I should have thought to ask for the key."

"He should have thought to give it," I said.

Dominic glared at the doorknob. "You could come down to the tavern until he gets back. I imagine you'd like supper."

I was on the verge of denying it, out of habit. My mother always forgot to eat, too absorbed in her work, and found it disappointing when I preferred regular meals. But I *was* hungry, in fact, and there was a pleasant smell of bread coming from across the alley.

"I would, yes." The words came out sounding defiant, and I glanced at Dominic in case he found it strange. He could have no idea whom I was defying by admitting a strong preference for food over hunger.

He lugged the trunk down the stairs again and down another set under the first floor. The tavern, it turned out, was a spacious vaulted cellar, sparsely inhabited, dotted with tables between the stone arches. Dominic pulled out a chair for me at one of them, then went to the bar in the back. I looked around while I waited and quickly noticed that I was the only woman here, as well. The few patrons were men, gentlemanly in appearance, but not in manners. They stared at me openly. I assumed my most forbidding expression, one I had practiced often on my mother's last patron before the Comte. It was a mixture of contempt and boredom that had usually frozen him quite effectively. I was still wearing it when Dominic came back, which perhaps explained why he left an empty chair between us and didn't try to make conversation.

A boy brought us a platter of food, some roast beef and boiled potatoes. After a few moments of attentive eating, I started to feel more warmly toward Dominic, despite the ill-mannered way he hunched over his plate.

"Thank you for supper," I said. He nodded, mouth too full to reply.

"So you aren't a student," I continued. "But you work with my—with Mr. Vellacott?"

Dominic looked up. He had caught my slip. However unpolished his manners, he had a sharp mind. He swallowed his food.

"I do," he said.

"Are you an alchemist, then?"

"Not really. Just a useful hand in the laboratory," he said. "How do you know about—about that?"

"Is it a secret?" I asked. Traditionally, alchemy wasn't considered a respectable science within the academy, but I thought Vellacott had made a place for his work here.

"Not exactly," said Dominic. "It's just not very well known. Most of the undergraduates think Mr. Vellacott only does chymistry. That's what he teaches them."

"Where is his laboratory, then?" I asked.

Dominic had another bite of beef, and he took his time chewing it. "I reckon you better ask him that," he said.

I sat back and regarded him. I was beginning to feel irrationally irritated.

"Is that why he employs you? Because you're so good at keeping your mouth shut you hardly know how to open it?"

"That's part of it." He looked at me steadily for a moment, unsmiling. "Mr. Vellacott does like his secrets."

I could hardly miss the challenge. It was on the tip of my tongue to tell him that it was no fault of *mine* that no one here knew about me, when my father came in.

"There you are, Miss Hope," he said. "I wasn't sure where you'd got to."

"The door was locked," I said. "Dominic was kind enough to buy me dinner."

"Ah, yes," said Vellacott. "Thank you, Dominic. Why don't we go—upstairs—"

Vellacott looked around the cellar, obviously nervous. I thanked Dominic, then left with my father.

Vellacott's rooms were rather spare—two bedrooms adjoining a parlor, where I sat while he paced around. There were two plush chairs around a small tea table and a window that looked out over the street. It was clear that he hadn't lived here long. There were few possessions in the room, no pictures or other such attempts to make the place a home. There was, however, a less faded square on the moss-colored wallpaper. So it seemed his attempts at decorating had extended just as far as removing a frame.

"I ordered tea," he explained, looking out the window. "It should be here any moment."

The professor's obvious discomfort had a strangely calming effect on me. He was afraid of me, and that meant I had some kind of power. I tried to put aside the disappointment nagging at the back of my mind and taking the form of the knowing voice of my mother. *Never pin your hopes on a man,* she always said, though she never took her own advice.

The tea arrived, and Vellacott set down the tray on the table.

"Sugar?" he asked.

"No, thank you," I said without thinking. I rather liked sugar in my tea, but we never took it that way at home.

Vellacott made a production of pouring the tea, stirring his own with more than the necessary attention. The silence stretched on long enough that I wanted badly to break it, to make conversation and put him at ease. But I didn't. I needed to know what he would say.

He sat back, his nervous glances at me becoming more frequent and obvious.

"I didn't catch your first name, Miss Hope," he said, finally.

"Theosebeia," I said.

His eyes widened.

"She—she named you that?"

Theosebeia was a pupil of the famous Egyptian alchemist Zosimos. My father would know that.

"Everyone calls me Thea," I said. Not quite everyone. Thea meant "goddess," and Will had felt the need to come up with another name for me.

Certainly you're a goddess, he had said. *But you intimidate me enough without that particular reminder.*

"Thea. You don't look like her." He was staring now, pretense abandoned. "If my memory serves me," he added, as an unconvincing afterthought.

People often said that, and it was not a compliment. My mother was everyone's idea of the perfect beauty. Petite, porcelain blond, and small-featured. I was her opposite: too tall, with wild dark hair, a long nose, and high color.

"Mother always said I looked like my father."

And that had never been a compliment, either, though now that he was before me I didn't mind it so much. Whatever else he might be, Vellacott was without doubt a handsome man.

"Your father," he repeated, and cleared his throat. "Ah. Yes. A Frenchman, I suppose?"

I shook my head slowly, and his hopeful look died.

"How—how old are you?"

"Seventeen." I looked him straight in the eye. He might be ashamed, but I refused to be. "My birthday is June the tenth, 1775."

Vellacott set down his cup very slowly.

"This is a jest of Meg's, I think," he said with forced calm. "She found a dark-haired girl of the right age—"

My jaw tightened as I swallowed my anger.

"No," I said.

"But she said—she said she lost it—"

Vellacott went very red, then very white, realizing, perhaps, that he was looking at *it*. He stood, his chair scraping the bare wood floor loudly, and crossed to the window. He gripped the sill, then turned back to me. He made a striking figure, tall and slim, with a profile well suited to dramatic poses. I assumed he was aware of this.

"This couldn't have come at a worse time," he groaned, and put a hand to his high, pale forehead. "You cannot stay here, Miss Hope. I'm terribly sorry, but it is simply impossible! If anyone knew—"

I couldn't look at him anymore. I took a sip of my tea and swallowed resolutely, though my throat was attempting to close.

"I'm close, very close to winning recognition for the official study of alchemy here," he said, with a note of pleading now. "I have a contract, you know, with the Royal Navy. To do what your mother did for King Louis! And a very distinguished alchemist recently arrived, one who has his own department of alchemy at the University of Bologna! We are very close to making a discovery that could prove to everyone— We could have a whole department. A department of alchemy at Oxford, Miss Hope, the first in England!"

I eyed my cup but couldn't help nodding. I understood the significance perfectly. To most scholars in the academies and societies, we were counterfeiters, charlatans, or fools. Things had only grown worse in recent years, as scholars sought more and more to purge their fields of superstitions and unsupported traditions. Many scientists took the continued existence of alchemy as an offense against their discipline. The support of an institution of Oxford's significance would be an enormous change—but not for me. I thought of the forbidding walls that I had been so briefly and begrudgingly allowed to enter. It was painfully clear to me that even if alchemy were allowed to make its home there, I would not be.

"The scandal this would cause! It's impossible— Your mother ought to know that much! What was she thinking of? Why did she send you?"

"She did not send me." My voice was brittle with cold. "And as for what she is thinking, I cannot tell you, for she has gone entirely mad."

"Mad?" My father turned to me, his pale face creasing with sudden, genuine concern. "Meg? What you do mean, *mad*?"

"Mad," I repeated. "Mad as mad can be. Violent. Her reason has deserted her. She doesn't know herself, or anyone else."

Vellacott's mouth worked some inaudible word as he stared at me. He lowered himself back into his chair, then in the same movement dropped his head into his hands.

"My God," he said after a moment. "My God."

Far from softening me toward him, this show of emotion irritated me. He had not seen her in seventeen years. He had not sought her out or showed concern for her welfare. He hadn't been there when the madness took her. And it had not been him she tried to kill.

"Where is she now?" he finally asked.

"In Normandy, near Honfleur," I said. "Her patron is caring for her. She could not be moved."

"But—there must be somewhere else you can go—some relative—"

"Surely you know my mother is an orphan," I said. "If I have other relatives, you will have to tell me who they are. I do not know them."

I stared coldly while my father's mouth hung open, trembling with failed speech, and considered my options. There were no relatives, true, but there was somewhere else I could go, although not with any sort of propriety. I had Will's letter in my pocket, with his latest address. My cheeks burned at the thought of showing up at his doorstep unannounced and unchaperoned. I could not bear to imagine what he would think it meant, what anyone would think it meant. And yet I wasn't sure I could bear to stay here with my disappointing father. My mother had been right about him. That was almost the worst part.

Still, he had a laboratory.

"Perhaps you do not know that my mother continued to pursue alchemy after she left England."

"Of course. Everyone heard of her contract with King Louis." He waved his hand. "The armor."

I nodded. The armor was what made Mother's reputation. Astonishingly light yet strong and impervious to rust. It was the sort of thing monarchs hoped alchemists would make, when they weren't calling us charlatans and passing laws against us. The armor gave her enough success that she could afford to scorn that kind of work now. We had focused all our energies on the Philosopher's Stone for several years.

"Yes, the armor. I helped her make it, you know." Of course he didn't know. His eyebrows lifted. I had his attention. "You said you were on the verge of some success. I assume you meant in your laboratory." *Think of him as a patron,* I told myself. *You do not have to like him. Indeed, when have you ever liked any of them, other than Adrien?* "My mother and I were also on the verge of a great success when the madness took her. I think you would find me useful."

"You—you helped her with her work?"

"Do you think my mother could have tolerated me for seventeen years if I did not?"

Vellacott gave a short, surprised laugh, and for the first time he looked at me with interest and not merely with fear.

"I can't picture her as a mother at all," he admitted. "But of course, she would train you, wouldn't she? And are you an adept?"

There was no way to answer this modestly. And anyway, this was no time for modesty.

"I am as good as she ever was, and with time I will be better."

He raised his eyebrows, and a small smile pulled at his mouth. "You are more like her than you look, I think."

I didn't smile back, though he clearly expected me to. Vellacott wasn't the first to think that likening me to my mother was the highest compliment he could give me. In fact, it had never occurred to anyone but Will to give me any other kind.

"You could say I am your niece," I said. "If you are unwilling to acknowledge me."

Vellacott's smile vanished.

"What must you think of me," he said quietly.

If I had been less tired, less heartsick, I might have managed to restrain myself.

"It's quite all right, sir. You are just as I was led to expect," I said. "You've spared me the inconvenience of revising my opinion."

The effect was immediate. His face crumpled and his head drooped. He looked as crushed as I could have hoped, though it gave me no satisfaction.

"I am rather tired," I said. "Do you have a place for me to sleep for the night? I would take my own rooms, but I don't have very much money."

"Yes, of course," said the professor, still downcast. There was an unmade bed in the spare room. He produced sheets and took the quilt from his own bed. I thanked him, excused myself, and shut the door of the room. The wrung-out, hollow feeling in my chest betrayed me. Despite what I told my father, I had hoped for a better day than this turned out to be.

5

I slept badly on a hard little bed in the cramped spare room. Morning light from the single window illuminated the peeling, water-stained wallpaper. As a patron, Vellacott left something to be desired. I spread out the papers I had brought on the bed. There was my mother's still-sealed letter to my father. I couldn't be certain what she had said about me in it. Her opinion of me always seemed to vary so much from day to day. I once more considered sneaking a look at its contents, but decided against it. The thought of my father knowing I had invaded my mother's confidences was more uncomfortable than not knowing what they were. I set it aside and picked up Will's last letter. I stared at the London address for several minutes. Only a day away by coach. I tried to imagine what he would say if I came to him. It would be some joke, probably, to put me at ease.

Fleeing war and revolution, are you, Bee? I knew you'd come find me once you had a good enough excuse.

Cleverer than that, of course, but something of the kind. I smiled and slipped the letter back into my dress. I wore my simple gray round dress today, without all the awkward padding of fashionable gowns. It had seen me through many hours of work. As a concession to respectability, I wore my stays, which I usually did not bother with in the laboratory. I did not want to give the Oxonians another reason to stare, or my father another reason to find me an embarrassment.

I smoothed the last set of papers, crumpled from being crushed in my pocket while I was held down and strangled. The memory sent my heart racing, and I put the papers down for a moment while I closed my eyes and waited for the sudden panic to pass. When it had, I forced myself to read my mother's cramped, hasty handwriting once more. These were the last steps she had taken to prepare the Stone, after she had evicted me from our laboratory. These were the steps that had worked, and that made these papers a treasure map—a map to a treasure greater than any pirate's. I had memorized them, of course, but I could not risk forgetting even the smallest step. I turned the first page over, almost against my will, and forced myself to look at the drawing on the back. The naked king stared at me with wild eyes. My mother wasn't much of an artist, but she had copied this image faithfully, along with the heading. A cold shiver of fear crawled up my back again, just as it had when I saw the picture in our laboratory.

"Cave Maledictionem Alchemistae," I murmured. Beware

the Alchemist's Curse. The warning could mean many things, and there were many theories. I had read and translated stories of adepts selling their souls to demons for the secret knowledge necessary to make the Stone. There were other stories, sometimes overlapping, of adepts who produced the Stone and found that unlimited gold and immortality proved a burden they could not bear—a curse. Some went mad from their endless striving and countless failures to produce the Stone. But my mother had succeeded. That, at least, was not what had driven her mad.

I looked closer. There was more Latin scribbled in the margins, in a cramped and hasty hand.

Alchemistam ultimam lapis elegit. Vae illi, qui non accipit.

The Stone chooses the last alchemist, but woe to whom it does not accept.

The last alchemist? I had never heard of that, or seen anything like this sentiment before. It made no sense, on its face. How could the Stone choose anything? It had to be some kind of metaphor—perhaps another way of saying that it took virtue and determination to succeed at making the Stone. One must be worthy. That was a common idea.

My eyes went from one warning to the other. If you put them together, it seemed to suggest that the Alchemist's Curse would befall the one whom the Stone had rejected. I could not tell if they ought to be taken together. The smaller warning wasn't in the text at all, just added by my mother. But perhaps she had a good reason to put them together. Foreboding stirred deep in my stomach.

Perhaps my mother knew something was going to happen to her. Perhaps she even knew why. She had made some mistake, maybe, and therefore wasn't "worthy" to be the last alchemist—whatever that was.

Or perhaps she was simply scribbling nonsense in those last days.

I pushed thoughts of my mother's madness aside, folded the papers carefully, and slipped them into my dress next to Will's letter. I looked doubtfully at the contents of my trunk, wishing there were some way to bring everything of value with me rather than leave anything here. I had brought as much as I could salvage from my mother's workroom, all that would travel. There was none of the White Elixir left, and the Stone itself had been wrecked beyond repair. But I had vials of metals, and in particular one of the fine ruby-red transmuting agent. I thought of the months it had taken to prepare and decided to bring that with me as well.

In the parlor, my father was staring at the breakfast tray. He jumped to his feet when I entered, and I handed him Mother's letter.

"I do not know what she wrote." I tried to sound indifferent, and was aware I did not succeed.

"Thank you." He took the letter tentatively, and his gaze lingered on her handwriting. She had addressed it, simply, to Edward. "Sit down, Thea, please."

We both sat, and he stared at the letter. He was obviously as eager to read it as I was hesitant.

"Read it. I don't mind."

He did so at once, while I served myself a piece of toasted bread from the tray. I examined the greasy eggs and bacon, appetite mingling with suspicion. We ate almost nothing for breakfast at home. Mother said heavy food interfered with concentration. I glanced up at my father in time to catch him wiping at his misty eyes.

"I want to apologize, Thea," he said. "For my dreadful behavior yesterday."

I stared down at the breakfast tray. One of the eggs had burst, and the yolk had pooled around it and begun to harden. I was at a loss. I had very little practice at receiving apologies, and even less at attempting to forgive.

"It is no excuse," my father continued. "But I was shocked—I have never been so shocked. To suddenly find out that I have been a father for seventeen years without knowing it."

But this sounded like an excuse, and one that did not fit his behavior. Last night, all his concern had been for his reputation, for the damage an illegitimate daughter would do to his position at the university. My defenses tightened again, and I felt more sure of myself.

"I hope you can forgive me," said Vellacott.

"You had every reason to be worried," I said. "But I think you will agree that saying I am your niece resolves your concerns neatly. I look enough like you that no one will doubt we are related. Besides that, I will keep to the laboratory. I assume my mother assured you of my abilities there?"

I could not restrain a nervous glance at him, and I was surprised to see him looking back at me with a bleak expression.

"Oh yes," he said, folding the letter. "I have no doubts at all on that score. But, Thea—"

Whatever he wanted to say, I was certain I did not want to hear it. I cut him off. "I'd like to get to work, sir."

I pushed the congealing eggs away. My mother had the right idea about breakfast.

My father nodded. We left the inn together, but very far apart.

We walked farther into the town, away from the college. We did not go far, but the scenery changed remarkably in that short time. Streets narrowed, as did the houses and shops. There was less stone and more wood, fewer high towers, coats of arms, and paned windows. Down High Street, and away from Oriel, we had clearly entered the part of Oxford that was inhabited by those of the town rather than the gown. There were more women here, house- and shop-wives, and my father grew visibly more relaxed the farther we walked.

Close to the edge of town, we passed down a narrow alley and into a wooden outbuilding, where a steady column of opaque pure white smoke poured from the chimney. I paused on the threshold to examine it a moment and to take in its scent. Vellacott cocked his head and watched me, and when I looked at him he wore a small smile.

"You know what it means, don't you?" he asked.

"The White Elixir." I was impressed in spite of myself. "You've almost made it."

"Almost?" Vellacott's high brow rose even higher. "You don't mean to tell me you've seen the finished product?"

I was tempted to tell him that I'd not only seen it, but watched it transform into the Philosopher's Stone itself. But an alchemist's instinct for secrecy held me back, and I merely nodded again.

Vellacott unlocked the door and held it open for me. I entered my father's laboratory. At once the familiar sights and scents filled me with assurance. Dominic was there, standing at a large table in the center and carefully measuring mercury into a glass vial. Against the wall was a large fireplace where another man stood over a brass brazier, which emitted the white smoke. The man was tall and broad, and he snapped bad-tempered instructions at Dominic in heavily accented English. Bookcases lined the farthest wall from the hearth, and several books lay open on the table. Dominic looked from one of them to his task, and back. Mr. Vellacott cleared his throat, and the alchemists looked up at me.

I met Dominic's gaze, and he smiled for half a second before dropping his eyes to his work again. The man by the brazier, however, scowled. I made a quick and careful study of him. He was middle aged, older than my father, also larger and less handsome. His eyes were a beady black and his strong-featured face had an unhealthily pale cast to it. His velvet waistcoat and feathered black hat were too fine for the laboratory, though he certainly moved and spoke like one who knew his business. As I watched him, his hand moved to a talisman that hung around his neck, a serpent staff of Hermes Trismegistus. My mother never wore talismans, nor let me wear one. It was the sort of thing that encouraged people to see alchemy as nothing more than an occult religion, a perception her sort of alchemists constantly fought. She scorned the whole legend of Hermes the Thrice-Great: the first alchemist, an Egyptian priest who became a god. But it never seemed contemptible to me. After all, it was the most honest account of the Great Work, no matter how we alchemists chose to describe it. The Philosopher's Stone offered endless wealth, perfect health, and immortality, and we dared to seek it. Didn't that mean we wanted to become gods, just as Hermes had?

"Professore Bentivoglio, this is Miss Theosebeia Hope," said Vellacott. "She is my niece, and has come to stay with me for a time until her mother arrives from France. She has extensive training in alchemy, and I believe she might be of help to us."

My father showed no discomfort at these lies, and I added this to my growing list of his unfavorable character traits.

"Miss Hope," continued my father, "may I introduce Professor Ludovico Bentivoglio. He has come at my invitation from the University of Bologna, where he is head of their recently established department of alchemy."

Ludovico did not bow, but continued to finger his talisman in an agitated manner. His sleeve dropped down as he did so, revealing scars on his forearms that could almost match mine. He stared at me with hostility.

"A pleasure," I murmured. I sank into a curtsy without lowering my gaze. Ludovico did not respond. "Bologna is in the Papal States, is it not?"

"Yes." The professor looked, if possible, even more peevish at this reminder.

"And yet yours is the only department of alchemy in any university in Europe," I said. "How was His Holiness the pope convinced to allow it?"

Professor Bentivoglio tossed his head, and his mouth curled into something like a smile.

"The Holy Father has many troubles," he said in his thick accent. "Your assurdo Revolution especially. Spies and traitors are everywhere, even in the Vatican. If alchemy can make help for him, then . . ." He held out his hands, flourishing his fingers as he did so.

"Complimenti, Professore," I said. As much as I might want to return his hostility with some of my own, there was nothing to be gained that way. "Your department is a great thing for alchemy."

The professor's beady eyes softened, and I seized this moment of lessened ill will to cross the room and examine the contents of the brazier. Closer up, I could see that the smoke had a faint tinge of silver to it. This had happened to me several times in my first failed attempts to prepare the elixir. I knew exactly what was needed next, and that the window to add it was small. I could feel the men's eyes on me, expectation in my father's gaze and suspicion in Bentivoglio's. I suppressed a smile. I was about to show them just what kind of alchemist I was.

I turned to Dominic. "Are you preparing the tincture of mercury to add next?"

He raised his eyebrows. "Yes."

"It won't work on its own," I said. "There is still too much sulfur in the composition. You will need to purify it with stibnite."

"The text says nothing of stibnite," said Bentivoglio.

I glanced at the book that lay open on the table. It was Brother Basil's *Twelve Keys*, the same we and Jābir had used as our starting place. Brother Basil was supposedly a sixteenth-century monk, though even that was shrouded in mystery. Even by the standards of alchemists, Basilius Valentinus was notorious for misdirection and secrecy. He was also famous for giving away immense amounts of silver to the poor. It made his works the most promising, and the most baffling to approach. It had also made me entirely determined to conquer them.

"Not in the receipt, but it is in the Decknamen," I said. Decknamen were figurative illustrations, useful for alchemists who wanted to keep their secrets, and extremely irritating to those of us who wanted to discover them. Sometimes the Decknamen were mere ornaments, but more often they were a code. Brother Basil's were the latter, and I had deciphered it.

"The Decknamen are a distraction," growled Ludovico. "They are like what fortune-tellers say—they can mean whatever you wish."

I shook my head. The Decknamen were frustrating, certainly. Some authors even put misdirection in them, to throw off unworthy adepts. But all of alchemy was frustrating. A true adept could not afford to dismiss any sources of knowledge because they were difficult to decode. But I left this aside.

"I have followed the instructions as written myself several times, and always reached this point—" I gestured to the brazier. "Before the composition broke."

"Ours broke last time, as well," said Dominic, earning a furious glare from Professore Bentivoglio.

"Are you saying you know what the Decknamen mean, Thea?" asked my father.

I went back to the table and opened Basil's book to the first woodcut, showing a king, a bridge, and a wolf jumping over a fire. An old man stood nearby, holding a crutch and scythe. I pointed to the king.

"The king of metals, obviously gold," I said, and Ludovico made an impatient noise.

"*Ovviamente*," he muttered. Obviously.

"Before his marriage, the composition, the king must be purified by the wolf—see how the wolf is jumping toward him over the fire with his jaws open? The fire is the purification process and the wolf is the substance that will devour the king before his 'marriage.' This"—I pointed to the old man holding a crutch and scythe—"is Saturn. He represents lead. See how the wolf springs from him? So the wolf substance is related closely to lead. What substance related to lead devours impurities?"

"Stibnite," said my father. He and Dominic shared a meaningful glance. "And you tried this, Thea? It worked?"

"It worked."

My hand went to my pocket involuntarily. My mother's notes began after this step, taking the White Elixir as a starting place and working from a different text. I scanned the shelves, but didn't see anything of Jābir's—nothing in an Arabic script at all. That wasn't unusual. Jābir was a Persian scholar and alchemist, and the reason my mother had seen to it that I learned Arabic. She'd been convinced that he had achieved the Philosopher's Stone itself, and that ignorance of his work was the reason no alchemists in Christendom had reproduced it.

I turned back and found Professore Bentivoglio's eyes on my skirts, where I clutched at my mother's notes. I released the papers and withdrew my hand from my pocket.

"You do not have much time before it breaks," I said.

Dominic was at the cabinet already, sorting through glass vials. He brought one out, but before he could bring it to me Professore Bentivoglio crossed the room and snatched it from him. He uncorked the vial and leaned over the brazier, so that his face was wreathed in the thick white smoke. With one last narrow-eyed glance at me, he tipped the stibnite into the brazier.

The result was immediate. The smoke ceased entirely, while the stibnite ate through the compound like wildfire, leaving it momentarily black. Bentivoglio whirled on me with a silent fury that was nonetheless obvious and threatening enough that my father stepped in front of me. I held up my hand.

"Watch," I said. "It isn't finished."

Dominic pushed past Bentivoglio and hovered over the brazier. He exclaimed, and the professor turned back to the hearth.

"It's kindled again, yes?" I tried not to sound smug. "When it has burned through, it will turn gray."

All three of the men now stood staring into the brazier. I stood back and took the opportunity to examine them. My father was the tallest of the three, and he looked out of place amid the dark and dust in his well-cut suit. Bentivoglio was broad and almost as tall, though not now, as he was hunched over the brazier with an avid gleam in his eyes. Dominic was the least physically imposing: slight, and not much taller than I. He stared at the composition without the keen, greedy look of the other two. He appeared interested, thoughtful, and serious; no more. He stepped back and turned to me before the others could tear themselves away.

"It's gray," he said. "Now what?"

"You keep the temperature constant for two days." I had stayed up watching it for nearly thirty-six hours before the Comte had come to insist I go to bed. That was the last I had seen of it. After I slept—for almost two entire days—my mother had barred me from the laboratory. "Simple enough, but tiresome."

"I will do it," said Professore Bentivoglio. I wondered how long he had been awake already. The shadows under his eyes suggested it was too long.

"Professore," said my father, evidently coming to the same conclusion, "this is drudge work. There is no need for you to exhaust yourself. Dominic can do it quite well, I'm sure. Perhaps . . . a rest? Certainly you deserve one."

Bentivoglio seized his talisman again and glared at Dominic. He muttered something in Italian that did not sound complimentary.

"I'll take care of it, Professore," said Dominic in a flat tone. Bentivoglio grunted and jerked his head toward me.

"Keep the zocolla away from it."

And then he left.

The three of us couldn't quite meet one another's eyes after that. There could not have been much doubt in any of our minds as to what *zocolla* meant, but as none of us had revealed a great knowledge of Italian to the others, we could pretend.

"Signore Bentivoglio is really very tired," said my father, with a tentative look at me. "I think he must have stayed up all night last night."

"And the night before," said Dominic.

I did not reply to this. I had gone without sleep for alchemy's sake many times and never behaved so rudely to those around me. My mother's patrons may have occasionally come in for a sharp word or two, but Bentivoglio had seemed nearly on the verge of violence.

"Well, well." Vellacott cleared his throat, covering my disapproving silence. "You certainly did not disappoint, dear Thea. If anything, your mother's letter may have sold you short!"

I looked up at him sharply. Sold me short? Then it was as I feared, and my mother had complained of my shortcomings to him. She must have mentioned her concerns about my lack of dedication, my occasional rebelliousness. Perhaps she had even told my father about Will . . .

"Alas, I can't stay." Vellacott pulled a watch from his pocket. "I have a tutorial in—oh dear—"

He cast an uncomfortable look in my direction. With another pang of disappointment, weaker this time now that I was becoming accustomed to them, I realized he did not want to be seen walking back to the college with me.

"I'll stay here, if you don't mind," I said. "I can help Dominic for a while."

"Oh." Vellacott's face cleared instantly. "I'm sure he would be quite grateful; thank you, Thea."

Dominic said nothing as my father took his leave. He placed a few more lumps of coal under the brazier and watched them catch the heat of the fire and glow orange.

"So you are Mr. Vellacott's niece?"

He did not look at me as he asked it. I knew, now, that this was his usual mode of address, but even so it accented the skepticism of his question.

"You heard what he said." At that moment, I did not feel inclined to lie for my father.

"Is your mother his sister?" he asked.

"No," I said.

"So your father is his brother, then."

Irked by his sarcasm, I kept what I hoped was a dignified silence. I wandered to the bookshelf to examine my father's collection more closely. A few minutes revealed that
my initial suspicion was correct. I saw nothing of the Jābiran corpus, the works from which we had collected our
instructions for the Stone. Of course, this could hardly be
the whole of my father's alchemical library. He would only
keep copies here, and the more valuable books were most
likely in his office.

"What languages do you have, between the three of
you?" I asked.

Dominic, who was crouched next to the fire, sat back
on his haunches.

"The usual ones," he said. "I'm not much use—just enough
Latin to keep up. Professore Bentivoglio has German be-
sides Italian, and Mr. Vellacott has good Latin and Greek.
And French, of course."

I suppressed a scornful laugh. Fewer than I had by
two, even among all three of them.

"No Spanish or Arabic?" I asked. "What do you do
about Jābir's texts, then?"

"Nothing," said Dominic. "We don't have them."

They were the usual Western alchemists, then. Too certain
of their superiority to look to other traditions—especially
Islamic ones. My suspicion confirmed, I turned from the
bookcase. The White Elixir was a great achievement on
its own. It had the power to change any of the base metals into silver. This was the penultimate dream of every
alchemist, one that most would never achieve. But it was
also the substance from which the Philosopher's Stone
was made. And my father and his friends would not know

how to continue—not without Arabic and Jābir. So, not without me.

I had come here intending to replicate my mother's notes and produce the Stone. But I wanted to do it for myself, take the credit, and return with it to France and heal Mother. I had no intention of handing over the fruit of centuries of labor to my unworthy father and his rude colleague, simply because I had no other recourse but to use his laboratory. It occurred to me that this was why my mother hadn't wanted to send me to him. She would want him to take credit for our work even less than I did. I thought of the Marquis. It was too late now, of course, to find him and accept his patronage. We had insulted him too thoroughly. But perhaps my mother had been right to prefer him to my father. I pushed the painful thought aside.

I had not thought it all through, it seemed. I hadn't reckoned on jealous, hovering alchemists marking my every move. For some reason it had not occurred to me that my father would certainly be as unwilling to yield the Stone up to me as I was to yield it up to him or anyone else. My hand went to my pocket again, and the page with my mother's instructions. Why work for my father's glory, when I could never benefit from it? His endowed chair, his department of alchemy would never be anything to me. I glanced at Dominic, still hunched over and staring patiently into the fire.

"Why do you work for Vellacott, if you can't be a student?" I asked Dominic.

Dominic didn't look up, but I could read his attention from the crease of his brow.

"Beats being a bargeman," said Dominic. "And he pays me well enough."

I couldn't stop myself from scowling at that.

"You work for an hourly wage so that he can have unlimited wealth?"

"Does he pay you better?"

"I'm an alchemist, not a hireling."

He raised his eyebrows into the fire.

"Then you gave him the White Elixir for nothing, not even my hourly wage."

I wanted to argue, but this was too much like my own thoughts. I considered leaving, walking back toward High Street. I had money in my pocket, enough for a coach to London. Will might have some kind of workroom.

"I plan to be a medical doctor," said Dominic with the reticence of someone making a confession. "Mr. Vellacott says he'll sponsor my studies in another year. Sooner, might be, if the elixir turns out as it ought."

"You don't want to be an alchemist?" I asked.

"No, miss," said Dominic. "I've seen enough of it to know I don't want to spend my life grinding and melting down metals in hopes of turning them into other metals. I'd rather be some use to somebody."

It occurred to me that I might have said something very like this to my mother in a rebellious fit, but that did not stop me from reacting to Dominic's dismissive summary with anger.

"Certainly, if that were all there is to it. But the true aim of alchemy is more than just transmuting metals, you must know that. The Philosopher's Stone brings power over nature herself. You could do more good curing the sick with it than any doctor could."

"You believe that?" Dominic shook his head. "One thing to say you can turn one metal into another metal. I don't understand it, but maybe it's so. But to have power over nature? That's magic, that is. And if that magic's real, then it's dangerous."

"You sound like a country priest." I had one in mind, in fact. A nearsighted, half-literate fellow who found out my mother's work and came around to condemn her for it in shrill preacher's tones. "Any great power is dangerous, of course it is. Electricity is dangerous, but that doesn't mean it shouldn't be explored and used."

"You're talking about the Elixir of Life, not electricity. That's not science. Mr. Vellacott says—"

"Mr. Vellacott couldn't read the Kitāb al-Rahma even if he had it," I snapped, thinking of the months I had spent poring over Jābir's texts. "He hasn't bothered to learn Arabic—he knows nothing of the whole Shi'a tradition. Don't quote him to me like he's some kind of master sage."

Dominic raised his brows at me again, and I clenched my jaw, worried I had said too much. He might be tight-lipped, but Dominic seemed loyal to my father, and might very well tell him whatever I said. Little though he could do with the information without Arabic, I didn't want to give him anything else for free.

I took down a book and flipped it open angrily. Dominic went back to his work. We did not speak for over an hour, until Dominic's stomach make a loud, discontented noise.

"Go, get something to eat," I said. "I can watch it."

Dominic glanced at the door, then at me, then back at the fire. He made no move to get up.

"Fine," I said, suppressing my irritation. "I will bring you something."

Out of the laboratory, the chill morning had turned to a damp afternoon. I thought I would wander a bit before going back to the inn for food. I pulled my shawl closer and walked down the narrow alley between the buildings, toward the street. My head buzzed with plans and schemes to make the Stone and abscond with it, none of them very practical. I considered whether I ought to tell my father the truth and make some kind of bargain with him. I could give him the texts with my mother's notes if he let me have the first Stone.

My mind was not on my surroundings as a man leapt from a shadowed doorway directly into my path. Before I could do more than gasp, he had dragged me into the doorway and pressed me against the wall.

It was Bentivoglio. I gasped against his hand over my mouth while his other delved in my clothes. I couldn't scream, but I pulled my head up just enough to bite down on his fingers. He cried out and pushed my head back into the wall. Pain exploded everything into whiteness, and I screamed until his hand clamped onto my mouth and nose, stifling sound and breath. I grabbed his hand with both of mine and managed to pull it down enough to gulp down air. His other hand fumbled against my thigh, but I was too much occupied with keeping my lungs filled to interfere. His face was inches from mine, and as I gasped I caught his breath full in my face. It smelled of sulfur.

"Professore!"

Dominic's voice sliced through the mist, sharp and commanding.

"Holy mother, what are you doing? Let her go!"

The professor let me go at once and ran. Without his body pressing me against the wall I slid to the ground. My legs had turned to liquid and pain blackened my sight. I put my hand to the back of my head and drew it away damp with blood. Dominic was shouting. I hardly heard, felt, or saw anything. The smell of sulfurous breath, real or remembered, blocked out everything else.

"Thea? Did he hurt you? I heard you scream—"

Dominic was beside me, crouched on his heels. I shook my head, then looked down at the blood on my hand.

"My head."

The pain was starting to come on in sharp, stabbing flashes. Dominic turned my head slightly to look, then frowned.

"We should get you inside. My mother's house is close by. Can you walk?"

It turned out that I could. I took his arm and walked without knowing where. The pain was beginning to fade to a dull ache, but without its immediate distraction my fear grew. Bentivoglio's attack was too much like another one.

We went down a flight of steps off the street to a below-ground door. Dominic unlocked it and helped me to the first chair inside. It was dark, the only light from the door and a narrow, high window that peeked out onto the street level. Dominic lit a kerosene lamp, illuminating a small but very tidy little home. There was a basket of knitting beside my chair, an emblem of domesticity that was as strange and fascinating to me as an alchemist's crucible might be to another girl.

Dominic brought a pitcher and cloth, and pulled a chair beside me.

"Do you knit?" I asked.

"What?"

I pointed to the knitting basket, and Dominic's face cleared.

"My mother's," he said. "May I?"

I looked at him. Part of my mind was racing, faraway. The part left in the room was stunned and lagging.

"Your head," he said. "I'd like to clean it and make sure the bleeding has stopped."

I nodded. The cool cloth on the back of my head stung, bringing me back to myself.

"The scrape isn't so bad," said Dominic. "The scalp bleeds a lot, but the wound is small. As long as you aren't concussed . . ."

"Cave Maledictionem Alchemistae," I muttered.

Dominic drew back.

"Sorry?"

"I thought you had enough Latin to keep up," I said.

"Beware—?"

"Beware the Alchemist's Curse," I said. Goose pimples pricked at my arms, and the chill fear I'd been pushing down washed over me.

"I'm a fool," I whispered. "I should have seen it."

"You aren't a fool," said Dominic. But he didn't know. He didn't understand any of this, and his face showed it plainly.

"This morning, Vellacott said Bentivoglio wasn't himself," I said.

"Yes," agreed Dominic, and his face flashed anger. "I wouldn't have believed him capable— But I was wrong."

"You were right," I said. "He isn't himself. And soon he will be even less so. It will get worse. I've seen how the Alchemist's Curse ends."

"The Alchemist's Curse?" Dominic looked from my face to the wound on my head, clearly concluding I was concussed after all.

"My mother," I said, closing my eyes against the memory. "She is mad now, completely mad. Her breath smelled like sulfur, and so did Professore Bentivoglio's. She tried to kill me."

Dominic's eyes widened even farther.

"But—but Bentivoglio wasn't trying to kill you."

"I told you, it will get worse. Look."

I reached into my pocket to show him the text with the Jābiran warning, and my mother's notes. But they were gone. The vial of transmuting agent was as well. All at once I understood why Bentivoglio had been rifling through my clothes.

"He took it! He has my mother's notes!"

I tried to stand up, but Dominic put a hand on my shoulder to keep me seated. Panic rose as I imagined Bentivoglio, red-eyed, copying down everything my mother had written, copying the text and my translation of it, taking all our work for himself. My head spun, and I doubled over.

"We can get them back," he said. "Please, don't fret."

"I have to get them back now, right now!"

Another thought occurred to me, making me gasp.

"It will make him worse! Vae illi, qui non accipit—woe to whom the Stone doesn't accept . . ."

I fell silent, working it through. If the same affliction had befallen Bentivoglio and my mother, then I could no longer brush aside the warnings in my mother's notes. It seemed they had both been rejected by the Stone— whatever that meant. Perhaps they had made the same mistake in their steps, or they were both unworthy . . .

Unworthy. My mind seized the thought with hope. Yes, that could certainly be the case. I thought of my mother, with her hot anger and cold contempt. Not so different from Bentivoglio and his insults. Both had benefitted from my work without acknowledgment or gratitude. And if it was that, then perhaps I was not unworthy, and needn't worry about falling victim to their fate.

"We have to go," I said, coming back to myself. "We have to get my papers."

Dominic's brow knitted, and he seemed to be consider- ing his next words carefully. I jumped to my feet, and this time threw off Dominic's hand.

"We should get Mr. Vellacott," he said. "I can't force Professore Bentivoglio to do anything on my own."

I hesitated, and my heart sank as my mind worked it through. We needed my father to get back my papers. My secret was over. He would see the papers, and if he broke the code they would show him how to follow the path to the Stone without my help. Even if he could not break the code, he would surely try to force me to translate for him. I would either have to flee or help him, and if I helped him, the best I could hope for then was that he might let me use it to cure my mother. My father would be the Stone's creator and discoverer, even if he did none of the work himself and thus avoided the curse. I would become a footnote, mentioned as an apprentice if at all. And yet I could not take on Bentivoglio on my own. He had already overpowered me thoroughly once.

"Yes, yes, all right," I said bitterly. "Let's go."

We walked quickly through the town, back to High Street and the forbidding walls of Oriel College. Spells of dizziness assailed me more than once, but adrenaline and Dominic's arm kept me upright. At the porter's gate, Dominic looked me over, uncertain.

"Maybe you should wait here," he said.

And indeed, if I had drawn stares yesterday with my French clothes, I would draw still more with blood all over them. I knotted my hands into my skirts, but the blood was dry now and didn't come off.

"No." I hadn't done this. A furious pressure in my chest was staring to release. I hadn't shoved my own head into a wall, any more than I had conceived myself out of wedlock. Let the right people feel shame. I wouldn't bear it for them.

I followed Dominic across the quad again. It was midafternoon now, and students wandered through it holding their books and staring openly at me. We went into a hall, up a stairway, and through a library. The library was gorgeous: wood-paneled, stain-glassed, and smelling of good leather and old paper. I forced down a pang of longing as we left it and stopped in front of my father's office. I heard voices inside. Dominic hesitated, his hand raised to knock on the door. He looked at me, wide-eyed and alarmed.

"Bentivoglio," he whispered. "He's inside with Mr. Vellacott."

My pulse rose, and I pounded my fist against the door. Inside, the voices stopped. My father opened the door. His eyes widened, then he stuck his head out the doorway to look up and down the hall. He pulled us inside and closed the door firmly behind him.

"Did anyone see you?" he gasped. He kneaded his hands together.

"Yes. A good many people," I said coldly. But I had no time to spare for irritation with my father. I fixed my narrowed eyes on Bentivoglio, who held my papers in his thieving hands.

"Those are mine," I said. "Give them back."

I stepped forward and tried to grab them, but Bentivoglio held them away. I examined his face, keeping my anger at bay. His eyes were red, but he was not quite mad yet. There was a trace of shame on his face. He hadn't yet left his own mind entirely.

"He attacked me." I said it to Bentivoglio's face. "He threw me against a wall and stole those papers out of my clothes."

"I am terribly sorry, Thea. I'm afraid there has been some . . . some misunderstanding," said my father. "But please, sit down, my dear. You shouldn't tax yourself—you've been hurt—"

"By him!" I exclaimed, whirling on my father. "I was hurt by your guest while he robbed me! I insist you make him give me back my papers!"

"Do not presume to order me around in my own study!" My father took my arm and conveyed me forcibly into a chair. Shock silenced me, and I stared up at him with hatred.

"You must calm yourself, Thea." My father looked abashed as he attempted to slow his breathing. "There is nothing to be gained by this shouting."

"Give me back my papers," I repeated.

Vellacott ignored this. He took his own seat, behind his desk, and rubbed his face with his hands.

"Miss Hope. I was rough with you, not like a gentleman. For that, my apologies." Bentivoglio inclined his head, then turned to my father. "But, Professore Vellacott, she may be a spy, perhaps of her mother's. These notes prove she lies to you."

"What?" I cried.

"No, no," demurred my father. He folded his hands in front of him on the desk. "I should not like to think you a spy, Thea. But clearly there is something to what Professore Bentivoglio says. It does at least seem you have not been telling me the whole truth."

Heat rushed to my face. My mind thrummed with outraged retorts. I wanted to scream at him, but I clenched my jaw shut until I was in control again.

"I am not the liar here," I said.

My father flushed.

"Sir," Dominic began. He was still standing by the door. I did not have to look at him to sense his unease. "Sir, I saw what happened. Professore Bentivoglio attacked her. Don't you see the blood, Professor? He did that—"

"Yes, thank you, Dominic," said my father, shooting

him a forbidding look. "I am quite aware of what has happened."

"But—how can you be, sir, when you've only had his word—"

"Enough, Dominic," said my father. "Thank you for assisting Miss Hope. You may go."

Dominic hesitated. I felt his eyes on me, but I stared ahead, stone-faced.

"Miss Hope—" Dominic said to me, but then my father was on his feet.

"Are you Miss Hope's apprentice or mine?" he demanded. "Get out!"

The door opened and closed, and I knew he was gone. Vellacott held out his hand to Bentivoglio, who handed him the papers with evident reluctance. I saw my letter from Will, removed from its envelope and unfolded. My stomach plunged.

"Where did you get this text, Thea? And the notes?" asked my father.

I ground my teeth together and said nothing.

"I assume the notes are your mother's? It looks as though—" He stared intently at the bottom of the paper with my incomplete decryptions. "It can't be, of course, but it seems as though Meg thought she had reached the final stage for making the Philosopher's Stone itself."

"She did," I said. "Right before she went mad."

"Mad? Oh yes. Do you mean that her notes are unreliable? The steps she took seem clear enough. Fascinating, in fact. She was operating under the mercury-sulfur theory of the elements—though in a form with which I am not quite familiar—and seems to believe that it worked."

I remembered the shining, ruby-red substance. It was exactly as every famous alchemist had said it should be. In another minute or two it would have hardened into the Stone, just as Jābir described.

"That's not what I mean." I sounded faint to myself, as if I were speaking from under a blanket. "She went mad after the notes. And he will, too," I said, looking up at Bentivoglio. My anger was draining out of me. "You can tell it's happening, can't you?"

The light from the stained-glass window behind him made Bentivoglio's dark hair glow orange. His eyes narrowed, but there was fear there, mixed with anger and hatred. No, he wasn't worthy to make the Stone. If it had rejected my mother, of course it would reject him.

"You need help," I said to Bentivoglio. "You do not want what is coming next. Believe me. I've seen it."

"What in heaven's name are you talking about, Thea?" Vellacott demanded.

"The curse," I said. "The madness. Cave Maledictionem Alchemistae, Professor."

Professore Bentivoglio's face twisted into an expression of rage that was too familiar. I did not smell the sulfur, but I could imagine it. My hands tightened on the arms of the chair. But it was only an instant, and then the lines of rage twisted again into an expression of terror.

He knew. He could feel it. But he stormed from the room, throwing the door open with a violence that made my father wince. Bentivoglio pushed past Dominic, who was standing just outside.

"Keep him out of your laboratory," I said to my father without looking at him.

"He needs rest." Vellacott sat heavily in his chair. "A good night's sleep will set him right."

"No, it won't," I said, but without energy. I was suddenly tired, too tired to fight a doomed battle to convince my father of things he refused to believe. He shifted in his chair and glanced at the door.

"Dominic—shut the door, will you?" he said.

Dominic stepped back inside the office and closed the door behind him.

"Miss Hope," my father began, twisting his hands together on the desk in front of him. "I have been thinking about your position here . . ."

I knew at once. He was going to try to send me away. My low spirits sank further.

"It's difficult, very difficult." Vellacott glanced up at Dominic and frowned. He seemed to consider sending him out again, but perhaps concluded that having a witness to the shameful things he was about to say was better than being left alone with me. "Even though you are my niece, there is a certain lack of propriety to your staying in my rooms. And there are no rooms to be spared at the Tackley for you to have your own, for the moment. And in any case, I find myself somewhat low on funds . . ."

I felt weightless, floating above myself. I belonged nowhere. I could drift away from the earth, into the void, and leave no mark behind. Merely some uncompleted work that my father would finish if he could, and take the credit for. I couldn't look at him. I couldn't look at Dominic, whose pity I felt from across the room. I looked out through the arched diamond window that looked over the grassy quadrangle below. What a lovely view my father had from his comfortable study. What a lovely life. Naturally, he didn't want me here, complicating it. Ruining it.

"I'll go," I said. "If you give me my papers, I'll go now."

"Ah," he said. "Yes. Well . . ."

I stared him down. He had no decent response to this. He simply would not do it. And I would not leave without them.

"But—" Dominic broke in, casting a wary glance at my father. "But where would you go?"

It was a good question. I knew only one person who might have me in England, and going to him would be a shameful impropriety. But he would at least be glad to see me. I pictured his face breaking into a smile of surprise and delight. My heart seized with homesickness for him at the thought. I would get the papers back, somehow, and then I would go.

"London," I said with decision.

I would bear the unseemliness. I needed Will more than I needed an intact reputation. He would help me. If he did not have a laboratory of his own, then he would know someone who could help me set one up. I needed a patron, someone to provide the funds and equipment. I did not need a father. And even if I did, I would not find one here.

"London?" repeated Vellacott hopefully. "You—you have family there?"

"You know I don't," I snapped.

"Then . . . perhaps . . . friends?"

I settled back into my chair and glared at him. Friends? No. I did not have more than one friend in London. If I had more than one friend in the world, I did not know who he was. He certainly wasn't Edward Vellacott.

"Sir . . ." said Dominic. "Maybe . . . maybe Miss Hope would be willing to stay at my mother's house. With my mother and me. Just until something else can be arranged."

Dominic stared at the floor, glancing at my father and then back down, like he was ashamed. Not of himself, I realized. Or of me, either.

"That's a fine idea, Dominic, yes," said my father, seizing gratefully on it. "Why don't you take her there at once. Miss Hope, you need rest. We will talk about . . . other matters . . . later."

I considered making an undignified scramble for my papers, but he had shut them in his desk. It was pointless. I stood.

"Give me back the letter, at least," I said, blushing. "It is personal. And nothing to do with alchemy."

My father had the decency to blush as well. He cleared his throat.

"Yes," he said, opening the drawer. "Yes, of course."

He took out the letter and handed it over. I had no doubt at all, from the way he avoided my gaze, that he had read the whole thing. It was not in its envelope. I took the letter and returned it to the pocket of my skirts. I went to the door.

"Thea . . ." said my father. "I'm . . . I am sorry about all this."

And he did sound sorry. Wretched, even. But he wasn't sorry enough to give me my papers back. Not sorry enough to offer me a place to stay. His wretchedness was of no use to me. I kept walking, and Dominic shut the door behind us.

We retraced our steps in silence, through the beautiful library, down the paneled staircase. Through the stone archway and down the stone steps that led into the green quadrangle, past the questioning, hostile stares. Back out the imposing gate, into the street where we belonged.

The sun was already setting. A gloomy mist had fallen,

thick enough to obscure the turrets of the college gate before we had gone a block. It wasn't until we were half-way back to his mother's flat that Dominic noticed I was lagging behind him and offered me his arm. A well-bred young man would have offered it at once. Will, for in-stance, would never have allowed the opportunity to pay me a kind attention pass by unfulfilled.

No, Dominic wasn't well-bred. I didn't like to think of myself as a snob. In this respect at least I fancied myself as good a republican as Will, as skeptical of aristocracy as he was and always ready to listen to his eloquence on the subject of the common man. And yet I had been very aware of Dominic's lower-class status, and close to dismissing him for it. His barely erased slum accent, his unrefined table manners, hourly wage, and underground, street-facing flat—they had all counted against him in my mind, even if I wouldn't have admitted it.

And yet now he was taking me in when my own well-bred father had turned me out. He'd protected me from Bentivoglio when Vellacott wished to pretend nothing had happened. He walked with his head bent toward the ground, and his arm was stiff and uncomfortable under mine, but when I slowed he glanced down at me with real concern, and a rush of fondness toward him flowed through me along with an unwelcome urge to weep.

"Just about there, Miss Hope," he said.

I nodded. The narrow, dim street we turned down looked familiar. Dominic pointed down the street, and in a few dozen more yards we stepped off the street and went down into his mother's flat. Dominic produced a basin of water, and I washed the blood from my hands.

"You might want to rest. Best to lie down a bit, for your head," said Dominic. "There's, ah, there's only two bedrooms. You can have mine. Just give me a minute—it's a bit of a mess."

Dominic vanished into a very low door off the tiny kitchen and the sounds of hasty tidying emerged: a chair being pulled along the floor, things being tossed. Dominic returned a few moments later looking rueful.

"It's still a bit of a mess," he said. "I wish I had somewhere better to offer you."

"It will be fine," I said. "Please don't worry about that. It's terribly kind of you."

"It's nothing," said Dominic, and shifted his weight. He hovered on the edge of saying something else for a moment, his mouth slightly open. Then he shook his head. "You take some rest. I'll go get your things from Tackley's."

I thought of him lugging my trunk down High Street and was ashamed.

"I'm sorry about all this, Dominic," I said. "You shouldn't have to do any of it."

"No, I'm sorry," said Dominic. "I'm sorry about Mr. Vellacott. This isn't how I would have hoped he'd act."

"You don't have to apologize for him." Now I was the one staring at the floor. "He isn't your father."

Dominic cleared his throat. "No," he said. "But he's my boss. He gave me a chance no one else would have, for no reason except he thought I might have promise. I . . . I thought better of him than this."

I didn't have a reply for that. I went to the door of his room, and he went out and up the stairs.

Dominic's bedroom was small, dark, low-ceilinged, and,

as he had warned, still messy. It had no window, so I left the door open to allow the faint light from the rest of the apartment to filter in. I dropped onto Dominic's short pallet of a bed. With my body's collapse came another interior one. I was too exhausted, too shaken to guard against it any longer. I wept long and hard.

I was still weeping when Dominic returned.

He pulled the trunk up to the door of his room and then stood there, uncertain. I tried to stop sobbing, but I had broken my defenses by letting myself cry. I couldn't put them back up quickly.

"I'm sorry," I wept. I turned my face into the pillow to at least muffle the mortifyingly broken sounds.

"No, don't be," said Dominic. He hesitated in the doorway a moment, then walked away with rapid steps. He reappeared holding a lit oil lamp. He set it down on a table in the corner, stacked with books and a ghoulish shape that made me gasp and sit upright.

"What's that?" I asked, pointing at what looked like a human skull.

"What?" He looked. "Oh. It's . . . ah . . . it's a skull."

"A real one?"

Dominic nodded.

The shock of finding myself in a room with someone's former head had knocked the sobs out of me. I took long, shallow breaths and looked from Dominic, to the skull, to Dominic.

"Why?"

"Memento mori," he said. "It was my grandfather's."

"That's your grandfather's skull?!" I asked in disbelief.

"No, no," he said. "I mean—yes, he owned it, but no,

that wasn't his head. He was a weaver. Kept it on his mantle to remind him, well . . ."

"That he was going to die?"

Dominic nodded again. He sat on a three-legged stool by the table and leaned toward me, his elbows on his knees.

"I shouldn't think that would be easy to forget," I said.

"Easier than you'd think," said Dominic. "If we all remembered death and judgment are coming, we'd be more careful how we live. Maybe I should give my skull to your father."

I looked at him. He knew it, and I knew that he knew it. But this was the first time it had been acknowledged between us.

"I can't believe you sleep in a room with a human skull," I muttered.

Dominic looked behind him, then around his dark hole of a room.

"I guess it's pretty gloomy in here," he said with a frown. "Not good for much of anything but sleeping."

And not much good for that, either, though I didn't say so.

"I don't think I can sleep," I said.

"It's close to suppertime. We could go to a pub. Are you hungry?"

I wasn't really. I felt spent and my head ached, but Dominic was right about his room, and I itched to get out of it. I rose from the pallet; answer enough.

"You'll want to change," said Dominic. "I'll get your trunk."

When he had closed the door behind him, I opened the trunk and sorted through my dresses by the light of the oil lamp. I had gathered by now that my stylish Parisian clothing raised eyebrows here in Oxford. The fabrics were too light, the layers were too few, and the whole effect was much too foreign. My simplest dress by far was the one I wore now, the gray round dress, but it was bloody. I pulled out an embroidered white muslin, the second simplest. Everyone was wearing gowns like these in Paris now. Floaty cotton muslin was seen as natural, unaffected, unaristocratic. Naturally all the aristocrats had adopted the fashion. I put on the dress and my green bonnet and was aware despite the dim light and lack of looking glass that I did not look like an Oxford lady. I sighed, picked up the lamp, and went out of the room.

Dominic stood by the front door, waiting, hands in his pockets. He looked up as I emerged, and his eyebrows lifted.

"You look very . . ."

"French?" I supplied with a sigh.

"Well . . . yes," he said. "Maybe a shawl?"

I agreed, and Dominic produced a brown knitted thing from his mother's room, which decidedly dampened the stylish effect of the outfit. When we climbed up to the street, I was glad to have it. The misty twilight had turned into a damp and gloomy evening. I pulled the shawl tighter, and we went west, away from Oriel College, through narrow gaslit streets. Not far away, but shrouded in thick fog, an even taller, even more aggressively walled fortress rose above us.

"Which college is that?" I asked, pointing to the highest of its towers.

"That's not a college. It's Oxford Castle. Used as a prison now."

We went around the castle and over the old moat that had been dug into a canal. Tenements and shabby store-fronts lined the waterway. Bargemen pulled a loaded vessel along the canal from the footpath. There were no under-graduates here. Dominic noticed my look and bit his lip.

"I hope it's all right with you, coming over this side of the canal," he said. "The pubs by the colleges are all full of stu-dents at this hour. I thought you might be tired of them."

I was. We went toward a square, three-story brick build-ing that spilled a smell of mutton over the musty scent of the canal. A sign hanging over the door read NAG'S HEAD, with a rough picture of a work horse under it.

I had never been to an English pub, of course. My mother had spoken of them occasionally, without fondness. She said the food was greasy and yet dry, and that no civilized person drank beer when they could have wine. I resolved to enjoy whatever the Nag's Head had to offer.

Dominic opened the door for me, and I stepped into a room not very much brighter though much warmer than Dominic's sleeping hole. A big brick fireplace was the central feature, with the bar to its side. Tables were se-questered by wooden beams that made each one its own little room. The wooden benches and low ceilings enclos-ing each table put me in mind of the cabin of a schooner. Dominic led me to the table closest to the fire, then went to the bar and ordered in a low voice. The bartender nodded my way and asked about me. Dominic murmured a reply I did not try to hear. He would surely find some way not to lie about me, but still, I was in no mood to hear any further half-truths to explain away my inconvenient ex-istence.

My head ached. I lowered it onto my hands and pictured my father, little though I wanted to. Poring over my notes. Decoding them, perhaps. And giving them to Bentivoglio. Cold horror pricked down my arms, despite the fire, and I clutched the shawl tighter over my shoulders. Dominic sat down across from me and his eyes widened with alarm at the look on my face.

"Are you unwell?"

"Dominic—do you believe me?" His forehead furrowed in confusion, and I continued on. "Do you believe me, that Bentivoglio is going mad? About the curse?"

Dominic looked away, back toward the bar.

"I don't give much credit to curses, Miss Hope," he murmured. "I believe you about your mother. And the professor isn't himself, sure enough. But a curse on alchemy . . ."

"What happened to my mother isn't natural. I didn't credit curses, either, but it's like you said: what we try to do *is* magic, and we believe it can be done because great alchemists have gone so far in the past—"

"*You* believe it can be done," said Dominic, shaking his head. "I don't. As for the madness, maybe it's something to do with the metals, with the smoke, something of that kind. But whatever drove your mother mad, there's some kind of explanation."

"No," I said. "You didn't see her. There was no natural explanation for that. It wasn't just madness. She was strong, stronger than her patron. Nature can't do that."

Dominic looked away again. "Maybe . . . the shock of it . . ."

Hopelessness gnawed at me. If even Dominic didn't believe me, I wouldn't convince anyone. Bentivoglio would work from my notes, following the same process that made my mother mad. There was nothing I could do.

"I'll talk to your father tomorrow," said Dominic. "See if I can get your notes back for you, at least."

"He'll have copied them by now," I said. At the thought of it, anger stabbed at me, fine and sharp as a needle. "And you don't have to call him my father. He isn't really. He didn't know I existed before yesterday, and he isn't going to acknowledge me."

"He might. He could change his mind. Come around. Realize what he's doing." Dominic glanced at me, then quickly away. "You're the spit of him, you know."

"That only makes me more of a problem," I said bitterly. "Harder to hide our relationship. He doesn't want anything to do with me, nor I with him. As soon as I get my papers, I'll go to London."

"What's in London?"

"A friend," I said.

Dominic waited for more, but I did not give it. Our meal came: cold mutton, brown bread, and two pints of watered ale. Despite my resolve, I began to doubt my ability to enjoy the pub's humble fare. I took a few bites, and a long sip of the weak ale.

"We moved here for the canal," said Dominic. "My father was a digger."

"A canal digger?"

Dominic nodded. "Then they finished the work, two years ago. There wasn't enough barging work for all the diggers. And he—ah—he wasn't the most reliable of them. He went back to London, said he'd send for us when he had work."

Dominic hunched over his platter, a knife in one hand and a fork in the other.

"I gather he didn't," I said.

"No," he said. "But I went after him anyway. Thought I could work, too, help him save up faster. Turned out he wasn't saving up anything, because he spent every half-penny on gin."

"I'm sorry," I said.

We fell silent and ate to the sound of forks scraping the pewter plates.

"Not sure why I told you that," said Dominic after a few moments. He sounded almost angry at himself.

"You're telling me you understand what it's like to have a disappointing father," I said. "It's kind of you."

"I suppose that's right," said Dominic with a sigh. "But my father drank himself to death last winter. He doesn't get any more chances. And even though I waited for him, and nothing came of it . . . Still, I'd give him another chance if I could."

My eyebrows shot up.

"You think my father deserves another chance?" I asked. The question came out sharper than I meant it, and Dominic looked up.

"No," he said, shaking his head. "Not that he deserves it. Just that you might want to give him one anyway."

"I don't." I set my fork down on the table and leaned back against the wooden wall.

"Give him a week," said Dominic. "Please. I think he'll change his mind. I know, it probably seems an eternity to stay in our place . . ."

"It is an eternity," I said sharply. "Not to stay in your

home, I don't mind that, but to wait on someone who doesn't want me, who has already rejected me—"

"That's your pride talking."

"Of course it is! Why shouldn't my pride have a say in this, if it will keep me from any further humiliations?" I demanded. "I have enough experience giving chances to a parent who doesn't deserve them and will only use them to hurt me!"

Dominic stared down at his plate. I bit down on my lip, regretting my outburst of emotion. Dominic would think I pitied myself, which was the last thing I wanted anyone to think. I opened my mouth to take it back, somehow, but he spoke first.

"You mean your mother," he said quietly.

I considered brushing it away, but Dominic was looking right at me, for once, with a calm sort of sympathy in his eyes. It wasn't pity, and I found I didn't mind it. So I nodded.

"Was she like that before she went mad?" he said.

"Oh yes. The madness had nothing to do with it, if that's what you mean," I said. "She was simply . . ."

I trailed off. There was no single word to describe Marguerite Hope. She wasn't simply anything. I sighed.

"She is brilliant," I said. "The only well-known woman alchemist in the world. She had to be ruthless. She never had time to be patient with anyone's weakness."

"Not even yours," Dominic said.

"Especially not mine," I said. "I had to be as good as she was, from before I could remember. Anything less wasn't good enough. And of course I was usually less. But then, once I started to be more—"

Dominic nodded like he understood. But he didn't, not

really. Even I didn't fully understand what had happened. Why my mother had turned on me.

"There was a time when I was simply a part of her," I said. "And she was hard on me because she was hard on herself. I understood that. I didn't mind it so much."

"But something changed?" Dominic asked.

"Yes."

I knew who had changed things, though not why he had changed them. It shouldn't have come as such a terrible shock to her that I, at sixteen, would find her charming young apprentice fascinating. She had thought Will was worthwhile enough to employ when he came to us and asked to learn from her. But the moment she caught me expressing an idea that had come from him instead of her, she started to look at me with horror. Like her own hand had started grasping things of its own accord, and without her consent. Finding us together that morning had only been the excuse. Mother had wanted to banish him from the first time I had smiled at him when she had not.

"She discovered that I wished to belong to myself, instead of her," I said. "And she found that unacceptable."

"When was that?" Dominic asked.

"About a year ago. I thought it might get better, over time."

After she threw Will out, I was angry, of course. Rebellious. As harsh as she was, sometimes. But I repented, too. I offered abject apologies more than once. I still remembered the smug expression with which she received them, and then stored them up to fling back at me the next time we quarreled.

"I humbled myself," I concluded. "And she only used it to make me more ashamed."

"But you're not the one who should be ashamed in any of this," said Dominic. "Your father is. And whatever he seems to you now, he knows that much."

I thought of my father's downcast expression as I had left, and I knew Dominic was right.

"His shame is no use to me if it doesn't change his actions," I said.

"That's true," Dominic said. "But I still think he might change. You're just the kind of daughter he would want. You're talented, and strong, and sharp as glass, and I know he sees that. He's going to regret sending you away. Maybe he does already."

I shook my head against the painful hope tightening in my chest. Unwelcome tears pricked my eyes. I scowled them away. Dominic had seen enough of those today. He wouldn't think I was so strong if I broke down in tears every time he said a kind thing to me.

"Please, Miss Hope. Just a few days. You need the rest anyway, before you attempt a journey," he said.

I cleared my throat thickly, and took a deep drink of my ale.

A few days wasn't so long. Dominic knew my father better than I did. Perhaps he would be sorry tomorrow. What harm was there in finding out?

"A few days," I agreed. "Just a few days."

I spent that night in Dominic's room. He took the skull
out and slept in the parlor. His mother would not arrive
home until well after we were both asleep. She worked
long hours, he explained. Came home late, left early. Once
he was a doctor, he hoped she wouldn't have to anymore.

I awoke the next day in darkness, to pounding at the
front door. I dressed quickly and opened the door to see
my father standing in the glare of noonday. I blinked furiously as my eyes adjusted to the light, trying not to be
irritated at Dominic that he had left me to sleep half the
day away.

"What do you want?" I demanded.

"Thea," said Vellacott. "May I come in?"

I peered at him and considered it. He appeared abashed.
A small hope nagged at me, planted by Dominic. I felt like

a fool to even find it in my heart. But there it was, small but insistent.

Perhaps he was here to apologize, and more importantly, to take me back in. To make it right. I glanced behind me, into the dismal, dim parlor, then back outside. It was a fine, warm day, of the sort I had assumed England never had.

"No," I said. "We can walk."

I stepped out and closed the door behind me. My father offered me his arm, and I pretended not to notice. We had turned off Dominic's street when my father spoke.

"I want to apologize, Thea," he said quietly. "For yesterday. For how I handled things."

I waited. An apology alone was not enough. He had apologized yesterday, as well, and still kept my papers, still turned me out.

"I hardly slept last night, thinking about it," he said. "I'm ashamed of myself."

I glanced at him and found that he looked it. My small, unwilling hope grew.

"I hope you will find it in yourself to accept my apology and come back to the Tackley." He shook his head in disgust at himself. "I should never have asked you to leave."

It was something. He sounded sincere.

"Will you give me my papers back?" I asked.

He hesitated a suspiciously long time before answering.

"Yes, yes, of course," he said eventually, letting his breath out in a rush. "They're at the inn."

But we weren't going to the inn. We had reached the alley where Bentivoglio attacked me. My footsteps slowed, and my pulse sped up. Whether consciously or not, our footsteps had been taking us to the laboratory. I stopped and narrowed my eyes at him.

"Why are you taking me to the laboratory?" I asked quietly.

Vellacott turned toward me, his eyes wide and innocent.

"I . . . I suppose I am. I don't know." He shrugged. "I didn't think about where we were walking."

He might have been telling the truth. Perhaps he truly had stayed up all night, suffering over what he had done. If so, the change had certainly been abrupt.

Or perhaps he had stayed up all night reading my mother's notes, and failing to crack the code. Perhaps that was what had changed his mind about the wisdom of having me under his roof.

I looked away from my father, around the alley. There was still a small dark blotch where my head had met the wall. Ahead, I saw the column of smoke from the laboratory fire, still an opaque white.

"Is Bentivoglio still in the laboratory?" I asked sharply.

My father pulled a pained expression. "Thea, I know. He attacked you, and I should have defended you from him—"

Yes, he certainly should have, but that was not my concern at the moment.

"Is he still working on the White Elixir?" I demanded.

"Well—yes, he is," said my father. "He slept well last night, and assured me that he was much more himself this morning. You know, he would never have treated you so roughly if he weren't under such strain, Thea. Bentivoglio is a fine man, a brilliant mind—"

But even if I'd had any interest in hearing my father sing the praises of the thief who threw me into a wall and took my papers, I had no time for it now.

"I told you not to let him," I hissed, and hurried through the alley to the laboratory.

I approached slowly, listening for voices. I heard none, so I tried the doorknob. It was locked, of course. I knocked. There was no answer.

"Thea!"

My father had caught up with me.

"Thea, I think it's better if we don't disturb the professor now . . ."

I ignored him and knocked again. This time, there was a faint groan.

"Dominic?" I called.

There was no response, no movement, no more groans. Something was very wrong.

"Give me the key, Father!" I demanded.

"Thea, I really don't think you should disturb—"

I cried out in frustration and ran to the west side of the outbuilding, where I pulled myself up on the high windowsill. I peered into the room.

The worktable was on its side. The cabinet doors hung open. Vials and metals lay in pieces on the floor. It looked much as our laboratory in Normandy had after Mother attacked me in it. At first, it seemed to be empty. Then, behind the table, I saw a man's leg.

I gasped and pounded on the window. The leg didn't move, but something else did. A small, dark puddle trickled past the leg and pooled around the table's edge. It was too dim in the room to see the color, but the liquid was thick and moved too slowly to be water. It could have been quicksilver, perhaps, but I knew it wasn't.

My mind whirred. The door was locked from the inside. That meant whoever had done whatever had been done was still inside the laboratory. Perhaps Bentivoglio had lost his mind and taken out his violence on his surroundings and then on himself. But then, where was Dominic? Not at home. He was meant to be here, tending the fire by himself. I peered more closely at the table. There could be two bodies behind it; it was large enough to block them both. I beat against the window pane again and shouted Dominic's name.

"Thea?"

My hand slipped on the ledge. My legs buckled under me, and I landed in an ungraceful tangle. My father came around the corner of the outbuilding. He extended a hand to help me to my feet, but I ignored it.

"What's going on?"

"I warned you," I said. Usually anger made me articulate, but I was having difficulty catching my breath. I pointed toward the window. "Someone is dead in there."

"What?"

"Or else dying."

My father went to the window. He was tall enough to look in without any undignified scrambling. He made a low noise, something between a moan and a sob, and dashed around to unlock the door. I followed, but hesitated on the doorstep.

They were both inside, Bentivoglio and Dominic, or what was left of them. I gasped and turned away, but not before I saw Bentivoglio's head smashed in like overripe fruit. I sagged, clutching the doorframe. My empty stomach roiled. I wanted to run, but my legs scarcely had the strength to keep me upright.

My father pushed past me and retched into the hedges.

"Dominic." I summoned my courage and looked in again.

Professore Bentivoglio was certainly dead. I tried not to look at the sloppy remains of his skull and forced myself to make my way toward my new friend. Dominic was covered in blood, collapsed at an angle to Bentivoglio's larger body. I knelt next to him. My hands hovered over him, but I hesitated. His eyes were closed. The thought that he, too, was most likely dead made me freeze, horrified to touch him.

"Is he alive?" came my father's hoarse voice from the doorway.

I stared at his body, my mind disorganized and fuzzy, until at last I saw his chest move. Encouraged, I put my fingers to his throat and let out a slow breath. His heart was beating.

"He's alive."

Vellacott said nothing, but crossed to the fireplace while I carefully touched Dominic's head, trying to discern his injuries. There were scratches on his face but no other obvious wounds. His eyes flickered.

"Dominic," I said. "Dominic, wake up."

He jerked up, almost slamming his head into mine. I sat back.

"The professor!" he cried. "It was like you said, Thea! He's gone mad!"

"I know," I said. I wished fleetingly that I could get Dominic away from Bentivoglio before he saw it—and then he did.

His shoulders collapsed and he seized his head, rocking back and forth.

"Oh no, no, no," he moaned. "Oh God, no, please no."

I reached my hand out toward his shoulder, but he shrugged it off.

"I'm sorry," I said. "It wasn't your fault."

"He was so strong," said Dominic into his hands. "I was only trying to get away."

"I know," I said.

And I did know. My throat was closing from the memory, from the thought of how easily I could have ended up like this, with my mother's brains and blood on my hands. I struggled for breath, my shoulders heaving as Dominic sobbed. I was no help, no use at all. I looked up at my father in mute appeal. He looked down at us from across the room. In the dark, I couldn't make out his expression.

"What happened, Dominic?" asked my father in a quiet voice.

"What I told you would happen!" I sat back and glared up at him. "Professore Bentivoglio went mad and attacked him, just like my mother did! Why didn't you listen to me?"

"I asked Dominic, Thea."

Dominic stopped rocking but didn't raise his head.

"I don't know," he said. "I don't know how it happened. But it was like Thea said—he went mad—like an animal—"

"He went mad," repeated my father. "And so you killed him?"

"I didn't mean to do it!" cried Dominic, lifting his head at last. His face was streaked with blood and tears, and his nose was running. His eyes were wells of misery. I wanted to throw my arms around him and comfort him, but my father clearly did not. He looked at his apprentice with angry appraisal.

"He was twice your size," said my father. "And I'm supposed to believe you killed him to defend yourself? No. No, you could only have done this by taking him by surprise."

"What? No—sir—why would I?"

"You were angry with him," said my father. "After the incident with Thea. Don't deny it."

Dominic's red eyes widened as he began to understand what I had already concluded. His mouth dropped open, and he shook his head. I stood up and took his arm, pulling him to his feet.

"Let's go," I said quietly. "We have to go."

"You may go, Thea, but Dominic may not," my father said. "Dominic will wait here until the constable arrives. There has been a murder. A great man was killed."

"This is your fault," I hissed at my father. "You could have stopped this if you had listened to me. I warned you, but you didn't listen—even after Bentivoglio attacked me—"

"Go home, Thea," said my father. "You were not a part of this. Go to my rooms at the inn. You can stay with me as long as you need to."

Now he offered that. Now, when there was no chance I would take it.

"I will not leave you to tell lies about Dominic!" I snapped.

Vellacott took a deliberate step toward us. He looked down at the mess that had been his colleague, then up at Dominic, his face full of revulsion.

"I am not the liar here," he said.

I met his eyes, unable to tell if he really believed the story he was spinning. Could he really believe Dominic had killed Bentivoglio in a quarrel over me, when he had known me for such a short time? It was an absurd idea, and yet it might sound more likely to the law than my story, about an alchemist's curse that caused violent madness. The despair in Dominic's eyes showed he was thinking the same thing.

"Sir—" Dominic's voice quavered. "I wouldn't—you must know I wouldn't—"

"I am going to get the constable." Vellacott went to the door, and looked back at us from the step. "I expect you to wait here, Dominic, so that you can explain to them what happened to the professor. His family will demand that at the least." His voice broke, and he looked down at the dead man with actual tears in his eyes. "Thea—"

I glared at him, and he inclined his head slightly. "You must do what you think is best. But I strongly suggest you go to the inn. You are overexcited, and making very little sense."

My father left, and I went to the fire. The composition was there, gray and curling around the edges. It was just about time to add the red transmuting agent. I couldn't simply leave it here. I glanced around. Bentivoglio had stolen the vial from my pocket. I only had to consider whether I was willing to go through his clothes to look for it for a moment, before I luckily saw it on the floor. It had not shattered when it had been thrown. I picked it up, tipped the correct number of minims of the liquid into the brazier, and then poured the whole composition into another, larger vial.

It was possible that this transfer of the substance would destroy it, but I preferred that to leaving it to my father. I put the vials in my pocket.

Dominic watched me with empty eyes, seeing nothing. I pulled him out of the laboratory into the sunlight, where he looked even more ghastly.

"He was a lord, you know. In Bologna. From a powerful family. They'll hang me for this." His voice was faint, and his eyes were already dull with resignation.

"They won't," I said, though they certainly would. A poor Catholic boy whose only defense for killing a rich man was a mad tale told by a bastard French girl? If Vellacott had not believed us, then no one else would.

"They will," I said. "But we won't let them. We can't stay here. We have to hurry."

I started to run, pulling Dominic after me. His mother's flat wasn't far, thankfully. He looked a fright, and drew stares from each of the few townspeople we passed. Once inside, he came back to life. He washed his face and hands in the basin, then went into his room to hastily change from his gory clothes.

"Bring whatever money you can," I said. "I have enough for the trip to London, but there won't be much left after that."

Dominic came out of the bedroom in fresh clothes, staring at me.

"London? What will we do in London?"

"Hide, for one thing," I said. "My friend there will help us. Please hurry, Dominic. We have to get away before Vellacott comes back with the constable. This will be the first place they look."

He stood there, staring at me. Shock had apparently dulled his mind. I seized his hand and pulled him to the door. He stopped me and yanked his arm away.

"Why are you doing this, Thea?" he asked. "If you help me run, they will think you helped me kill him. You had nothing to do with this."

I stared at him. "Nothing to do with this? Those were my notes he was following! And I am the only one who understands . . . it could just as easily have been me!"

Dominic was shaking his head. "I can't let you do this. I will turn myself in. I will tell them what happened. And you can ask your father to speak for me."

"He won't. You heard him. Don't be stupid, Dominic. I have nothing to stay for anyway, not after that." I seized his arm, and this time he went with me.

We went down backstreets to the coach station, walking as quickly as we could without drawing attention. The next coach to leave for London was mercifully soon, and I bought us both inside passage and nearly forced Dominic into the carriage. An elderly gentleman, already dozing, was the only other passenger. We pulled away.

I watched Oxford go past with hatred. I had never enjoyed a place less. I resolved not to come back if I could help it, then realized at once that the resolution was unnecessary. I couldn't come back now that I was fleeing with a fugitive, unless it was under guard, to stand trial.

8

I spent the journey trying to get a glimpse of the road behind us, expecting the constabulary to catch up at any moment. But when the first few hours had passed, and it became clear they would not catch us on the road, at least, I turned my anxiety to Dominic.

He sat next to me. His head leaned back against the boards, his hands clenched at his sides. His eyes were closed, but he wasn't asleep. His chest was alternately still and heaving. His face was tinged green, and I didn't think it was from the coach's movement. The elderly gentleman across from us, on the other hand, snored violently. I placed my hand over Dominic's tightly curled fist and leaned toward him.

"Everything will be well," I whispered.

Dominic's head tilted toward me, but he didn't open his eyes.

"My mother." His voice caught. "She'll think . . . What will she think?"

"She'll know you're innocent."

"I shouldn't have run. I should have stayed and told them the truth."

"They would not have understood."

"Then they never will," he said. "They will catch me sooner or later."

I couldn't argue with that. I had no plan to hide him beyond getting away from Oxford and throwing him into Will's hands. I didn't know if Will could hide him, really. What if I hadn't saved Dominic at all, but only made it worse? My stomach turned over at the thought.

"I'm no criminal," Dominic said, finally opening his eyes. Only a few inches from mine. "I don't know how to hide."

I swallowed hard and summoned my resolve.

"Leave that to me."

"You're no criminal, either," said Dominic. "How do you know how to hide?"

"I don't," I admitted. "But I know someone who does."

It was the middle of the night when we arrived at the staging post in London. All I could see of the city were glimpses of the wide river and dark, tall buildings on narrow streets. The staging post was on a crowded street outside a church whose shadowy spires sliced into the night sky. Dominic looked up at it. Small hackney cabs were parked on the street, and a young man came toward us almost the moment we disembarked, offering his services.

I knew Will's address by heart, but hesitated to give it

to the cabdriver. Up to this point, we had left an easy trail to follow.

Dominic, standing beside me, spoke into my ear, too quietly for the cabdriver to hear. "I need to see a priest."

"We can find one tomorrow," I said.

"No," said Dominic. "Now."

I decided not to argue.

"Do you know of any Roman Catholic chapels hereabouts?" I asked the cabdriver.

It was dark, but I could see his eyebrows shoot up. I suddenly realized what an unusual request this must be here in the heart of the Anglican religion. I had forgotten, in my exhaustion, that England was not France, where a priest could be found on every street corner even in these enlightened times.

"There's one on Warwick Street. The one they tore up in the riot," he said after a moment. "But it'll be locked up tight at this hour."

"It's almost morning, in any case," I said, though morning was several hours off. I knew I couldn't give this cabdriver Will's address. He'd be sure to remember us now, when the law came looking. "How much to take us there?"

I counted out the amount, and despite the lightness of my coin purse I tipped him lavishly, hoping to buy some small portion of loyalty.

We climbed onto the open bench and drove west, to a well-tended section of the city with tidy paved streets and tall, dignified buildings surrounded by high iron gates and walls. It was a respectable neighborhood. But even here the night air was heavy with a sooty fog. Will's address was well to the east of here, which was good. When the constabulary showed up at the staging post, they might follow us here, but I would make sure they could not follow us farther.

We stopped outside a row of unassuming brick buildings.

"This is it," said the cabdriver.

"This? Which one?" I asked. There were no markers, no crucifix or statues or even a sign.

"This is the Bavarian house, what has a chapel," said the coachman with a shrug. "I'd try around the side if I was you. Want me to wait?"

"No, thank you," I said. From now on, we would have to walk.

Dominic had already leapt from the coach and knocked on the front entrance. When there was no answer, he hurried around the side street. I followed him.

The cabdriver seemed to have the right idea. A small cross hung over the side door. Heartened by this, Dominic pounded on the door, paused a few moments, and pounded again. I looked around the alley, wincing at the noise. Despite the presence of the Roman chapel, this looked like the sort of street whose inhabitants might not take kindly to being woken well before dawn.

Dominic took a few steps back, peering up at the window on the second floor.

"Dominic, maybe we should go," I said. "No one seems to be waking. The priest might not even live here."

But Dominic picked up a handful of gravel from the street and starting flinging it at the window. It was quieter, at least, than his pounding on the door had been.

And in a moment it proved more effective as well. Light glowed through the window. Someone had lit a lamp.

In another minute, the door opened. A bald, middle-aged man in a dressing gown peered out.

"Are you a priest?" asked Dominic.

"I am," said the man. He was bleary-eyed and half awake but did not seem irritated to have been woken.

"I need to confess, Father."

The priest nodded and beckoned him inside. Dominic went in without a backward glance, and then the priest noticed me.

"Come in, my dear. Are you also in need of a confessor?"

"No, thank you—Father."

My tongue tripped on the title, enough for the priest to smile slightly and understand that I was not one of his flock.

I followed him in, and I noticed with gratitude that he locked the door behind us. I looked around in the uncertain light.

It was not a big chapel, but that much I knew from the outside. There were a dozen or so rows of pews facing a set of stairs and an altar. Nothing burned but the light the priest carried and a red lamp hanging in front of a screen beside the altar. The close air was thick with the smell of stale incense. Dominic knelt and crossed himself, facing the altar, and then didn't get up. The priest hung back a moment. I heard a muffled, wet sound. Dominic was crying.

The priest put a hand on Dominic's shoulder and murmured something in a low voice. Dominic got up and followed the priest into a dark, curtained box. I knew enough to recognize it as a confessional, though I had never been inside one. My experience with church was limited to a few solitary forays, fueled by curiosity. My mother had no religion but her own, and that was alchemy. Her patrons had been men of liberal religious sentiment, believing it a beneficial practice for a certain sort of person—though naturally not enlightened, rational men such as themselves. Even Will, who was so different from those men in so many other ways, was just like them in this.

I wondered what any of them would do if they unexpectedly found themselves a killer. I wondered what I would do.

Inside the confessional, Dominic's voice had turned to sobs. My own throat started to feel tight.

I sat in the pew farthest from the confessional. I heard Dominic, but the words were indistinct, as were the priest's murmured replies. A wave of exhaustion hit me. Just across the room from me, Dominic was laying down a burden, giving it to someone else who was sworn to take it, and to tell him he was free of it. There was no one like that for me. If alchemy was our religion, then we were its priests. We held the power, and we would reap the rewards, but the burdens were ours alone. No one could take them from us. If my mother had been judged unworthy by some god of alchemy, then there was no priest who could make her better. I simply had to be good enough to pass the test, to make the Stone and save her.

But good enough at what? There were no Ten Commandments of alchemy. Adepts had brought their own moralities and religions to the practice and claimed they were essential, but my mother and I had never given credit to any of that. Perhaps I should ask Dominic to teach me. He seemed to be well versed in the practice of being good. If I couldn't learn from him, then I would have to count on my natural moral instincts, because the only virtues I had been trained in were those of diligence and honesty. The latter, not because an adept should not lie, but because my mother refused to be lied to.

Gone was the exhilaration I had felt at the thought of making the Stone myself, proving myself to my mother and the world. I had seen the path to success, steep and treacherous. I had seen a man fall from it to his death. The cost was too great. Now all I felt was its weight, pressing down on me so heavily that I considered lying down on the bench to escape it in sleep. But I knew I couldn't. We had to leave as soon as Dominic had his absolution. I glanced at the door and tried to estimate how quickly the police might have found out where we went. Surely the coach station would have been one of the first places they went after they didn't find us at the laboratory. And the station master would have told them we took a coach to London. From there, all it would take was for our London cabdriver to tell them we had gone to the chapel. We had taken the last coach of the day out of Oxford, but the police could surely have commandeered one. It was possible they were only an hour or two behind us. Not enough time.

I fidgeted. I watched the confessional, expecting Dominic to emerge at any moment. I should have told him to hurry. I should have told him how little time we might have. He was intelligent enough to work it out himself, surely, but his mind was clearly not fixed on escape. All he cared about right now was making things right with his God. It occurred to me that he might very well emerge from the dark wooden box and declare his intention to turn himself in. Perhaps the priest would insist on it. That seemed to me like the sort of thing a priest might do.

Well, if that happened I would simply have to talk Dominic out of it, as I had before. The thought of him swinging from a rope for this made my stomach turn and my knuckles whiten on the pew in front of me. And that wasn't counting the trouble I would find myself in. I didn't know what the penalty for abetting a fugitive was. Not death, probably, but perhaps quite a long time in prison. I swallowed, and my throat felt very dry.

Dominic's question came back to me. Why was I helping him? He had been very kind to me, but we had not known each other long. My father clearly hadn't considered that I might have done something as foolish as this, or he would not have left me alone with Dominic while he went to the authorities. But at the thought of my father, I found my answer. He had not hesitated to throw his innocent apprentice to the gallows, because he cared for no one but himself. I was not like him, no matter what my mother had sometimes said. Surely this proved it. My resolve hardened again.

Dominic emerged, the priest behind him. I jumped to my feet and went to them.

"We have to go," I said. "They might not be far behind."

The priest looked steadily at me for a moment, then to my surprise, he nodded.

"Do you have anywhere to go?" he asked.

"We do," I said.

"I will not ask you where," he said. "And I cannot promise you that it will be safe for you to return here. But I can give you a little money, and I will pray for you both."

Dominic's eyes were red and his face blotchy, but he was calmer now. He took the coins the priest offered and slid them into his pocket.

"Thank you, Father," he said. "I hope this doesn't bring you trouble."

"It won't," the priest replied. "If they come, I will tell them the truth: that you came, that you left, and that I do not know where you went. Go now. God be with you."

I took Dominic's hand and pulled him from the chapel, but once we were in the street, he didn't need any more prodding.

"What now?" he whispered. "Where is this friend of yours who knows how to hide?"

"I only have the address," I said. "Twelve Sharp's Alley, St. Giles."

"St. Giles?" Dominic's face flashed alarm.

"Is something wrong with St. Giles?" I asked.

"It's a slum. Everything's wrong with it," he said. "Though I reckon a slum is what we need. It's not so far."

We ran at first, eastward, until I was too dizzy and breathless to run any longer. Dominic took my arm, and we walked. The smell of the streets started to thicken unpleasantly, and the paved roads gave way to dirt, then mud. As the hazy sky lightened with the dawn, we came into a large intersection with a tall pillar in the center. The sun peeked past the buildings that faced the road. The one across from us was clearly a public house of some kind. The one next to us was as well, I realized, when a drunk man stumbled out of it and nearly tripped over another passed out at the foot of the stairs.

"Seven Dials," said Dominic. "Seven streets meet here, a gin shop on each."

Squinting at each of the intersections, I realized he wasn't exaggerating. The sun was coming up on more ine-briated men than I had ever seen at once, even in Paris. A loud, drawn-out retching noise came from behind me. I stopped myself from turning to look. I was beginning to understand where the terrible smells were coming from.

We skirted the edge of the circle, and I pulled my shawl over my bonnet. There was nothing I could do to hide my dress, which was much too fine for the neighborhood, but at least it was dusty and rumpled. In any case, the only people out of doors seemed too bleary-eyed to care. The only exception was a woman in a ragged, low-cut dress, whose drunken exhaustion didn't prevent her from seizing Dominic's arm and attempting to pull him inside a dilap-idated doorway.

"Been a long night, hasn' it, lovely?" she cooed at him with a ghastly, forced smile.

Dominic jerked away, cheeks aflame. The woman made another grab for him, but he threw her off.

"Don't touch me," he spat. The woman made an obscene gesture and stepped toward him again, this time with her fists up. I pulled Dominic behind me.

"He didn't mean any offense," I said.

The woman bared her teeth at me like a dog, and for a moment I thought she might actually bite me. Then she laughed. I had never heard a sound with less amusement in it.

"Best o' luck to you, dearie," she said. "They're never much fun on their first time."

We hurried away. Three blocks later, Dominic's face was still burning. The neighborhood didn't grow any more pleasant as we went farther. Dingy laundry hung across the narrow streets, which were little more than a muddy slush of excrement. The smell was horrible, piss and vomit and other waste I tried not to identify. We passed more gin shops, more drunks, more ragged prostitutes, and a shop that seemed to be selling rats and birds out of cages. For what purpose, I shuddered to imagine.

No one paid us any further attention. We turned, at last, down a particularly narrow alley. Sharp's Alley. Advertisements for syphilis cures plastered the walls. They were all mercury based, and therefore all poison. My mother had made sure I was aware there were no cures for syphilis that didn't kill you nearly as quick as the disease itself.

Twelve Sharp's Alley was a tenement building with sagging eaves and ill-fitting windows. The front entrance was unlocked, and inside we found a set of steep stairs, one going down and one going up. The smell in the hallway was more damp than the alley, but little different otherwise.

"So does he live up in the fire trap or down in the plague hole?" asked Dominic.

I laughed nervously, but Dominic remained stone-faced.

"You do not like it here at all, do you?" I said.

"Do you?" He shoved his hands deep into his coat pockets.

"Of course not, but you seem to hate it more—" The word that occurred to me was *intimately*, but I hesitated to use it. "More," I finished.

Dominic shrugged, seeming to shrink into his coat as he did so. "My father died in a place like this."

"Not here, though?" I couldn't stop myself from asking. "In St. Giles?"

"Yes, in St. Giles," he said. I opened my mouth to say something sympathetic, but he cut me off. "Up or down, Thea?"

"I don't know," I said. But I couldn't picture Will going down the stairs into that dark, dank cellar every day, so I allowed my optimism to guide me. "Up. Let's try up."

Dominic didn't question it. We climbed the stairs, which creaked so noisily I was afraid they might not support our combined weight. A low doorway, no taller than me, perched at the top of the steps. My hand trembled as I knocked.

There was no answer. I knocked again.

Several conflicting fears warred within me. The first was that he was not here, that he would not open the door because he had moved on, and that we would not be able to find him. But almost as bad was the idea that he would open it. I had pictured this address, 12 Sharp's Alley, a hundred times. I had not pictured it like this. I knew he had fled from Germany and was hiding without much money left, but I had never imagined Will living in poverty so ugly, so abject. This was not a place where people lived, it was a place where they died. I needed to find Will here. But, oh God, I didn't want to.

I knocked again, and heard a movement inside—something hitting the ground.

"Will?"

I put my ear to the door and heard a slow, quiet footstep. Someone was hovering behind the door, hesitating.

"Will, it's Thea," I said. "Thea Hope."

"Bee?" came a quiet, incredulous voice, followed by a low cough. The door cracked open, and I caught a glimpse of his face in the semidarkness behind. "What are you—" He opened the door a touch farther, then saw Dominic. "Who is with you?"

I didn't like the way his voice sounded from behind the door, strained and sharp with suspicion.

"He is a friend of mine. His name is Dominic. We need help, Will. I'm sorry, but I didn't know where else to go."

There was quiet a moment. I could hear his breathing. It sounded wrong. It was too labored, and at the same time too shallow, as though he had been running. But he hadn't. There was no room to run here.

"Is it really you?" he asked.

"It is," I said. "I swear."

He finally opened the door fully. "You'd better come in then."

We went in and paused while our eyes adjusted to the dim light from the fire. I was relieved to find that there was one, at least, with the familiar brazier standing over it. A chest sat open a few feet away, with base metals and a crucible inside. I glanced at Dominic, who was staring at it.

"An alchemist?" Dominic asked in a low voice. "You didn't say he was an alchemist, too."

"Everyone I know is an alchemist," I replied.

"I'm not," said Dominic.

"Then you are the only exception," I said. "And not much of one."

Will had turned his back on us and gone toward the fire. I stared at him, trying to make out what had changed. Disappointment was uncurling inside me like a waking animal. He didn't want me here. Even Will didn't want me.

He turned back toward me and ran his hand through his blond hair, cut ragged around his ears. Now that he stood by the fire, I saw what I had already heard in his voice. He was thin, much too thin. His face was hollowed out and shadowed in ways it hadn't been before. His cheeks and chest had sunken in. The room was cold and damp despite the fire, but Will's forehead shone with sweat. He coughed, pulling out a handkerchief as he did so and quickly hiding it away when the fit had passed. But I saw the streak of red in it that he was trying to conceal.

"Will—"

He met my eyes for the first time.

"Ah, Bee. Don't look at me like that," he said, managing a shadow of his old sly smile. "I won't have it. I'll send you right back out on the street."

"But—is it—?"

"Just a touch of consumption," he said. "It's trying to

kill me, but it will have to hurry if it wants to beat the Prussians."

He let out a short laugh that quickly turned into another cough. When it had finished with him, he sat down by the fire. Not on a chair, as there were none in the room, but on the bare floorboards.

"Do make yourselves comfortable," said Will, with a grand sweep of one hand while the other tucked his handkerchief away again. "That may seem a difficult thing to do, but you'll find the floor quite pleasant once you're very tired of standing."

I went forward and sank down across from him. I untied my bonnet and pulled it off, holding it in front of me. I fiddled with the ribbons and forced back the panic flooding through me.

"Will—" I began again.

"So you didn't know where else to go," Will interrupted. "But last I knew you were still in France. It seems I've missed a few rather significant developments in the life of Theosebeia Hope. And you know that isn't a story I like to fall behind on."

I smiled, even though my heart was heavy as lead. I never could resist smiling when he set his mind to making me.

"I sent you a letter," I said. "You didn't get it?"

Will reached into his front pocket and took out a letter—my letter. My pulse quickened. He kept it in his pocket, just where I kept his.

"This one?" he asked. "I got it, Bee, but I hadn't the faintest idea what to make of it! Your mother is mad? You're leaving France? I thought it was some joke."

"Not a joke," I said, and my smile faltered at the thought of all the miserable things I had to relate. "I don't know where to start."

"You left France, it seems," prompted Will. "Why? I thought we agreed you should stay and bring down the ancien régime."

I smiled again, wryly this time. Will liked to joke as though I were even more a revolutionary than he, though in truth I was a great deal less. I'd never thought about politics carefully until Will came, and the seven months he'd been with us hadn't been quite long enough for him to convince me.

"We never agreed on that," I said. "And anyway, you left."

"What an unfair way to put it," said Will. "I didn't leave, I was unceremoniously thrown out. And if you'll recall, that was quite as much your fault as mine."

A flush crept up my cheeks. Dominic watched me, a slight frown on his face.

"In any case," I said, to change the subject. "The Revolution doesn't seem to need our help."

"That's what Lafayette wants you to think. The Revolution's all done, plebs, pack up your pitchforks and let the liberal aristocrats take it from here!" He coughed again, deep and painful, but kept talking afterward as if there had been no interruption. "But the people won't have it, you know. A citizen king and a constitution written by rich men? The Revolution isn't finished yet, not even close to it. You'll see."

"A Jacobin alchemist," muttered Dominic. He sat down next to me.

"An excellent summary of me." Will's brilliant smile moved to Dominic, turning unfriendly. "It seems you know me completely now, but I know nothing about you except that you seem to have gotten my Bee into trouble."

"*Your* Bee?" asked Dominic.

"He didn't get me into trouble," I said hastily. "It wasn't his fault."

"Don't tell me it was yours, Bee," said Will. "I won't believe you."

"No, it wasn't my fault, either. If anything it was my father's."

"Your father?" Will asked. "You mean the Oxford fellow? I thought you'd never met."

"We hadn't," I said. "The Comte sent me to Oxford after—well—"

The scent of sulfur came back to me, and my throat seemed to constrict like my mother's hands were around it again. For a moment I couldn't go on.

"How far are you?" asked Dominic abruptly, nodding toward the brazier over the fire.

"Far?" Will asked. "Do you even know what you're asking?"

"I know what alchemy looks like. Have you made the White Elixir?" Dominic continued.

"The White Elixir?" repeated Will, incredulous. "The substance that turns all metals into silver? Do you think I would be hiding away in this hovel if I had?"

"We did," said Dominic. "Or almost did. With Thea's help."

Will's mouth fell open, and his hostility dropped with it.

"You—*you* made the White Elixir?" He turned to me. "Bee?"

I swallowed and drew a shaky breath. "They did."

"But then—" Will seemed to grow taller, even as he sat. "But that's the final step before the Philosopher's Stone!"

"It is," agreed Dominic. "And Thea got close—"

"Got close!" exclaimed Will. His eyes flashed with a brilliance almost like before. "My God! Do you mean you know how to make it?"

"*I* don't," Dominic said, glancing at me. "But . . ."

"Will, listen," I said. "It isn't as simple as that. There was a . . . a problem."

A problem. I winced at the feebleness of the understatement. My mother was insane. Professore Bentivoglio was dead. Dominic and I were both fugitives from the law. It was more than a problem. It was a curse.

"The process causes madness," said Dominic. "Thea's mother went mad in France in the last stages. Then someone else, in Oxford—a colleague of Mr. Vellacott—he went mad as well."

"Mad?" The avid light in Will's eyes dimmed. "Truly mad? You said so in your letter, but I didn't think . . ."

I swallowed hard, then nodded. "She was gone, Will, completely gone."

"You don't mean—"

"She attacked me," I said. "She nearly killed me."

"What?" Will's eyes widened in horror. "My God, Bee!"

"But that isn't all," I said. "It wasn't just her, it's the work, the alchemy. A curse, or . . . a . . . a judgment on unworthy alchemists." Will's eyebrows lifted skeptically at this, so I hurried on. "Professore Bentivoglio, my father's colleague, he did the same thing. He attacked Dominic, and then— and then—"

"I killed him," Dominic finished for me. He looked at his hands.

"He didn't mean to," I said. "And he was only defending himself. But my father didn't believe it. He went to the police. He was going to blame it all on Dominic. Bentivoglio is a powerful man, from a noble family, and Dominic . . . isn't."

Will nodded slowly, looking from Dominic to me.

"So you ran away. I sympathize. I've recently found myself on the wrong end of unfair accusations. Breach of contract, in my case, rather than murder, though strangely it carries the same sentence. But nevertheless." He paused to cough, and when he was finished he looked straight at Dominic with undisguised hostility. "I have missed the part of the story that explains how it was not you who got my Bee into trouble."

"And I missed the part where she belongs to you," said Dominic. He didn't raise his voice, exactly, but seemed close to it.

"I suppose you didn't stop to think how bad this could be for her now?" Will said. "Especially with those fools in Parliament making speeches about the dangers of the revolutionary French every night?"

Dominic's eyes flitted to me and filled with guilt.

"I didn't ask her to help me," he said.

"He didn't," I agreed. "Don't badger him, Will, please. He isn't to blame for any of this."

Will looked at me for a long moment. He opened his mouth, then closed it again. He ran his long fingers through his messy hair. It was a familiar enough gesture to bring on another flash of memory: his hand taking mine while we talked.

"If you say so, of course," he sighed. "But I don't like seeing you here."

"I was going to say the same of you," I said. "Will, wouldn't it be better to go back to your parents? They wouldn't send you away, not when you're sick like this."

Will shook his head.

"I agreed not to badger your apprentice," he said. "So I must ask you not to ask about my parents."

"But—"

"No, Bee."

His tone was final enough that I could not mistake it. I didn't press, and he pushed himself laboriously to his feet.

"I suppose it's been a while since you ate," said Will, slightly out of breath from the effort. "I'll go out and get some food, shall I?"

I was starving, and Dominic's stomach rumbled at the suggestion. I handed Will my coin purse as he went to the door.

"It's all I have left, I'm afraid," I said. "But it should be enough to feed us for a while."

Will gestured to a sad, rumpled pallet in the corner. It was the only piece of furniture in the room that wasn't alchemical in nature.

"That's the only bed, I'm afraid. One of you should probably take a turn on it, if you've been traveling all night. There's another room." Will pointed to a low door off the entryway. "Just a closet, really. It's empty except for the rats. But you can take the bed in there if you want quiet."

He slung a coat over his shoulders. I recognized it. It had been a fine coat once, a double-breasted dove-gray garment, cut slim and long. It was ragged and dirty now, but still he looked a bit more like himself as he buttoned it up. He caught me looking at him and smiled.

"This isn't how I pictured our reunion," he said. "But I *am* glad we're having one, even so."

He took my hand in his, and warmth spread through me that could not be explained by his hands, which were cold as lead.

"Don't open the door while I'm gone," he said as he left.

I locked the door behind him.

"You should sleep," said Dominic. "I'm not sure I can."

The shadows under his eyes, dark as bruises, said otherwise.

"You take the bed and I'll sleep by the fire," I said. This seemed to me a reasonable division of the scant comforts available. But he argued, and in the end I sank gratefully onto the pallet. The last image I saw before sleep took me was Dominic kneeling by the fire, looking into the brazier.

10

In my dream, someone was watching me.

I didn't know who. I didn't know why. My eyes were heavy, and it was a struggle to open them even a sliver. Whatever watched me was behind me, though I couldn't see it. I kept turning; slowly, then suddenly. But it slipped away each time. I could not catch it. Then my eyes closed and I could not open them. From behind me, hands closed around my neck, slow but firm. Almost gentle. But all the same, I couldn't draw breath. I choked, and woke up.

I threw myself upright and reached for my neck. I gasped, tried to scream. I tried to peel the hands off, and found there were none.

Someone was beside me, murmuring something. I threw up my hands, but realized at the same moment that he wasn't trying to hurt me.

"Just a dream, Bee," he said. "Just a dream."

Will. I remembered. I started to breathe again, melting into his chest. It was thinner than before, hard like bone instead of muscle. But somehow his arms around me felt as they always had before. Even in this damp garret, it was the same. The only place that had ever felt like home.

"You're all right. I'm here."

"I know," I said. "I know that."

Something started to soften in my chest. Feelings I had sent into hiding started to creep out, feeling safe for the first time since he had left. I tried to stop them, but I couldn't, not when he was holding me. I wanted to sob into his chest and see how he would comfort me. He would, I was sure of that, no matter how pitiful and messy my weeping made me. *I should pull away,* I told myself. But I didn't. Then he started to cough.

It wasn't bad at first. It could have been a normal cough. It started in his throat, but quickly went deeper. It took hold and shook him, tearing him from me. I pulled back in alarm as he folded, fumbling with his handkerchief, turning away. He wanted to hide it, but there was no hiding this.

When the coughing finally subsided, he did not look at me. He couldn't meet my eyes, couldn't make a joke. I understood then, though deep down I had known from the moment he opened the door. Will was dying.

It was worse than everything else. Worse than my mother's madness, my father's rejection, Dominic's trouble, worse than fleeing from the law. The thought of Will had been enough when everything else had disappointed. I could face losing the rest when finding Will was still ahead of me.

"Have you seen a doctor?" I asked.

"I never met a doctor who could cure consumption."

"If you got out of this horrible place—"

"I would still be dying."

His flat tone sent a chill down my spine. I opened my mouth to protest, but Will cut me off.

"Your friend." He nodded toward the wall. It took me a moment to realize that Dominic must be resting in the other room. "He went to work while you were sleeping and I was gone. I got back to find him melting something in my brazier."

"What?"

Will nodded toward the fireplace, an oddly careful look on his face.

"See for yourself."

I pulled myself to my feet, taking the hand Will offered for support, and took a deep breath to fight down a spell of dizziness. I recognized a sharp, fresh scent.

"The White Elixir?" I asked Will. "But I thought you said you hadn't made it?"

"I haven't. Your friend brought it with him. He was transmuting some of my lead, and it seems to have worked."

I crossed the room and stared into the brazier. The White Elixir was pooled like quicksilver around a large lump of glittering metal that was distinctly not lead. I felt in my pockets for the vial I had brought, and found it missing. Will held out tongs to me. I reached in with them and pulled out the lump, which was about the size of a fist. The White Elixir released it, coming together again and losing its liquid shine. I touched the metal. It was warm and pleasant to the touch.

"You said this was lead?" I asked Will. "You're quite certain it was lead?"

"Quite certain. I spent my last silver a long time ago," he replied.

I knew this was what the White Elixir was supposed to do, but I had never seen the results before. Now I held them in my hand. Silver, made from alchemy. I passed it from one hand to the other, rubbed my thumb over its smooth, warm surface. I wanted more.

"Do you have any more lead?" I asked. "Or tin?"

Will went to the chest against the wall, full of a familiar array of instruments, vials, and metals. He took a dull gray block, pewter, and dropped it into the brazier. We watched, entranced, as the elixir parted around it, then slowly began to bubble and spread across its surface. The bubbles turned to steam, and a thick smoke rose into our faces. I fanned it away, entranced by the process I had only half believed was truly possible completing itself before my eyes.

I took Will's hand without thinking. For a moment, it remained cold and unmoving in mine, and I panicked, imagining he was about to draw away. Then, to my relief, his fingers closed around mine and squeezed. We watched wordlessly, hand in hand, until the steam slowly thinned and the elixir parted again. This time I lifted the newly created silver from the brazier and dropped it into Will's outstretched hand. He stared at it for a very long moment.

"I had almost despaired," he said quietly. "I had almost resigned myself to believing what they all said about us. That we were either fools, or frauds."

"It is real." I knew exactly how he felt. We had talked

of it once. We were both young enough to abandon alchemy as a failed pursuit and choose something else. I had considered it, and so had he. I had met alchemists who had spent their whole lives looking for this and never found it. Talented men who could have done anything. But they had done this, and failed. The waste of it.

And now I held what they had died striving for in my hand. That meant we had been right not to abandon alchemy. But even more than that, they had all been right not to. Because this was not just silver that I held in my hand. This was proof that the basic elements of the world could be changed. Our detractors believed we sought this only for riches, and to be sure, most of us did. But the best alchemists, the ones I admired, who went the furthest— they saw past riches, past fame. They knew what it was to stand outside of society, to look at the world and wish it were different. Better. If we could turn pewter and lead into silver, then we didn't simply have to take the world as it was given to us. We could change it. Lead into silver was only the beginning. Next was silver into gold. Sickness into health. Death into life.

"You said you had almost succeeded," he said, not taking his eyes from the silver.

I didn't know what he meant at first.

"The Philosopher's Stone. You said you had almost completed the process to make it."

I met Will's eyes, and for a moment I felt the desperate need that I saw there inside myself. We both needed the Stone. There was so much we had to heal.

"What are you doing?"

Dominic stood in the doorway. He crossed the room

in three rapid steps, seized my arm, and pulled me away from the brazier. "What are you thinking? Do you want to go mad, too?"

I shook his hand off my arm. I wheeled on him, an angry outburst on my lips. His usually hooded eyes were wide with surprise.

"I'm sorry!" he exclaimed. "I wasn't trying to— I only meant— You can't use the Elixir. It isn't safe."

"But you're the one who started it going," said Will. Dominic made a confused noise, but Will pressed on. "No, don't deny it. Where did it come from if you didn't bring it with you? I didn't have it. The White Elixir was in the brazier working on the lead when I came back from the shop."

Dominic's eyes widened farther, and his slumped shoulders drew back, pulling him upright and defensive.

"He didn't bring it," I said, an edge of accusation in my voice. "I did. It was in my pocket. You took it from me while I was sleeping."

"I didn't!" he said. "I don't think . . ."

He reached into his coat pockets and dug around for a moment before pulling out an empty vial. He stared at it, then at the brazier.

"I didn't," he repeated, but with less certainty this time. He looked back at me in appeal. "Was it— You didn't put it there?"

"Of course not. But I'm glad you thought to get it going. Our money troubles are solved, at least."

"No, no, no, no," muttered Dominic. He angled past Will and stood between him and the brazier. "We can't use it. We can't."

"Why not? It's the next part of the process that causes madness. Making the Philosopher's Stone." But as soon as I said it, I knew it was wrong.

"No," said Dominic. "We hadn't started on the Stone when Bentivoglio attacked you in the alley. And I . . ."

He put a hand to his forehead, and his head dropped. His mouth moved, but no sound came out.

"Dominic?" I asked. I glanced at Will in alarm. He caught my look, and his fingers tightened on the heavy silver in his hand.

"I don't remember burning the elixir," Dominic said without raising his head.

"You're tired," I said. "We were up all night. You had a terrible shock."

"No," he said. "No, Thea."

"Then—" I thought as quickly as my sleep-starved mind would work. "Then we'll keep you away from the work. We'll stop. We have enough silver for now. Mother and Bentivoglio—neither of them lost control right away."

"But if I've started to do things without knowing it—"

"We will watch you," I said. "We will keep an eye on you. You might get better without more exposure."

"He was so strong, Thea," Dominic said in a low voice. "It wasn't natural, how strong he was."

I started toward him on some instinct to offer comfort, but Will took my arm and held me back.

"I can lock you inside the other room," said Will. Dominic looked up at him with a glimmer of hope.

"If I get worse, I don't know if the lock will hold," he said.

"If you get worse we will know, won't we?" said Will. "Oughtn't we have some warning?"

"Yes," I replied. "Professore Bentivoglio wasn't himself for days before he became violent. You said that, remember?"

Dominic nodded slowly. He glanced behind him at the brazier.

"You won't make any more? You won't go further?"

I met Dominic's earnest gaze. I had not known him long, but I had seen enough of his goodness to know that if the Stone had rejected even him as unworthy, then the standard was too high for me to meet. My last hope that I could finish the Philosopher's Stone without falling prey to the madness crumbled.

"Thea," he said. "You've seen it. You know what will happen to you."

I thought of my mother's empty eyes and her feral scream. I thought of Bentivoglio throwing me into the wall, then lying in a pool of his own blood, his head smashed in.

"I won't." The words tasted like poison in my mouth. Like a curse I was putting on myself, almost as bad as the one I sought to avoid. "I know we can't."

Dominic nodded and pushed past us, his head down. He went into the side room and shut the door firmly behind him. While Will fished the key out of his chest and locked him in, I took down the brazier from the fire. The steam was a faint mist now, but I tried not to breathe it in all the same. I put the brazier in the corner and covered it with a filthy rag from Will's alchemy chest. I didn't want to touch the elixir. I thought, for a moment, of taking it out and throwing it in the trash, but an involuntary spasm of horror at the idea prevented me.

Will and I sat by the fire, sharing a loaf of bread between us. The elixir hovered between us, though I had banished it to the corner. The second time I caught him gazing in its direction, I shook my head.

"We can't, Will," I said with as much certainty as I could muster. "You haven't seen what it does. Death is better than what happened to my mother."

"I don't agree," said Will quietly. "There isn't a cure for death, but there may be one for your mother."

I grasped in my mind for some comfort to offer him. But there was none: only the Stone, which had slipped through my fingers. My mother had made it. She had succeeded. If only I had seized it and run.

"If only she hadn't destroyed it," I groaned. The memory of the glass ovum shattering where she had thrown it was suddenly as fresh and wrenching as it had been then. Will set down his bread, barely touched, and took my hand. He ran his thumb over mine, staring down at it. Pricks of pleasure ran up my arm, but with the pleasure was some alarm. Will hadn't touched me like this before, so casually. Some boundary seemed to have been breached, and since I did not yet know what it was, precisely, I could not feel entirely at ease.

"What did she destroy?" he asked.

It took me a moment to understand what he meant.

I closed my eyes and winced at the thought. "My mother made the Stone. She destroyed it when she attacked me."

Will's thumb went still, and his grip on my hand tightened. When he spoke, his voice was thick and desperately quiet.

"She made the Stone. You saw it."

I tried to pull my hand away, but he didn't let go.

"I saw it, yes. Just before my mother nearly killed me."

"Why?" His voice was a low growl of despair. "Why would she?"

"Why?" His grip on my hand was almost painful now. His fingernail pressed into my palm. "Will, have you not been listening? She was mad! She was destroying everything! The Stone, me, nothing mattered to her!"

I tore my hand free and stared at him. He caught sight of my expression and his face flooded with regret.

"I'm sorry, Bee," he said. "I didn't mean it. Forgive me. It's just . . . the Philosopher's Stone!"

He started to cough, and in the several minutes it took for the violence of it to pass, my anger at him had faded away.

"I know," I said. "I understand. Believe me, I have asked the same questions myself." I put my hand on his knee. It felt awkward and strange, and I wished at once that I hadn't. But I left it there a moment before drawing it away.

"You know how to make it, don't you?" he asked.

I sat very still while I considered how to answer. I did know how. I had the White Elixir. My mother's notes were in my mind, each step more deeply imprinted than the last, as they grew closer to the goal of every alchemist, of all the work I had ever done.

"Bee. It is the only thing that can save me. It is the only thing that can save your mother."

"I don't know that for certain," I said without believing. "We have no proof that it will do what the corpus says it will."

"We had no proof the White Elixir could turn base metal into silver, either," said Will.

I shook my head and shut my eyes. It was dangerous to let him talk, dangerous to look at him and know he was dying. Everything he said was too much like what my own heart told me.

"We'll go mad, Will," I said in desperation. "We'll kill each other. We will never get to use the Stone."

I looked away, trying to shake off the memory of sulfur. I tried to arm myself, ready for him to argue again as I felt certain he would, perhaps should do. But instead his arms closed around me again.

"I'm sorry, Bee," he said. "I don't want to push." His voice was gentle, like his hand on my arm. I didn't want to fight with him. I didn't want to deny him anything at all, and certainly not his life. A sob caught in my chest.

"There must be another way," I said, knowing there wasn't.

"It doesn't matter," said Will. He laid his cheek against the top of my head and let out a long sigh. "I'm so glad you're here. I'd started to think I was never going to see you again."

The sadness in his voice was more than I could bear. I dropped my head into his chest and breathed hard, desperately fighting not to weep and losing the battle.

"Don't, Bee." Will put his hand on my head and ran his fingers through my hair. "I hate making you cry. I've wanted to make you laugh since the first moment I met you."

I exhaled sharply and turned a sob into a strangled laugh.

"I didn't know that," I said.

"Oh yes," said Will. He coughed again, but moved past it quickly. "You looked at me with those big, serious eyes of yours, and I took it as a challenge. I wanted to see what you looked like with a smile on your lovely face, one I put there."

I turned my face up to him. I could almost smile at him. "And what did I look like?"

"Beautiful." His smile was as warm as summer grass. "Happy. You should have so much happiness in your life, Bee. So much more than you've had."

I laid my head against his chest again. I couldn't look at him smiling at me like that, with the proof on his own drawn face and hollowed cheeks of how little happiness was left in life for him.

He helped me to the pallet and lay beside me. I leaned my forehead against his sternum. He laid one hand on my hip, still but in a way that suggested it might move at any moment. I held my breath. I didn't know if I wanted his hand to move or not. I wasn't sure if I liked it where it was, if I wanted more or less of what he might do. Something was different than it had been in France, when every small increase of intimacy had been an exquisite thrill. I hadn't asked him to lie next to me, but I had come to his door without a chaperone. I had asked to sleep under his roof. I wasn't sure what assumptions he had made, or what he thought I wanted. I didn't know what I wanted myself, but it felt too late, somehow, to tell him that now.

But when his hand did move, it was only to stroke my hair. I breathed in deeply and let the tension leave me.

"I missed you, Bee," he whispered.

"I missed you, too."

And slowly, I fell asleep, even with the disquieting rattle of his breath against my ears and the feeling of his thin, hard body against mine.

11

I woke up with a new plan. I couldn't let Will die. I couldn't let my mother waste away in madness. I was frightened of the curse, of course I was. With what I had seen I could hardly be eager to subject myself to it. But Will was dying. I reached for him as I surfaced from sleep. I would do what we both knew he needed me to do, though he wouldn't ask for it. I would make that sacrifice. And when I had made the Stone, whatever had happened to me, Will could use the Stone to cure it. We would be as before, but stronger. We could go anywhere together. Be anything we wanted. We would have each other, and we would have the Stone. Will, the Stone, and my mother cured and grateful but far away. It was all I could think of to want.

I opened my eyes, ready to tell him. My chest was tight with terror. I would tell him quickly, get it over with before I could change my mind. But he wasn't there. I pushed myself up and squinted at the tiny window. It was layered so thickly with grime that I could not be certain, but it appeared to be twilight. I had slept all day, and I felt no more rested. I glanced at the brazier in the corner, still covered with the rag. I went to it and stared at the White Elixir inside. It was stunningly beautiful, dense white and shining. Like an opal, but more so. I should write down my mother's notes, so that Will could continue if I went mad before it was finished. Then I would need to check his stores. He most likely didn't have everything we would need. When he got back, I would send Will out with the silver to buy the supplies. And Dominic could—

It was the first time I had thought of Dominic since awakening. My stomach twisted with guilt as I went to the low door and knocked quietly. When there was no answer, I called his name.

"Thea?" he answered.

"How are you feeling?" I asked. "Are you . . . are you hungry or—?"

"Or deranged?" he asked. His voice sounded closer now. He was just behind the door. "No, not yet. I've got a fever, though."

I slid to the ground and leaned my head against the doorframe. My mother had been feverish.

"Perhaps you are just ill," I said.

"Bentivoglio had a fever," said Dominic.

"Do you feel—" I tried to imagine what it would feel like, to fall the way my mother and Bentivoglio had. "Aggressive? Or violent?"

Dominic was quiet a moment. I could hear his rough breathing, just beyond the door. I pictured him there, his head leaning against the frame just as mine was.

"Yes," he said finally. "I keep thinking of your friend. I keep seeing his face and wanting to hurt him."

"You want to hurt Will?"

"Yes. And I heard . . . something that wasn't there. A voice."

"What voice?" I asked, dread churning my empty stomach.

"My father's," he said, very quietly. "Telling me to do things he wouldn't have told me to do. It's him, but it's not. He wasn't a very good man, but he wasn't like . . . like this." He was quiet again, breathing hard. He might have been crying. "Don't let me out, Thea. Promise me you won't let me hurt you or anyone else. I'd rather die than be a murderer again."

"You aren't a murderer, Dominic," I said. "You don't really think that, do you? Don't you know none of this was your fault?"

"I know that a man is dead because of me. I know that his family has lost him because of me. He had children. They won't see him ever again."

"But you had to defend yourself!"

"You defended yourself from your mother without killing her," said Dominic. "I should have been more careful. I could have, if I'd thought more quickly. Like you did, didn't you? You're quick."

I didn't want to think about how quick I'd had to be the night my mother tried to kill me. I had been very quick indeed—quick to strike. I recalled the Comte's face as he looked up at me from my mother's side. *Mon dieu, Thea, you could have killed her!*

"I had help," I said. "My mother's patron was there. We overpowered her together. But even so, I nearly killed her. It was only a happy chance that the blow I struck wasn't fatal, and an unhappy chance that yours was."

We fell into silence again. I put my palm flat against the door, wishing I could send some peace to him that way. He was a good man, to take this so to heart. I hadn't spared a thought for the blow I'd dealt my mother since I left France. It occurred to me that it might have killed her, after all, by some delayed effect. That sometimes happened with head wounds. And in her altered state, who knew what damage I had done her?

"You're kind, also," said Dominic, interrupting my line of thought going in quite the opposite direction.

"I'm not," I said. "I'm afraid you do not know me very well."

"I feel I know you better than I know most people," said Dominic. "I know you risked yourself to help me when I am no one to you."

"You aren't no one."

"I didn't mean it that way, I just meant that you barely know me. You don't owe me anything."

I chewed my lip and considered this. We hadn't known each other long, but I did feel he deserved loyalty. I sorted through what I knew of him, what he had done to make me feel that way.

"You defended me from Bentivoglio," I said. "You took my side. You took me in when I had nowhere to go."

"Anyone would have done that."

"My father didn't," I said.

"Your father—" Dominic's voice dripped with disapproval, but he stopped himself from pronouncing a condemnation.

"My father is like most men. He only cares about himself."

Quiet again.

"Do you really think that?" asked Dominic after a moment.

"That my father only cares about himself? Surely you wouldn't argue—"

"No, no. Not that. That most men are like him."

"Oh." I had said that without giving it much thought. It was a truism of my upbringing. I made a few mental exceptions. Will, of course. Dominic as well. "Do you not?"

There was another long silence. I was beginning to understand why Dominic thought I was so very quick, by contrast.

"I suppose I do, but maybe not like you do. Men are selfish; women, too. But we don't have to be. We aren't meant to be. We could always repent. Even your father, even now . . ."

I had almost believed this when he'd said something similar in the pub. But since then my father had behaved even worse. I'd felt a fool for hoping even then. Now, that small hope was dead.

"No," I said quietly. "I've seen enough. He won't get any more chances from me."

Dominic went silent again, though I had the feeling he wanted to say more. Then the front door opened, and I looked up, expecting Will.

It wasn't Will.

I leapt to my feet. Three large figures stood in the shadowed hall. It was the police, I thought in a panic. Then one of them stepped inside and spoke with a heavy accent.

"You are Miss Hope?" he asked.

"Who are you?" I demanded, willing Dominic to be silent.

"I am Valentin Wolff. I am looking for Miss Theosebeia Hope."

He pronounced my name very precisely, as though he had practiced. And surely he must have, as he got it right, which no one ever did without practice. He was German, from the accent. Prussian, no doubt. Will's employer had found him.

But why was he looking for me?

The Prussian walked toward me slowly, and in the darkness I distinguished his broad, heavy shoulders and the walking stick he held in his hand. He surveyed the room, looking me over the same way he did the dying fire, the chest, the brazier in the corner.

"Alles," he said to the men behind him. "Wir brauchen alles, sagte er."

All this. We will need it all, he said.

"You are Theosebeia," said Valentin, returning to English. "You will come with us."

"I would rather not."

Valentin paused, and I thought he might be smiling. It was hard to tell in the darkness.

"You are a clever girl, he said," said Valentin. "He said you would come. If you cannot help your friend, we will kill him."

There was little point in pretending, but I did it anyway, just in case.

"What are you talking about? What friend?"

He took another step toward me, and now he was close enough that I could just make out his smile.

"William Percy. He is a thief and a fraud, but he thinks you will wish to help him. But perhaps you do not?"

I glanced at the door, where Dominic stayed quiet. I would go, of course, but what to do about Dominic? He might die of thirst before we were free to come back for him.

"What do you want me to do?"

"You will help William Percy pay his debt to Burggraf Ludwig. If this debt is discharged, William Percy's life will be spared, and you will of course be free to go."

"And what does William Percy owe to Graf Ludwig?"

"He owes him the Philosopher's Stone."

A chill swept over me. My breath wouldn't come. I forced out words without it.

"And Will . . . told you I would make it?"

Valentin inclined his head in assent.

I reached for the doorframe. Suddenly I wasn't sure my legs would hold me. Could Will have told them about me, to save his life? I had thought he wouldn't ask it of me. But if this were true, then he was not even going to ask. He had forced my hand.

My mind recoiled at the thought. I wouldn't believe it. I couldn't.

"You're a liar," I said to Valentin as calmly as I could. "But I will come."

"Thea, don't!" cried Dominic from behind the door.

The Germans pushed me aside and rattled the door

that hid Dominic. When they couldn't open it, one of them stepped back and began to kick it down. Another decision was made for me.

"Who is this?" asked Valentin when his partner emerged, pulling Dominic with him. "And why did you lock him up?"

"Thea, you can't." Dominic looked at me with desperation. His forehead shone with sweat in the last of the firelight. "You know what will happen. Will shouldn't ask this of you."

"Perhaps not," said Valentin. "But, if you do not choose to help him, we will find another way to convince you."

"Don't hurt her!" exclaimed Dominic.

Valentin bowed his head and frowned at the thought.

"I hope that will not be necessary," he said to Dominic. "Perhaps we could hurt you instead."

Valentin glanced at me to gauge my reaction. Whatever my face showed seemed to satisfy him.

"Wir nehmen ihn auch," he said.

We take him also.

Dominic had told me he didn't know German, but he seemed to know well enough what this meant. He lashed out against the man holding him, landing a punch to the jaw before the German had time to react. Valentin took my arm and pulled me back. Each of the Prussians was half again as big as Dominic, and yet Dominic felled one of them with another blow. When the second pushed him into the wall, Dominic threw him off. Valentin watched dispassionately while his two fellows got up and tried again. He drew me close to him and leaned his head down to my ear.

"Is it some of your alchemist's witchcraft, that he is so

strong?" he asked in a low voice. His face brushed mine, and I shuddered and jerked away, but Valentin held me.

The two Germans had finally realized they had to coordinate their attack. Each seized one of Dominic's arms and threw him face-first to the ground. I winced as his head bounced off the floorboards with a sickening crack. I tried to pull free of Valentin, again without success. The other Germans produced rope and bound Dominic's hands behind his back.

"Please, let me see if he is hurt," I said to Valentin.

"There is a surgeon at the Burggraf's house who will see to him," said Valentin. "You should have warned us that you had enhanced his strength with your sorcery."

"I didn't," I said. "He is sick, and he is going to get sicker."

"Sick with strength? An unusual sort of sickness."

I watched helplessly as one of the Prussians threw Dominic over his shoulder. Dominic's eyes were closed, and his mouth leaked blood. Valentin escorted me out after him, while the third German stayed behind to gather up the supplies. Valentin's grip on my upper arm was vise-tight and painful, but it wasn't what made me follow him.

Outside, twilight had deepened into night. A carriage waited, stylish and out of place, and looking much too large on the slum's narrow street. Valentin lifted me in and climbed in beside me. He released my arm and grasped my hand instead. I tried to pull it away, but he tightened his grip.

"I am sorry for this—" Valentin cocked his head in thought. "Unverschämtheit."

"Impertinence." I translated without thinking.

"Sprechen sie Deutsch?" he asked.

I tried to look confused, and shook my head.

"This is an impertinence. I thought that might be the word you were searching for."

"Ah, yes." Valentin's eyebrows relaxed. "I am sorry for this—impertinence." He said it as carefully as he had said my name. "But I must be certain you will not attempt to throw yourself from the carriage."

I edged away from him but left my hand lying limp on his leg, where he held it. I stared at Dominic, unconscious and bound across from me, and then out the window as the muddy alley rolled past. The tall wooden tenements blocked the last of the day's dying light, and a dirty fog fell over us. I was starting to feel as though it was never daytime in London.

"I won't," I said.

The streets grew steadily broader and cleaner as we passed out of the slums. Burggraf Ludwig's house was in the West End of London, which seemed like a different world than Will's, not just a different neighborhood. The streets here were paved with tidy cobbles instead of muddy slush. Tall gas lamps cast soft yellow light at regular intervals along the way. Instead of cramped wooden tenements, too close and tall to show the sky, the streets were lined with grand houses, spacious lots, and tall iron gates bearing proud brass crests. One of them swung open to let us in. The Burggraf's house stood back from the road, shrouded in stately trees. Valentin released my hand when the gates swung shut behind us. I stepped out of the carriage and glanced back at the manned gate and high walls and concluded that he was right. There was no need to restrain me now. Well trained as I was, no one had ever thought I might need to know how to scale a wall. It had not seemed a skill necessary for the successful practice of alchemy, until now.

I stepped inside the white marble entryway, where a sparkling chandelier hung down from two floors above, casting the bright, clear light of dozens of candles. Fluted Greek columns flanked the graceful, curving staircase. The stately, black-and-white-checked floors gleamed with polish. Everything was light, white, and sparkling clean. The contrast between Will's den and this house could not have been more pronounced. In spite of myself, I drew in a long breath of clean, fresh air. Then I turned to Valentin.

"I want to see Will," I said. My voice rang off the high ceiling that soared above us.

"You may see him when the surgeon has finished tending to him," said Valentin. "You will not want to see him until then. We left him somewhat messy."

I glared at Valentin. "What have you done to him?"

Valentin cocked his head at me and looked surprised. "Did you think your friend gave us your name without resistance?" he asked.

"Do you mean—" My stomach lurched with horror and hope. "You tortured him? That's why he told you about me?"

The relief I felt to have proof that Will had not betrayed me willingly died quickly as I imagined what it meant. *Messy*, Valentin had said. I glared up at him. In the light of the chandelier, I saw his face clearly for the first time. He looked younger than I expected, younger than my father. Much younger. He could not have been much older than twenty-five. He was not ugly, despite a scar that ran down his forehead and through his eyebrow. His hair was the color of dry dirt strewn with straw, and his straight bearing and dark blue waistcoat gave him a military look. If I had seen him first on the street instead of uninvited in the garret, I would have trusted him by instinct. It was strange to notice that at the same moment I learned he had tortured Will.

"What did you do to him?" I demanded again, my horror rising. "How could you? He's not well, surely you saw that!"

"No, he is not well," said Valentin. He looked at me, his eyes a little wide, as though he, too, were seeing me clearly for the first time. "It seems alchemy is not a healthy profession. You are very young," he added without pausing.

"I . . . what?" I snapped.

"Forgive me," said Valentin. "You are . . . not what I had thought. Permit me to ask, what is Will Percy to you?"

"As you said, he is my friend."

"Forgive me," he said again. "But you live with him."

My face burned crimson, but I forced embarrassment from my voice.

"I do not."

Valentin stared at me a moment longer, looking as though he was about to say more. Then he thought better of it and extended his arm to the staircase.

"This way," he said.

We climbed two flights, my hand trailing on the elegant bannister. I looked up and saw the sky through the glass dome that capped the ceiling. I had been in many fine houses—enough to know that this was not merely grand, but stylish as well. Just below the dome, a balcony guarded by a gleaming bronze balustrade looked down on us. I caught movement out of the corner of my eye and saw the swish of skirts just disappearing from view. On the third floor, we crossed the broad length of the house, passing a German sentry standing as still as the gray-dappled marble columns that overlooked the staircase. Valentin made for one door, while across from it the German who had carried Dominic in stood guarding the other.

"Dominic is in there?" I asked Valentin.

"Dominic," he repeated, and I realized with chagrin I had given him a name he didn't know. "Yes. Dominic is in there."

A pang of worry shot through me.

"Is he hurt?"

"I think not gravely," said Valentin. "He may have lost a tooth. The surgeon will see to him in a moment."

"If he becomes violent, please don't hurt him again," I said.

"Do you expect him to become violent?"

I glanced at the burly German guarding Dominic's door, the one who had thrown him to the floor and knocked out his teeth. I noticed with satisfaction that he bore his own marks from the encounter. An enormous bruise blackened one of his eyes, and his lower lip was swelling and split. But he stood tall despite that, ignoring his painful face, his arms straight at his side. His hair was pulled back as neatly and tightly as Valentin's, and his clothes were nearly identical to those of the guard across the hallway.

"What are you people?" I asked, turning back to Valentin. His hand was on the doorknob, but he hadn't opened the door.

"We are employees of Burggraf Ludwig, who owns this house, as I have told you," he replied.

"You are soldiers," I said.

Valentin inclined his head in assent. "Once we were."

"But you kidnap women and torture sick men," I said. "Have you no honor?"

"You believe we are men of honor, because we were soldiers?" asked Valentin.

He opened the door, and placed his hand on the small of my back, steering me into the room. A library opened before me, inlaid up to the high ceiling on every wall with dark mahogany bookcases. Rich red curtains were pulled back from the tall windows, which let in just enough light to read by. The pleasant smell of good leather, paper, and pipe smoke was cut through by something else, something sharp and ugly.

Will sat in a burgundy chair by the fire, trembling and pale. I wasn't sure what it was I smelled, but it came from him. He looked up at me, an expression of agony on his face.

"I'm sorry, Bee," Will groaned from the chair. "I'm so sorry. I didn't want to tell them. I didn't mean to tell them anything."

I walked toward him more quickly than I wanted to, forcing down my hesitation. I knelt beside his chair and tried to take his hand in mine, but he winced and jerked it away. His fingers were covered in white bandages.

The smell—strong, unhealthy, and chemical—was coming from them. It was some kind of disinfectant.

"Oh Will, what did they do?" I whispered.

"Nothing," he said. "It doesn't matter. The surgeon said they'll grow back. That isn't why I told them—"

"Don't, Will," I said. "I understand. I don't blame you."

And I was resolved to try not to, though a twisting, hollow feeling inside made me wonder if I could. I tried not to consider whether I would have betrayed him after merely having a few fingernails ripped out. If I had let myself dwell on it, I would have had to admit that I did not believe I would.

"You don't understand!" It was nearly a shout, and proved too much for him. He started to cough. His whole body convulsed with it, and I looked away. It hurt to see him so broken down. It was a dull ache that hadn't left me since he opened the door, one that flared up into acute pain with every convulsion. When he was finished I forced myself to look at him again. He was wiping blood from his mouth, breathing hard and shallow.

"They knew you were at my house," he said in a hoarse whisper. "They saw you go in. They said they would hurt you until I made the Stone. So I told them I didn't know how, but you did." He broke off again, staring down into the bloody handkerchief in his unbandaged hand. "I'm sorry, Bee. I shouldn't have, I know I shouldn't have. But I couldn't bear for them to hurt you. The things they said they would do—"

He broke off again. His coughs were wet and deep and painful. I shot another angry glare at Valentin. It felt good, and easy, to be furious with him. He was a monster, torturing Will and threatening me until he told them what he had told them. Valentin frowned and looked away, but he didn't deny it.

"Fortunately you are willing," said Valentin with a trace of irony. "So no outrages will be necessary."

There was a quiet knock on the door, and Valentin stepped out.

Will's dark blue eyes locked on to me with an open intensity I'd never experienced before without a bottle of champagne to prepare me. They were still beautiful, but their usual intelligence was overshadowed with fear so deep I could have fallen into it. It wasn't fear of Valentin, or fear of torture. Those things weren't the worst terrors he faced. It was fear of death, and it began to thread its way from him into me.

"I'm dying anyway. Another month or two of my life isn't worth your sanity."

His words were flat. They were lies. He was no more ready to die than I was ready to let him. Valentin slipped back into the room, and I stood to face him.

"I can make the Philosopher's Stone for your master," I said. "But the process will cost me my mind."

Valentin's eyebrows crawled up his forehead as far as they could go. "That seems unlikely."

"I've seen it twice now. Almost three times, if Dominic is not far from that fate. There is a curse on it."

"How unfortunate," he said. His straining eyebrows did not relax.

"What?" I snapped. "You'll torture a man to make him

produce a legendary substance that produces unlimited wealth and cures any malady, but you balk at the idea that the process might have an ill effect?"

"You mistake me, Miss Hope," said Valentin. "It is my employer who believes in the legendary stone, that, as you say, produces such wonders. I am not paid to believe."

"Fine. Your master and I believe, let that be enough. I will give him what he wants, though you doubt it, and when I do he will grant me a few favors. First, he will allow Will to heal me of my madness, and then . . ." I did not look at Will. I did not need to in order to feel the desperate hope coming from him. "And then you will allow Will to heal himself. And Dominic. Then you will take the Stone, and Will's contract is fulfilled. Do you agree?"

"Certainly," said Valentin with a wry smile. "It seems a most acceptable arrangement. If you have gone mad, and the stone you produce can heal you, then it will be proved to be what you say, will it not? And naturally the wonderful object would discharge William Percy's debt."

"And—" I tried to sound confident, though I knew this was likely too much to ask. "And we will need to go to France. My mother is there, also mad. I must cure her, as well."

"That will not be possible," said Valentin. "But if you are able, you may bring your mother to Burggraf Ludwig's estate in Prussia. The magical substance can heal her there as well as in France, one presumes."

"Fine," I said. "And you may mock me all you like, as long as you take the necessary precautions. You saw how unnaturally strong Dominic was, and his madness has only begun. It would be a shame if I killed you because you did not believe me."

"I shall have chains made that would restrain the most fierce monster," said Valentin.

"Good," I said.

"Let me do it, Bee," said Will, pushing himself forward in his chair. "You can tell me what to do, but stay out of the room."

My heart constricted with affection, and hope flickered inside me briefly before I was forced to snuff it out. Will's hands had not been as steady as mine in the best of times, and now one was tormented beyond use, and the other trembled just lying in his lap. I shook my head.

"I can do it," he said. "You never saw what I could do, Bee. Marguerite never gave me a chance. I'll make it, and then you can cure me of the madness and the consumption at once. And that way if it doesn't work, at least you are spared."

"Even you do not believe it will work, Percy?" asked Valentin.

"I believe whatever Miss Hope says," said Will. "As should you. But it could go wrong. Alchemy is very—"

"Precise." I let my gaze rest on his bandaged fingers, then met his eyes, which welled with misery. "It has to be me, Will."

Will lowered his head. He closed his eyes, and from the way his chest rose and fell, I knew he was trying not to cry.

"You brought Will's supplies? And the brazier?" I asked. Valentin inclined his head in assent.

"Bring them here," I said. "We will need more supplies, I think. I will give you a list. The substance in the brazier is the most important thing. If that is damaged we will have to start over. It will take months longer."

"Nothing was damaged," said Valentin. "We shall do exactly as you say, Miss Hope. After dinner."

"Dinner," I repeated, as though I had never heard of it. I was hungry, but for once I did not want to eat. Food would pull me back into myself, banish the heedless energy that I needed to propel me forward. If I did anything as sane as sit down to a meal, I might decide I could not face madness after all, even for Will.

"Yes, miss, dinner," repeated Valentin, firmly. "Dinner, and then a good night's sleep. We will begin in the morning."

Terror rose in me at the thought of lying awake until dawn, waiting. I could do it, but I could not spend a night contemplating it.

"I slept all day," I said, and heard a note of pleading in my voice. "I would rather—"

"Tomorrow we will do things your way, Miss Hope. Tonight, you will join me at dinner." He extended his arm. I hesitated to take it. His face tightened, reminding me that this man had ordered Will's fingernails pulled out. He might even have done it himself, and in any case did not seem to have been troubled by it in the least. I took his arm but looked back at Will. Will laid his head against the high back of his chair. His body was slack with resignation as he watched us go.

"Is Will coming?" I asked.

"The maid will bring him some soup. The men do not

like to dine with a man whom they were required to torture, at least not on the same day."

"Yes, I can imagine how unpleasant that would be for them."

Valentin escorted me out of the room and closed the door behind him. "We are wicked, in your eyes," he said.

"Oh, not at all." My sarcasm fell flat, even to my own ears.

"And it does not concern you that your . . ." Here he glanced at me. "Your friend defrauded my employer?"

"It seems to me your employer could afford it," I said, but without energy. The thought of sitting through dinner with this man and his cohort made me feel bone weary, and at the same time filled me with dread. I couldn't think of any good reason Valentin insisted on forcing me to eat with them. I imagined them eyeing me the way he did, assessing my virtue, perhaps drawing different conclusions than Valentin had.

He led me down the stairs and into a spacious and handsomely appointed dining room. The walls were a pale spring green, with recesses on three sides for marble busts of unattractive men. Four of Valentin's soldiers stood clustered around a wide, gleaming sideboard, pouring themselves aperitifs from a crystal decanter. They each wore similar suits of dark blue, and though they had not changed for dinner, all but one of them seemed comfortable in these genteel surroundings. The biggest of them, a ruddy, simple-looking fellow, held his glass as though he was sure his grip would break it. They froze in the midst of their actions when we came in, staring at me bluntly. I wished I were wearing a less crushed and dusty gown, and then sternly reminded myself that I did not care.

"Miss Hope, may I introduce you to Herr Martin," said Valentin, indicating the German nearest us. The tall, dark-haired man made a shallow bow without setting down his sherry. His smile curled up on one side, showing teeth like a wolf. I looked away quickly.

Valentin introduced me to each of the men in turn, and I in turn immediately forgot their names. I said nothing. I did not curtsy. If the men noticed, they pretended not to.

We took our seats around the table, Valentin across from me and the man called Martin on my right. The chair at the head of the table was empty. I glanced at Martin, and my eyes fell on his fingers. They were long, rough, and pink from a recent and vigorous scrubbing. Perhaps they'd recently had blood on them. Perhaps the blood had been Will's.

I felt Martin's eyes on me, but I refused to meet them. Instead I glared at Valentin. He had seated me next to the torturer. How did he expect me to eat?

"Is she coming?" one of the men asked in German. Valentin glanced at the door.

"She said she would," he said. "She wanted to meet Miss Hope."

As if on cue, the dining room door opened, and a young woman in a fashionable satin gown appeared. The men jumped to their feet at once and folded themselves into bows quite a bit more respectful than the ones they had made for me. The young woman nodded her perfectly coiffed and powdered head at them, then made her way to me. Another woman, older but with an unadorned, severe beauty, followed her in. I rose slowly to my feet, more to prevent them from towering over me than from courtesy. The younger woman was an inch or two shorter than I, which left her still above average height for a woman. Her face and hair were powdered, a fashion my mother had never let me indulge in, nor one that much tempted me. Her cheeks were much pinker than natural. She was good-looking, but with a stern set to her jaw and a coldness in her eyes that might make it hard to call her pretty.

"So," said the woman in English. "You are the young lady who 'as come to rescue William Percy. What did you call her, Valentin? Theo—?"

"Miss Theosebeia Hope," said Valentin. "Meet Miss Rahel, the older daughter of Burggraf Ludwig."

"And this is my companion, Miss Berit. You have a strange name," said Rahel.

"My mother is an alchemist," I said.

"I know that." Rahel nodded. "And your father?"

I thought of my father. I imagined him in his beautiful Oxonian study, poring over my notes, trying to break my mother's code. Or perhaps he had broken it already. Perhaps he was in the laboratory, performing the steps that would soon drive him mad. If he was, it was his own fault. I had warned him.

"I have no father."

Rahel pursed her lips, looking for a moment like an unhappy German governess I once had. She had stayed less than a year, but she was the reason I spoke German with a Bavarian accent.

"Some man caused your birth, whether he accepted the responsibility or not."

"He did not," I said. "Hope is my mother's family name."

Rahel nodded thoughtfully. "Ein hübsches uneheliches Kind. Einfach zu nehmen."

A pretty bastard child. Easy prey.

Rahel raised her eyebrows at me for a moment, and I held back my anger and attempted to look puzzled. Rahel seemed to accept this and moved to her place at the head of the table. The men all sat as she did, and Berit sat beside her. Rahel began to speak to the men in German, and for the moment I was forgotten.

Dinner was veal in a heavy cream sauce, served with lavishly buttered potatoes and boiled peas. It was delicious, but I decided to find it too rich. It was useful to have the occupation of pushing food around on my plate while I listened intently to the conversation and pretended not to understand it.

They spoke of their king, Frederick William II, and his plans to join with the Austrians in the invasion of France. The leaden mass of dread that had settled in my stomach turned over at the talk of war. The Germans rattled off the names of the nations allied against France with easy certainty that this war was theirs to win. Prussia, Austria, Britain: the great powers of Europe saw France in its time of weakness and circled like vultures. The only thing left to be determined, in their minds, was who would take which part.

"Frederick William should not let Austria march first. He is too occupied with Poland—he does not see what can be gained in France," Rahel said in German. She took as avid an interest as each of the former military men at the table.

"Austria may be too much tempted to give France back to its fool of a king," said Martin.

"Perhaps," said Valentin. "But there is no doubt that Leopold made promises to his sister and her husband, and even more to the émigrés. Louis is not a bad man."

"No, but he is incompetent. There is no worse crime for a king, and his incompetence has left all Europe in danger," said Rahel. Her eyes flitted to me, and I trained my own back on my plate. "The Bourbons cannot deal with the revolutionaries. It is no kindness to give them another chance to fail."

Valentin stared at his plate with a small frown but said nothing. It seemed that the Graf's daughter tolerated only so much disagreement, and Valentin had reached his quota. She changed the subject.

"I take it our young magician is much diminished since we saw him last." My gaze was carefully lowered, but I felt her eyes on me.

"Consumption," agreed Valentin. "He doesn't have long. His young lady believes she can save him with alchemy, poor child."

His pity held an edge of contempt. I felt my anger redden my cheeks.

"Be careful what you say, Valentin," said Rahel. I looked up at her before I could stop myself, and found her smiling directly at me. "The young lady understands every word."

I froze, with what I feared was a very foolish expression on my face. Rahel made a short, sharp laugh. The game was clearly up.

"How could you tell?" I asked in German.

"You have no skill at feigning stupidity, my dear," said Rahel, in her own language.

I raised my chin and tried to will the blush from my cheeks.

"I feigned well enough to fool your captain," I said with an angry glance at Valentin.

"That is no accomplishment!" cried Rahel with another bark of a laugh. "Men are always willing to believe in the stupidity of women. Though perhaps that is not their fault, when women are so quick to make themselves fools for men. Your mother, for instance."

Valentin widened his eyes meaningfully at Rahel, the universal expression for *Stop talking.* She took no notice.

"I know of her, of course," she said, nodding at my shocked look. "My father's obsession with magic is impossible to avoid when one lives in the same house. I have learned the most famous names, your mother's included. That armor of hers was quite useful, I recall. I know that she could be rich in her own right if she chose her patrons on the merits of their offers rather than the merits of their faces."

"My mother is a scientist," I said as coldly as I could. "Money is not what she cares for."

"Perhaps not, though if that is true then it is strange indeed that she pursues the 'science' of turning everything into gold."

I bit my tongue. I did not want to argue the value of alchemy with this woman, and still less did I want to defend my mother to her. I speared the last several pieces of veal in front of me with a force that made an unpleasant scraping noise on the china, and shoved them into my mouth. If I was chewing, I could not talk.

"Nothing is so disappointing to me as an intelligent woman who makes herself stupid for a man," said Rahel. Her wry, even tone was beginning to falter. A flush rose under her carefully powdered face. I noted, with some surprise, that she was actually upset. "And it seems there is no end to the disappointment. Tell me, my dear, what is it about our young magician that earned your devotion?"

I chewed furiously. My mother, alchemy, Will. This woman seemed determined to probe everything and everyone who occupied a painful place in my heart, and I did not understand why.

"He is good-looking, of course, in that careless way that will not last," she said. "And perhaps that much is over already?"

I thought of Will's wasted body, his thin, hollow chest. The shadows under his eyes like purple bruises. He was still handsome, but she was certainly right that it could not last much longer. The meat stuck in my throat. I reached mechanically for the glass of wine in front of me.

"He had confidence, I saw that at once," said Rahel. "He was used to charming women. He expects us to love him, to do anything for him, no matter how little he deserves it."

"We must be grateful that Miss Hope feels he is deserving of her help," said Valentin to Rahel through a very still jaw, "or we would not be able to give Burggraf Ludwig what he desires."

"That is your concern, not mine," Rahel snapped. "My

father has promised *me* nothing, whatever he may have offered *you*."

There was something strange here, some dynamic at play that I did not understand. Rahel hated Will, that much was clear. And yet somehow I could not believe the easiest explanation, that Will had spurned her.

"If you do not want your father to get the Philosopher's Stone, then why are we here?" I asked Rahel.

"You have not answered my questions, Miss Hope," said Rahel. "Why should I answer yours?"

"Will's family is rich," I said, seizing desperately at a slight chance. "They have a large estate in the north. If you don't care about the Stone, send word to them. They would surely pay Will's debt."

Rahel shook her head and snorted. She reached for her glass and took a long drink of wine, her eyes never leaving me.

"We have appealed to the Percys," she said when she had set down her cup. She was calmer now. "They have the measure of their son more than you do, Miss Hope."

"You mean—" I thought of Will's forbidding face when I had suggested he go to his parents. "They will do nothing for him?"

"Some debts cannot be paid by anyone but the debtor."

I frowned at Valentin in mute appeal. There was danger here, danger in this woman's anger. But I didn't understand why, and I didn't see what it might change.

"I am to make the Stone," I said. "Valentin and I have an agreement. I will make the Stone and give it to Valentin. That will pay Will's debt."

Rahel fingered the stem of her wine glass, a smile playing at her lips.

"I have to know that our agreement will be honored," I said. "If it isn't certain, then I won't be able—"

My throat closed on the words, but it didn't matter. None of these people believed I could do what I said, or that I would suffer what I knew I would in consequence.

"And Valentin gives my father what he wants, gets who he wants in return, and Will is free to live out the rest of his days in your arms. A happy ending for everyone. Who am I to stand in the way?"

"I don't understand," I said. "Why would you want to stand in the way? What do you want?"

Rahel threw her napkin on the table in front of her and pushed back her chair. The men stood as she did, but I kept my seat.

"I wanted to see you, my dear," she said. "And now that I have, I am quite content."

She left, and Berit followed. The men retired to the next room for cigars, and Valentin offered to escort me to my room. We climbed the stairs slowly. I was more exhausted than I had expected. My head ached, reminding me how recently it had been pushed into a wall. Valentin kept pace with me silently, patiently. At the top of the stairs, I stopped to catch my breath. I looked up through the domed ceiling far above me, into the gray English sky.

"If I asked you what all that meant, would you tell me?" I asked Valentin without looking at him.

He shook his head slowly. "I cannot."

"Did Will—" I didn't want to ask this. I had a cowardly

impulse to banish the question, not just from the tip of my tongue but from my mind as well. "Did Will hurt her, somehow?"

Valentin was quiet for a long moment. His teeth worked against each other behind his closed mouth.

"No," he said. I waited for him to elaborate, but he did not. We continued down the hallway, and I counted the doorways as we passed, wondering who and what was in each. We were on the second floor, below the rooms where Will and Dominic were being kept. Perhaps they felt I was less likely to leap from a window in an attempt to flee. If so, they were right, though it wasn't my skirts that would prevent me from trying it.

Valentin unlocked a door and held it open for me. Inside was a lovely, high-ceilinged room decorated in soft shades of blue and gold. The bed dominated, a beautiful brocaded affair, with a blue satin canopy draping down from a gold filigreed circle. The paneled walls were papered with blue and green chinoiserie, and a broad window and large gold mirror seemed to expand the room outside itself. I crossed to the vanity, letting my fingers trail over the ribbons and beads from a broken necklace as I passed. I threw open the closet doors, where several delicate gowns reflected the same feminine sensibility as the decor.

"I do not believe those will fit you," said Valentin from the doorway. He watched me with a guarded, flat expression. His fists were closed tight. "But you are welcome to try them on."

I touched a petal-pink silk gown, and from the still set of Valentin's jaw, it was clear that I was not only unwelcome to wear it, he did not even like me to look at it.

"Whose room is this?" I asked.

"For now, it is yours," he said.

I sat in the chair in front of the vanity and opened a drawer. A letter box lay inside. I touched it. Valentin's posture tightened. His whole frame was dense with restrained action, but he was in control. He wouldn't stop me. But I pushed the letter box to the back of the drawer. It was not mine, and I was not the sort of person who read letters meant for others. I pulled out an ivory-handled comb. A long black hair was threaded through it. Deliberately, I took the hair between my thumb and forefinger.

"Not Rahel," I said. "She is blond. And I rather doubt all of this would be quite to her taste."

"You asked if Will Percy had hurt Rahel," said Valentin. He barely opened his clenched jaw to say it. "You thought he might have. And yet you mean to make such a sacrifice for him? To give up your reason, as you believe you will?"

"I asked, and you told me he hasn't hurt her," I said. "You declined to say more. Should I turn on my dearest friend because the man who abducted us both seems to hate him for no good reason?"

"Your dearest friend." His words dripped with contempt. "Is that what he is to you?"

"Not only my dearest friend." I thought back to the day when he first came to the chateau. He had bowed to my mother but smiled past her, right at me, thinking about how he would like to make me laugh. "My only friend."

"Your only friend?" repeated Valentin. "What about the other one? Dominic?"

"Dominic is my friend," I agreed. "But I met him only

four days ago. So you might call him the exception that proves the rule."

I picked up the beads on the vanity and rolled them on my palm. I felt Valentin's eyes on me and wished he would leave.

"You've had a lonely life," he said.

I looked up at him in surprise. The contempt was gone from his voice. He sounded softer, thoughtful. Like he had actually considered, for a moment, what it might have been like to be me.

I hadn't meant to invite pity. I never meant to do that.

"I suppose so, before Will came," I said. "All my friends had been dead hundreds of years."

Valentin's expression tilted in confusion.

"My friends," I explained. "Paracelsus, Ortolanus, Jean de Meung, Jābir ibn Hayyān."

"Alchemists," he said, his confusion clearing. "You're an odd girl, Theosebeia."

"I should be more like this one, I suppose?" I asked, holding up the dark-haired girl's beads and gazing around her room. If Burggraf Ludwig kept a house in London, perhaps it was so that his children could attend the social season. Rahel did not seem the type for balls, but she must have a sister. A younger one, as Rahel was the older.

"You should have had more than one friend," said Valentin. It sounded more like an accusation now than sympathy. He was stiffening already, withdrawing his pity. Good.

"Like she did?" I asked. "This girl has plenty of friends, doesn't she? And time to spend with them. Balls and dances and whatever it is fashionable girls do."

I searched Valentin's face, but it had turned to stone and gave nothing away.

"You might find it hard to believe, Herr Wolff, but I don't envy her. I might have been lonely growing up, but I was never bored. I had purpose. Can this girl say the same? Did anyone ever teach her to be more than an ornament?" I asked. "Did they give her a chance to use her mind?"

"What about your mind?" he asked through a very still jaw. "You prize it so much, yet you will give it up for him?"

"Tell me what happened, if you want me to hate him," I said. "Tell me whose room this is. Tell me why you hate that I am sitting in her chair."

Slowly, and with effort, Valentin peeled his fingers from his palms. He released his breath in a long, silent stream. He loosened his shoulders and jaw. He let go of something and said nothing.

"Good night, Miss Hope."

He closed the door behind him, and the key turned the lock.

How convenient. Someone had evidently found it necessary to lock this door from the outside in the past. I added another stroke to the picture of the black-haired girl I was forming in my mind.

12

The next day I rose, ill-rested and sore of head. I looked at my dirty robe à la polonaise, lying crumpled on the floor, and concluded that I could not face the day in it. I decided to test Valentin's assertion that the black-haired girl's clothes wouldn't fit. I took out each of the gowns and laid them on the gilded brocade bedspread. The petal pink was too girlish, I decided, and another was clearly a ballgown, and much too elaborate for daily wear. The most practical option was a sprigged, egg-blue muslin. I tried it without my stays, and couldn't close the thing. With a sigh, I laced myself into my undergarments and forced the dress closed over them. I was taller than the girl it was meant for, but without the hip pads, the dress fell to a respectable length. I tightened the ribbons that drew the neck closed and examined myself in the mirror. I stretched my arms forward, and though it was tight I could move well enough.

I would have chosen a more dignified dress to meet my fate in, if there had been one. This was a dress for a young girl going for a walk in the park on a suitor's arm, or to a picnic on a fine spring day. It looked wrong on my nervous, taut frame. It didn't suit my wan face or my heavily shadowed eyes.

I considered taking it off and suffering the future in my own, sullied dress. There was only a little blood on the hem. Perhaps I could wash it out in the basin.

But it was too late. There was a knock at the door, and I answered it still in the robin's-egg muslin. Valentin started to say good morning, then saw what I wore, and his voice failed him.

"Good morning," I replied. I no longer wanted to change. The stricken look on Valentin's face was worth a little incongruity. "Do you have the supplies I asked for?"

Valentin opened his mouth but didn't use it. He nodded. Even that seemed to cost him something.

"Good. And where would you have me work? I will need somewhere with a good space and a fireplace of suitable size."

Valentin turned his head away. He stared resolutely at the wall as he answered.

"The library."

I raised my eyebrows, but Valentin did not see. No adept would have suggested a library. Between the smells, smokes, and occasional explosions, books were not safe in an alchemist's workroom. But these were Burggraf Ludwig's books, and therefore I felt no particular desire to protect them.

"I'm ready," I said. "Lead the way."

Valentin did not take my arm and walked farther from me than he had before. We climbed the stairs and I saw that the room where they held Dominic was still guarded, this time by the large, florid German.

"Guten Morgen," I said to him. Valentin held the library door open expectantly, but I ignored him and continued in German. "How is the prisoner today?"

"Well enough, I think," said the German, with a hesitant look at Valentin.

"His fever? Is it worse?" I asked.

"Nein. Better. He ate quite a breakfast."

Better. I scarcely dared to believe him. I turned to Valentin. "What did your surgeon say?" I demanded. "Did he see him?"

"Yesterday," grunted Valentin. "The surgeon said he could do nothing."

"If he is better, I need to know," I said.

Valentin continued to stand, holding the door, pretending not to have heard what I said.

"I have agreed to make the Stone for you, and lose my reason so that your Burggraf can have what he did not make and did not deserve, and you can have your reward, whatever that is."

Valentin looked at me sharply, and I made a note of the raw feeling in his eyes at the mention of his reward. I continued with more confidence.

"But before I do this, I will see my friend. And I will have assurances from you of his well-being."

"Which friend?"

"Both." I met his eyes in challenge. He was the first to look away.

Valentin nodded at the big man, who opened the door to Dominic's room. It wasn't locked, I noticed. There must have been a limit to the rooms that were equipped to serve as prison cells.

The room was some sort of servants' quarters, not as large or prettily decorated as the others in the house that I had seen. Dominic sat on the floor, back against the wall, hands chained to each other through a pipe that stood out from the floorboards. He looked up at me as I came in, and to my surprise, he smiled. I went to him and knelt by his side.

"I don't know for certain," he said to me. "But I think the fever broke."

I felt his forehead with the back of my hand. He wasn't hot. He wasn't sweating as he had been before. There was no scent of sulfur on his breath. The heavy weight of my dread lightened. The fever had broken.

"What about your mind? Do you still feel . . ."

"I feel like myself. I didn't, last night. There were moments . . ." He shuddered. "But this morning I woke up myself. I must not have gone far enough into it. Whatever it was. I haven't heard the voice all morning."

I sat back and gazed at him with relief.

"Although I admit I still feel a bit like hurting that friend of yours," he said. "But I don't think that's anything to do with the Alchemist's Curse."

"Not you, too," I sighed. "Poor Will certainly has a knack for making enemies."

"You aren't going to do it," said Dominic. His chains clinked against each other as he leaned toward me. "Tell me you're not going to make the Stone. Whatever they threaten us with. I'm not afraid to die, not now."

"You don't mean that," I said. "Everyone is afraid to die."

"Maybe I am. But I can face it. I've confessed."

I stared at the manacles on his wrists. They were tight, and I could see red marks where they had rubbed the skin raw. I thought about lying to him. But I waited too long.

"Thea, no!" His clear eyes widened. "Whatever they do to Will or me, or even you, none of it is worse than the curse! It was like . . . it was like hell, Thea. It was torment. There were other souls there. Like the souls of the damned."

I stared. "Like hell? But . . . surely you don't mean . . ."

"I mean it, Thea!" he exclaimed. "There were other minds there, other victims. It couldn't truly have been hell, but it was as bad as I could imagine. I only felt the edge of it, but that's enough to know I'd face anything else first!"

I jumped to my feet. My heart felt as if it were punching a hole in my chest. I had to get out. I couldn't listen to more, or my courage would fail.

"He'll cure me," I said from the doorway without turning around. "With the Stone. When I've made it. You know I don't really have a choice. They have you, they have Will. They have all the means they need to force me."

"Don't do this for me," cried Dominic to my turned back. "Do you hear me, Thea? I don't want it. Don't do this for me!"

"I won't, then," I said. "Not for you."

I shut the door before he could reply. I turned to Valentin, still waiting in the hallway.

"When I have done as your Graf requires, I want you to take Dominic to Germany. He will need to be kept from the attention of the law here. And he will need money for training. He wants to be a medical doctor."

"You ask a great deal," said Valentin.

"Not at all," I said. "I will give your Graf unlimited wealth and immortal life. In return I ask only a few paltry favors."

And paltry favors they were; my mind, Will's life, Dominic's freedom restored. Small things indeed, when set against the value of the Philosopher's Stone.

Valentin grunted again. He seemed more prone to it this morning than he had yesterday.

"If it is not merely a fantasy, what you promise," he said.

"If it is, the deal is off." I was out of patience. "But I tell you, I've seen it. It is no fantasy."

Even now the thought of the deep red mass, hardening into the stone in the ovum, stirred something like lust in me. Despite the cost, a part of me wanted nothing else but to make it, and only hoped that I would not lose my mind before I could see it done.

"You have seen it," repeated Valentin. "But have you seen it do what you say? Have you seen it turn all metals into gold, heal all ills?"

All I had seen it do was smash against the wall, but I couldn't dwell on that. It would work. Everything I had ever done pointed to it. The same book promised it that warned of the Alchemist's Curse. And I had certainly seen the curse. Why would something so dreadful guard the Stone if it wasn't all that the writings said it was? No, the Philosopher's Stone was real. It had to be.

I pushed past Valentin, making sure to brush his arm with the fabric of my dress, and went into the library. I gathered my tools, arranged my metals, stoked the fire. I uncovered the White Elixir and found it unharmed.

It was time to get to work.

I kept my mind on the tasks in front of me. Carefully heating the Elixir, preparing the gold tincture and the antimony sulfate. Even with my heart stuttering and my body pulsating with anxiety, I ground and mixed the metals with the steady hand my mother always envied. I knew she envied it because she never mentioned it, neither to praise nor disparage, except indirectly. The thought of her reedy, resonant voice pushed away the image of the mad thing she had become.

Thea. This anger of yours is growing tiresome.

It was my mother's voice, so vivid I looked over my shoulder to see if she was behind me. She wasn't.

It is weakness to dwell so on the faults of others. And you cannot afford to be weak, my darling.

I stood and spun around, more for something to do than from a hope of seeing her. She wasn't there. All I saw was Valentin, sitting in the corner, his eyes trained on me.

"Miss Hope," he said. "Is something wrong?"

"Did you hear someone?" I asked him.

Valentin shook his head slowly.

Why would I speak to him? my mother asked. *And what did I just tell you about showing weakness?*

I turned back to my work and tried to calm myself. Whatever this was, whatever it meant, I did not have attention to spare for it now.

There was a knock at the door. I turned and stared at it in alarm until Valentin rose to respond. He had heard that, then.

A German stood outside, the tall, dark-haired one. The torturer.

"What is it, Martin?" Valentin asked.

"The Fräulein wants to see her," said Martin in German.

Valentin nodded. "I'll take her at once."

"No." A slight smile crossed Martin's face. "I am to take her."

Valentin stared impassively at Martin.

"Miss Hope," he called, without looking at me.

I approached slowly. I would not have liked the idea of going to see Rahel, in any case, but I liked it less for the malicious smile on Martin's face and the wary look on Valentin's. I stopped at the doorway.

"Why does she want to see me?" I asked. "Didn't she say what she wished last night?"

"It seems not," said Martin.

I glanced up at Valentin. His expression was stony, but he gave me a slight nod.

"Keep the heat even," I said to him. And then to Martin, "I will have to be back before the hour is out to complete the next step."

"I doubt the Fräulein will have use for more than an hour of your company," said Martin, his wolfish smile curling into a definite leer.

I stepped through the doorway. Martin started to follow, but Valentin seized his upper arm and leaned close.

"If any harm comes to her," he said in a low voice. "You will answer to me."

Martin pulled back, but Valentin did not let go.

"I answer to Fräulein Rahel," Martin said.

"I will be clear," said Valentin. "In this, you will answer to me."

They exchanged a long, unfriendly look before Martin turned away, and Valentin released his arm.

Valentin watched from the doorway as we walked down the hallway, and it wasn't until we had passed the wide, open stairway and crossed out from his sight that Martin took my arm. I tried to shake him off, but his grip tightened.

"Our captain likes you," he hissed in German.

"I doubt it," I replied. "More likely he simply dislikes you."

Martin stopped abruptly, released my arm, and slapped me across the face.

I staggered back, my mind shocked to a blinding white. I put a hand to my face. It felt hot, and then began to sting.

"There," said Martin. "Not so clever now, are you? Valentin never did know how to handle a mouthy woman."

I turned back to him, slowly, desperately wishing for a mouthy retort. But all I could do was stare, eyes wide. My cheek was tingling now, and the pain was growing. I had a sudden and alarming urge to cry.

"Valentin will punish you for this," I said. My voice sounded very far away, but at least it did not tremble.

Martin laughed. "You think Valentin will care about a little smack?"

"He said you're not to harm me."

"He did." Martin stepped close to me. I tried to back away, but he seized my arm again and pulled me toward him. His smile had something worse behind it than mere mockery. "But you are more innocent than you look if you think that was the harm he meant."

I stared at him in horror. His words were like another slap to the face, shocking me back into silence. I couldn't miss his meaning. I swallowed hard, and lowered my hand from my face with effort.

Martin smiled again but made no further threat, apparently satisfied that he had put me in my place. He pulled me after him, down a corridor emitting faint piano music. He knocked at an ornately paneled door. The music stopped, and Rahel's voice invited us in.

The door opened on a spacious and lavishly decorated parlor. Floor-to-ceiling high windows draped in heavy burgundy curtains let in all the sooty light London had to give. A thick Persian rug spread across the marble-tiled floor, and an emerald-green velvet sofa stood diagonally across it. Rahel lay on the sofa, a book in her hands, facing the piano, where Berit had just stopped playing. She watched as Martin conveyed me into the room and pushed me into a plush chair across from her. If she objected to his handling of me, or noticed the redness on my cheek, she did not say so. She merely sat upright, swinging her silk-clad legs over the side of the sofa and laying her book open on its spine in her lap.

"Ah, Theo-see-bee-ya," she said, pronouncing it carefully and wrong. "I have been reading. Berit, you may go."

The older woman rose silently from the piano bench and slipped out of the room through an inner door. Martin turned toward the door we'd entered through, but Rahel stopped him.

"No, Martin," she said. "You will stay."

I didn't look at him. I didn't have to, to picture the look on his face.

"So, as I said, I have been reading," Rahel said. "And I came across a passage that reminded me of you."

She lifted the book so I could just make out the cover. *A Vindication of the Rights of Woman.*

"Women are everywhere in this deplorable state," she read in English. "Men have various employments and pursuits which engage their attention; but women, confined to one—that is, the art of pleasing men—seldom extend their views beyond the triumph of the hour. But was their understanding once emancipated from the slavery to which the sensuality of man and their short-sighted desire has subjected them, we should probably read of their weakness with surprise . . ."

Rahel trailed off, gazing meditatively at me.

"It made me think of you, Theo-see-bee-ya," she said, reverting to German. "I thought to myself, I have an example of such a woman as Miss Wollstonecraft would like to see. You were not raised with a view to pleasing men. You were given employments, pursuits beyond the cultivation of your beauty, even if those pursuits were . . . well . . . of questionable value. And I should indeed be surprised to hear you called 'weak.' And yet . . ." She shook her head sadly.

"And yet what?" I snapped. My patience was frayed. Had I been brought here, subjected to abuse and threats, just to listen to Rahel express her disappointment in my character?

"And yet you fall victim to a worthless man with a

handsome face just as easily as any other girl," she said. "I should not like to think Miss Wollstonecraft is wrong. Yet here you are, forced into servitude out of nothing but misplaced devotion."

"I am sorry to have disappointed you," I said coldly.

"Help me understand, Theosebeia," she said. "How does a young woman such as yourself choose to throw herself away on a man? If you were not raised to it, then are we as a sex simply doomed to this foolishness? Perhaps Rousseau is right, and we should accept it as our nature. Fashion ourselves into pleasing playthings."

"I do not think so."

"Something must have gone wrong," said Rahel. "You were lonely, perhaps? Or simply so sheltered and innocent that you did not recognize a scoundrel when you saw one."

"Will is not a scoundrel," I said.

"If it was that, there is no easy cure," said Rahel. "Except, I suppose, more experience with scoundrels."

She glanced to the door, where Martin stood. I sat straighter in my chair and gripped the arms.

"That isn't necessary," I said. "I am perfectly aware of the failings of men."

"My dear, you misunderstand me," said Rahel.

"I understand that you are threatening me," I said. "Though I do not understand why."

"I do not threaten you," said Rahel with a dismissive flick of her fingers.

"If you dislike scoundrels so much, why do you employ him?" I didn't need to point to Martin. Rahel knew who I meant. Her eyes lit up as though I had asked exactly the question she had hoped for.

"Because I know the use of scoundrels," she said, bending toward me. "They are to be employed, as you say, channeled. If you had some purpose for Will, I could not fault you for your association with him. But instead, he makes use of you. You suffer for him. And you will get nothing for it. Nothing."

Her voice was rising, and so was my pulse. I did not have to understand her anger to know it was dangerous.

"So what use is it to threaten you? You submit to worse than what Martin could do to you, and yet you submit to it willingly."

"Tell me, then." My knuckles whitened against the arms of the chair, but I kept my voice calm. "You bring me in here to chide or punish me for believing in Will, but you won't tell me why I shouldn't. Tell me—stop me, if you can. Or don't tell me, and let me be."

Rahel's hot look turned cold. She placed a hand on top of her splayed-open book and curled her fingers against it.

"I want only to understand you, Theosebeia," she said. "But it seems you don't wish to understand yourself."

A retort sprung to my lips, and then another one, but I kept them both back. I knew what she wanted to hear, but I would not tell her that I believed Will a scoundrel, that he was not worthy of my love. And she would not, perhaps could not, tell me why she wished me to believe it.

There was a loud knock at the door. Martin opened it, revealing Valentin.

"Excuse me, Fräulein, but I must take Miss Hope back to her work. The composition is smoking."

I bolted up from my chair and went to the door. Martin

stepped forward and placed a hand against my shoulder to halt me. I flinched away.

"The Fräulein has not dismissed you," he said.

"Oh, let her go," said Rahel. "We wouldn't want her precious composition to catch fire. It might burn up the library."

I pushed past Martin and hurried out of the room. When Valentin shut the door behind us, I allowed myself to shudder.

I walked quickly, Valentin following after me.

"What did you do to the composition?" I asked sharply. "It shouldn't be smoking."

"It isn't," said Valentin.

I stopped, glancing at him in question. "You lied to Rahel?"

"I thought it was time to collect you," he said simply.

Once we returned to the library, I resumed my place by the fire, and Valentin his chair. He looked at me with a carefully blank expression.

"What did she want?" Valentin asked.

I considered this. "To inspire me to discover whatever it is that neither of you will tell me," I said, and then sighed. "Or perhaps merely to toy with me."

Valentin frowned and said nothing. I went back to work, pushing this new fear to the back of my mind, where it joined the others.

I worked as long and as attentively as I could, until I was wrung out, exhausted, and slightly sick. Valentin left to bring me food and I sank into the tall armchair where Will had sat, tortured and trembling. I tried to push that image away as I pushed away Mother's voice, and to remember him as he'd been in France, hale and handsome and happy. Full of dreams and plans and ideas. There had always been so much to talk about. Not just alchemy, but what alchemy could be for. He had read all the scientific texts, and other books my mother never bothered with. Philosophy, politics, literature. I didn't know, until Will showed me, that I would love reading Rousseau and Voltaire, dissecting their arguments, debating their merits with him. He understood my world completely. But more than that, he expanded it. I tried to remember that feeling of horizons widening. Of finding that the world was bigger than I knew, and that I wasn't alone in it.

Will had given me that once. But here in this room, it was contracting again. All I could find in myself was fear and anger and suspicion.

I didn't want to suspect him. It felt like giving Rahel a victory, to let her hatred plant seeds of doubt in my heart. And yet something had caused her hatred. Will had, somehow.

I had to know. Even if it meant admitting my doubts. Even if it meant doing what Rahel certainly wanted me to do.

Valentin brought me a tray of food and examined the slowly melting mixture in the brazier.

"Is this how it is meant to look?" he asked.

I nodded, then examined my dinner with distaste. The tray contained several boiled eggs sliced and slathered with mustard, some sort of pickled cabbage, two pieces of rye bread, and a cup of tea.

"Somehow I do not imagine this is what Rahel had for dinner," I said.

"Fräulein Rahel did not dine in this evening," said Valentin. "I assure you the rest of us ate no better than you."

The sour scent of the cabbage turned my already sour stomach. I had gone too long without eating, but for a moment I considered refusing the tray. Valentin heaved a sigh and leaned over me. He picked up a fork and scraped some of the cabbage onto the bread, then placed the slices of egg on top. He set the fork back down on my plate. I looked at it.

You could pick it up, said my mother's voice. *Stab him in the eye.*

"Here," he said. "It's best like this."

I looked from the fork to Valentin, pictured myself striking. He would be so surprised.

I shook myself. It was a pointless thing to do, and anyway, the food did look a little more appetizing now that he had piled it up. I took a tentative bite, and was surprised to find that I enjoyed it.

"Thank you," I said to Valentin, and regretted it at once. I did not owe my captor gratitude for providing me with edible food, even if I did feel slightly guilty for thinking about blinding him. But he accepted the thanks before I could think how to retract them.

"You're welcome." Valentin sat in a wooden chair across from me, watching blank-faced while I ate. Whatever discomfort it gave him to see me in the black-haired girl's dress, he seemed to have overcome it. I took another bite, and then another before the last was swallowed. The bread had a rich, tangy flavor. I finished it quickly and started piling the remaining cabbage and eggs on the other piece of bread.

"I have to see Will," I said when I had swallowed my food. "You may bring him here, or bring me to him."

Valentin snorted.

"Somehow you have become convinced that I do your bidding, when it is the other way around."

"If I can't see Will, I'll stop," I said. It was not a threat, but a fact, and one outside my control. Valentin's mouth twitched. He seemed to see it.

"If you require persuasion, we could bring your other friend here. The one who still has fingernails that he does not need."

It was a bluff, but a chilling one.

"Surely it would be easier to let me speak to Will than to torture Dominic," I said. "Dominic owes no debt to your Burggraf. You have no right to hurt him."

Valentin's eyes flashed their agreement even while the rest of him remained still.

"Perhaps you would do it anyway, but you wouldn't enjoy it," I said, testing a theory. "Though you didn't mind torturing Will at all."

No one but you would mind torturing Will, said my mother.

I shook her out of my head again.

One corner of Valentin's mouth twitched up. Far from minding my attempt to pry into his mind, he approved it.

"Not quite right," he said. "I did not think I would mind torturing William Percy. But in the end I found there is no pleasure in hurting a defenseless man, no matter how much he may deserve it."

"You can't help yourself, can you?" I asked. "Whatever it is you think Will has done, you want me to know what it is. And yet, you also don't. You and Rahel both. Why?" He didn't answer, so I continued, thinking out loud. "It's because you want me to continue with the work, isn't it? You were hired to find Will and make him fulfill his debt, and you feel obliged to do your duty. And you think whatever you are hiding might turn me against Will, don't you? You think I would stop loving him, and leave him to his fate if I knew. If I knew . . . what?"

His eyes flicked down, I thought, to my chest. But they continued moving down my bodice, over to the sleeves. He was looking at my dress. At the dark-haired girl's dress.

"The Burggraf has another daughter, doesn't he?"

Valentin sat quietly for a moment. Whatever struggle there might have been in his mind did not show on his face, except for a forced blankness there. Finally he stood.

"You may speak with Percy," he said.

I stood as well. I set aside the tray and brushed my hands on the sprigged dress.

"Tell me her name," I said.

Valentin held the door for me in silence, and we proceeded up yet another flight of stairs. These were at the back of the house, hidden behind a low door. The fourth floor was little more than an attic: cramped, low-ceilinged, and drafty. These were servants' quarters, unadorned and markedly colder than the lower floors. We stopped in front of the narrowest door at the end of the corridor.

"Ada," said Valentin.

I didn't understand at first. I thought perhaps he had begun to say something in German, and stopped. Then I realized he was answering my question. Ada was a name. It was the dark-haired girl's name.

"Ada," I said again, pronouncing it with a soft "A" sound,

as he did. It sounded childish with that accent, like baby babble. One might think my own preposterous name would have taught me to be forgiving of the names of others, but no. I felt a stirring of entirely undeserved hostility. I did not like Ada. I did not like her silly name or her ribbons or her girlish, gilded bedroom. I did not like the reverent way that Valentin said her name, and I could not stand—would not stand—the thought that Will might have something to do with her.

"Thank you," I said to Valentin, and ducked into the room.

It was colder than the hallway. I drew my arms across my chest and turned to berate Valentin for keeping Will in this frigid space, but he had shut the door behind me. Will lay on a narrow bunk under a small window, wrapped in blankets and facing the wall. The room was not much bigger than a closet, and I crossed it in two steps. I knelt beside Will and put my hand on his shoulder. He didn't stir. I shook him, then without waiting touched his face—cold— and then in a panic began to feel at his throat. Before I could find a pulse, his eyes snapped open and his hand found mine. He turned toward me, stifling a cough that shuddered through his body.

"They are trying to kill you, keeping you in here," I said with fury. "I will tell Valentin that this is unacceptable."

Will pushed himself upright, and his eyes kindling with happiness to see me were the warmest things in the room. I pulled my hand away and seized the blankets that fell off him as he rose. I draped them over his shoulders and tucked them snugly around him, covering his tortured, bandaged hand. I didn't want to see it.

"I didn't think they would let me see you," he said, still smiling at me in a sleepy way. His eyes caught on my dress and flashed alarm. My stomach clenched.

"What is that ridiculous thing you're wearing?" he asked. "Why have they dressed you like this? Are they trying to freeze you to death, too? Here—"

He took one of the blankets and clumsily wrapped it around me with his one good hand. He put his arm around me, pulling me close beside him on the bed. In spite of myself, I leaned my head against his chest. I closed my eyes for a moment. There was something indefinable about his scent that hadn't changed, that still smelled like home. Like something to hold on to.

"There's no one like you, Bee," he said. "No one in the world but you is brave enough, or brilliant enough to do this."

My breath came rough. I didn't want to be brave. I wanted to be safe and happy with him. Away from here, away from all these ugly doubts.

"I don't feel brave," I said instead.

"You probably don't feel brilliant, either. Or at least not as brilliant as you are."

If I were truly brilliant, I would have thought of a way out of this that didn't involve losing my mind while Will tried not to die in this attic. But I didn't say that, either.

"It's her fault, you know," he said. The fingers of his good hand moved on my arm under the blanket. They were cold, but they were his. My skin pricked at the touch. I wasn't sure who he meant. My mind flicked, unwillingly, to Ada. "I hated the way she would talk to you. I should have done more to contradict her. I thought about that constantly after she threw me out."

Ah. He meant my mother.

"You did contradict her." I'd been shocked the first time he stood up to her for me. No one else had ever done anything like it, not even the Comte. "That was the real reason she threw you out, in the end."

"I was afraid she might turn on you after I left, be even worse to you."

I was quiet. She had turned. Suddenly I had become a thing outside of her, someone whose mind and desires were different from her own. She said things I would never forget. She left memories that still seared at their touch.

And you did not? she said. *Do you think you hurt me any less than I hurt you?*

I closed my eyes tighter. I pushed down the panic that flared in me at the implications of hearing her voice. I heard Will's heart beating fast, felt the faint warmth of his chest. I sank into it and stilled my mind.

"You were too full of things for her. Too much life, too much love. Marguerite couldn't stand for you to love anything but alchemy and her. She would have kept you her captive forever if she could have. And I can't say I blame her."

"You can't?"

"Not for that," said Will. "Not for wanting to keep you all to herself, or for being afraid to lose you. I might do the same if you let me. I missed you more than I would have believed, Bee."

"I think I missed you more," I said.

"Not possible." His lips brushed my forehead.

"I was alone with her." I wanted to sound calm, but a slight tremor in my voice betrayed me. "You weren't alone at all."

Will's hand went still on my arm. His shallow breath caught in his chest.

"Tell me about Ada," I said.

Will let out his breath in a long, slow sigh. He coughed, but not violently.

"I wondered if they might say something about that," he said. "I thought perhaps not, but that Prussian brute was always half mad where she was concerned."

He sounded calm. I let his calm wind its way into me. There was an explanation, of course. He would tell me, and we would both sigh at the unfairness and folly of other people.

"She is Graf Ludwig's daughter," I said.

He nodded. "The younger one. He has two. The older is different."

"Rahel is here," I said. "I met her. She invited me to dinner."

"Of course she did," said Will with a note of bitterness. "She would be quite interested in you."

I passed over that, intriguing though it was. I had started this. I had to finish.

"But Ada is different," I prompted.

"Very," he agreed. "As soft as her sister is hard. As naïve as Rahel is cynical. Sheltered, young. About your age, I suppose, though she seems much younger."

I nodded. "They are keeping me in her room. I saw some of her things. This dress is hers."

"Of course, I should have guessed. Just her sort of thing."

Will fell silent a moment. I felt him thinking, arranging what he would say. I didn't like that.

"What happened, Will?" I asked in a low voice.

He sighed again. "Nothing happened," he said. "That's why it is so hard to explain. Nothing happened, and yet everything resulted. Do you see?"

"No."

"No, of course not. I suppose I should start at the beginning. I met the Graf here, in London," he said. "His wife is a cousin of Queen Charlotte, so they keep a house here, attend the social season. He hired me, though my official contract didn't begin until we went to Prussia. At the time I didn't think much of that, though of course in hindsight I realize he waited so that I would be bound by the stricter Prussian laws."

This was off course again, though I had to suppress an urge to scold him for being so careless. The Germans were famously harsh to failed alchemists. Prussia was the only place in Europe that still hanged them. Will must have been truly desperate for work to take it there.

"One night there was a ball, and Ada's escort fell ill. They asked me to accompany her in his place."

My heartbeat slowed and struggled, like the blood pumping through it had suddenly thickened to mercury.

"She is pretty," I said.

"Oh, yes, she is pretty," agreed Will. "And charming as well, for about a half an hour. After that she has used up all her conversation, and starts over again. It's not her fault, of course. Not all seventeen-year-old girls can have your mind, or your education. But I couldn't help comparing. I had left you so recently."

"So you went to a ball with her," I said. With every false start, every attempt to veer away from the destination of the story, my anxieties thickened.

"Yes," he agreed. "And I . . . well . . . I tried to be an agreeable partner."

I knew perfectly well what that meant. I could imagine his smile, the small jokes that assumed they understood each other. And if that was only a month after he left France, then he still would have looked like himself. Tall, slim but well built, beautiful blue eyes that crinkled when he laughed, finely molded features that glowed with health.

"And she fell in love with you," I said. It was the obvious conclusion.

"I didn't know until we were all settled in Germany," said Will. "I got to work, I didn't see her very much at first. But then she started coming by the outbuilding where I worked. She came in and asked questions—stupid questions, but of course they would be. She knew nothing of alchemy, despite the fact that her father had employed one alchemist or another almost all her life."

He coughed again, and this time didn't stop quickly. He pulled his arm from my shoulders and fumbled for his handkerchief. I winced at the violence, the horrible wet tearing sound of the cough. When he was finished, there was too much blood on the handkerchief to hide. He bent over, breathing hard. I wanted to tell him it was all right, that he didn't have to go on. That I trusted him.

But I didn't. Not completely. Not anymore.

"I didn't know how to make her leave," he said quietly. "I should have found some way. I should have known it would be trouble. But she was my patron's daughter. I didn't want to offend her. I tried to be polite."

Unbidden, an image of Will flashing a dazzling smile at a pretty dark-haired girl came to my mind. I imagined him explaining patiently as she bent over a crucible in a low-necked gown like the one I wore now.

"In the end she . . . she threw herself at me. I turned her down as gently as I could, but . . . she didn't take it well."

There was a darkness behind his words. My heart sped up again.

"What did she do?"

"She became hysterical," said Will. "She started threatening me, breaking things. In the end I had to send her out in no uncertain terms. I was harsh with her. I pushed her. I . . . I insulted her."

Will bowed his head and chewed his lip.

"So." I couldn't stop myself. "So she went to Graf Ludwig. She told him—what?"

Will shook his head slowly. "No," he said. "She tried to kill herself."

I gasped. My skittering heart stopped. My hand flew to my throat, imagining a noose. "How?" I breathed.

"She filled a bath and cut her wrists," Will continued. "When they found her, she was nearly dead. I don't know if she told her father it was for my sake, or if he drew his own conclusions. But after that—"

"My God," I whispered. "But why? Why would she do something so desperate, simply because you rejected her?"

"I don't know!" he said. "I never imagined she would,

or I would have been more careful! I wouldn't have said some of the things I said. I was harsh, Bee. I don't like to think about the things I said to her, now, knowing how hard she took them. I have to conclude that she isn't quite right, isn't healthy in her mind, but I don't know. I don't know."

"But she lived?"

"She did," he said. "I think. She was alive when I fled."

"You mean you don't know?"

I pulled away from him to stare at his face. He shook his head. He looked as miserable and guilty as I could have hoped. I thought of Rahel's bubbling rage, and Valentin's under his steely self-control. It made sense. Will's story fit with what I knew. But it was not the only explanation that did.

A hole seemed to open in my chest. I could either fall into it, or I could stay back. Keep doubting Will, or trust what he told me. This was dangerous ground. If I refused to believe Will, then what? How could I do what I needed to do? My doubt could kill him, quite literally. I put it aside. I stepped back from the chasm.

"She must have died," I said. "If she had lived, surely she would have told her father the truth."

Will's forehead crinkled quizzically. "The truth?"

"The truth about you," I said. "That you didn't seduce her."

His face cleared. His shoulders sagged with relief that I had decided to believe him.

"I don't know that she would have," he said. "I think she may well have lied about me. She wanted to punish me. That much I know."

I nodded slowly. It made sense. It explained everything. And it fit with what I knew about Will, good and bad. He would have charmed her. Whatever he said, I was certain of that. He would have enjoyed her attention at first, until she began to get in the way of his work. Until she started to make him nervous and threatened his place as the Graf's alchemist. He was like me. Quick to turn, like mercury. Ada would have been shocked. She would have been hurt. Then furious.

"You shouldn't have gone to Germany," I concluded. "That was stupid, Will."

"It was stupid," he agreed. "But it wasn't so easy to find a patron once your mother turned me out and started spreading stories. I considered myself lucky that Graf Ludwig hadn't heard them yet."

"Perhaps if he had, he would have kept a closer eye on his daughter."

Will looked at me. He was still waiting. Waiting for a sign of my forgiveness, my acceptance. I didn't want to meet his eyes, but the chasm still beckoned. I couldn't stand on the edge any longer, and I wouldn't jump.

I took his hand in mine. I traced the long, calloused fingers and the scars from fire and metal. I had the same scars. No one who didn't have them could understand us, how hard and long and dangerously we worked, with only a slender hope of success. How much trust we had to give to something so uncertain that it would look like madness to anyone not like us.

"We have to be good to each other," I said.

"Yes," agreed Will. "If we aren't, no one else will be."

He understood. Tears pricked at my eyes.

"When this is over, we'll go wherever you want," said Will. "We can give up alchemy if you like. There are other things you could do. With your mind, your abilities. I'll make all of this up to you, Bee, I swear I will."

"Where would we go?"

"What about the New World? New Spain, perhaps? Florida? You speak lovely Spanish, and mine is passable. You could improve it on the voyage."

"The New World," I repeated. The words conjured up a jumble of fevered images. Steaming jungles mixed confusedly with the names of the battles of the American Revolution, the plantations of the English settlers and the fabled gold of the Aztecs.

"France isn't the only place for revolution," said Will. "And alchemy isn't the only way to pursue it."

His eyes had begun to kindle again, and I was brought back to our long talks about the philosophers over coffee or champagne. My mother was so impatient with us. She wanted alchemy for its own sake, but Will had always seen more possibilities. After all, wealth was an invention men used to deprive one another, and gold was just the glitter of legitimacy they gave to their theft. *The fruits of the earth belong to us all, and the earth itself to nobody,* Will had quoted. Make gold as abundant as lead, and it would be just as valueless. Revolution.

He began to cough again, pulling me back to the present. None of that was to be if he wasn't. I put my arms around him and laid my head against his heaving chest. His heart, stuttering alarmingly fast, was the only one on earth that truly knew mine. I would not let it stop beating.

Not much later, Valentin knocked. I rose, resolute. Reluctant as I was to leave Will, I had what I came for.

"If he is dead before I can cure him, the deal is off," I snapped at Valentin. "Put him somewhere warmer. You know how sick he is."

"And would you also like me to wipe his brow and spoon him hot soup?" Valentin asked.

"Yes, indeed. That is a fine idea."

Valentin glowered and again forced his mouth shut. I knew the tale he wanted to tell me now, the one he thought would make me turn on Will if I knew, something Valentin both wanted and could not want. We descended the stairs, first the cramped, hidden ones, then the broad, elegantly banistered set.

"Did she live?" I asked, when we stood in front of Ada's bedroom.

Valentin started, then stared at me in open shock.

"Yes, he told me," I said. "But he didn't know if Ada survived her attempt on her own life."

Valentin's brow furrowed in deep consternation. "You know," he said. "And you still defend him?"

I could have told him that his precious Ada was a flirt and a liar, but I did not. Let him think I believed Will a reprobate, and still loved him. Nothing else would still his desire to denounce Will to me.

"Does she live?" I repeated. I sounded calm, though my heart had sped up in fear of the answer.

"She lives," said Valentin.

"And you love her," I said. Feeling flickered on his face, and I connected it to something Rahel had said at dinner about his reward. "You love her, and Burggraf Ludwig has promised her to you, hasn't he, if you bring him the Stone. I suppose he thinks you are an acceptable choice now that her reputation is beyond repair."

Valentin opened the door to Ada's room and pushed me into it. He started to swing the door shut, then paused, pinning me with a narrow, furious gaze.

"I will have other clothes sent to you," he said. "Do not wear hers again."

13

I dreamed someone slept in the bed with me, and woke gasping for air.

It took longer than it should have to convince myself it was only a dream.

I rose to dress, taking deep breaths to steady myself. By the door, a clean, simple gown and shawl lay folded on the floor. Valentin had been as good as his word. I was glad enough to leave Ada's frilly dresses in her closet. I felt as much revulsion at the idea of wearing the girl's clothes as Valentin felt at seeing them on me. All the gilded, fanciful touches in her room made me feel inexplicably furious, and faintly ill. I turned away from them and went to the window. There was a trellis under it, covered in vines. It would be easy to climb down, if I wanted. If that were any way to escape.

It was very early, and the sun hadn't yet risen above the

grand houses on the eastern side of the street. I brushed my hair, staring out at the garden and gate, and tried not to think how often Ada must have done the same. She had left a presence here that I could feel. I had slept in her bed and hadn't quite felt alone. I didn't feel quite alone now. I glanced over my shoulder on a nervous instinct.

And someone was there.

I spun around, my whole body trembling. There was a figure in the corner, in shadow.

"Who are you?" I demanded. "How long have you been there?"

The figure rose slowly. It wasn't so very dark in the room, but I could make out no features. Was it a man or a woman? I couldn't tell. Cold horror pricked up my arms.

"How did you get in here?" I demanded again, backing away from it. I clutched the window behind me.

The figure didn't answer, though somehow I knew it heard me. It took a step forward, into the light, without becoming any more illuminated. I held a hairbrush in my hand. I threw it as hard as I could.

The brush hit the wall across the room with a ringing sound of brass on papered wood. It dropped to the ground. It had hit nothing, because there was nothing there.

I turned away and leaned my forehead against the windowsill, bracing myself. I was not sure what would be worse to see when I turned back again: that the figure was still there, or that it was not. I took a deep breath and looked.

It was not.

I nodded. Nothing was there. Nothing was watching me. That was good. It was only the madness, beginning to finger its way into my mind.

That was not good.

Things are not always so simple, Thea. You think that because you do not see a thing this moment, it is not there?

I turned back to the window again, ignoring my mother, staring determinedly at things I knew were truly there. The trellis. The oak tree. The gate. Someone outside of the gate.

I squinted harder at the gate in the uncertain light, seeing movement. The guard was pointing away, talking and gesturing in an aggressive manner to a figure on the other side. The figure was tall and slim, dark-haired and familiar. He seemed real; I could make out particulars, and that was reassuring. He did not leave, despite the guard's threats. The black-haired man folded his arms across his chest and turned, looking up at the house.

My heart lurched. I jerked back from the window, into the shadows.

It was my father.

Questions pelted my mind like grapeshot. Was it really him? Had he seen me? He couldn't have, could he? But how did he know I was here? How could he have found us? Were the police with him? Would the Germans let him in?

On the latter question, at least, my mind was soon put to rest. When verbal threats failed to remove him, the guard took his musket from his shoulder and pointed it at my father's heart. Vellacott put up his hands and backed away. He left, with a searching backward glance at the windows.

I dressed as quickly as I could and rattled the door to my room. For the first time, the lock infuriated me. I was trapped in this haunted room. This room that mocked me with every silly feminine flourish, that still smelled like her perfume. No wonder I was seeing things that weren't there. Of course my mind was twisting, locked up in here with ghosts while my father hunted me. A yellow mist of panic clouded my vision. I had to get out, I had to. I swore at the lock and began to pound on the door, shouting profanities in every language I knew.

It worked. Heavy steps pounded down the hall.

"Quiet!" hissed Valentin from behind the door. "You will wake the ladies with that filth!"

"Let me out of this donnerwetter dollhouse!" I shouted back. "If you leave me in here another moment I will break everything in here that she ever touched, n'est-ce pas? Je merderai on all her pretty little things, I'll—"

Valentin threw the door open, a thunderous look on his face. He seized my shoulders and shook me until my teeth rattled.

"Quiet, you wild creature! What is the matter with you? Have you gone mad?"

Abruptly, he stopped shaking me. He pressed the back of his free hand to my forehead. My eyes widened, locked on his. His question repeated itself in my mind.

Have you gone mad? Have you gone mad? Have you gone mad?

The yellow mist began to clear. The door was open now. The wild desperation began to recede. Valentin was solid in front of me, his strong hand on my arm thick and real: no figment. He lowered his hand slowly, and his grip on my shoulders loosened. I didn't want him to let go; his touch was an anchor. I sucked down a deep, steadying breath.

"Is there a fever?" I asked.

Valentin tilted his head. "Yes."

"It's—" I tried to think of an explanation for my fit.

It had seemed quite natural at the time, not mad or even out of proportion. But now I could not sort out the jumble of thoughts from the wild rage that had taken me. I would not tell him about the figure in the corner; I was not ready to see his alarm at that revelation. I seized on the last certain thought I had. "There was a man at the gate." *My father.* That had been real, surely? "I think. He wanted something. The guard sent him away. I have to know what he said. I have to know what he wanted."

Valentin peered at me, and it was clear enough what he was thinking. I quelled a powerful urge to shout that I was not mad and took another deep breath. I uncurled my fingers, flattened my face. I met his eyes and tried my best to appear sane.

"I became overexcited." My calm, slow voice sounded to my own ears like it belonged to someone else. "I apologize."

Valentin snorted.

"Now I am certain you have lost your mind," he said. But he released my arm. "I was going to escort you to breakfast. Your friend Dominic is well enough. Fräulein Rahel said you might both eat in the dining room this morning, if you like."

"Will Rahel be there?" One meal under her smoldering glare was enough.

"She takes breakfast in her room."

I hesitated, and Valentin went on. "I will ask Karl who he sent away from the gate. Come, you must be hungry. You ate almost nothing yesterday."

I could not suppress a small, wry smile at his concern. One might call it motherly, though not if one had my mother in mind. The almost nothing I ate yesterday would have seemed a great deal to her.

"There are sausages and strudel," Valentin continued, starting to sound impatient. "And your friend Dominic is already there."

If the truth were told, I didn't want to see Dominic much more than I did Rahel. He would certainly attempt to convince me to stop work again, something Valentin ought to have known considering how loudly Dominic had shouted his objections the other day. And I was afraid of what he might see on my face. On the other hand, I was suddenly ravenous for sausages and strudel. I nodded and followed Valentin.

I slipped into the dining room quietly. It was full of men again. This time they hovered over the sideboard helping themselves to pastries and sausage rather than liquor. Dominic sat at the table, slouched over a cup of coffee, not a scrap of food left on his plate. He eyed the sideboard, evidently planning his second course. He hadn't seen me come in, so I was able to observe him unobstructed for a few moments. He looked disheveled and somewhat under-slept, as one would after spending a few nights chained to a radiator, fending off madness. But his eyes were clear. His color was healthy. He seemed well. I straightened my shoulders and hoped I could give him the same impression.

"Good morning, Dominic," I said.

He looked up at the sound of my voice, eyes wide, and jumped to his feet.

"Thea!"

I crossed to the sideboard, ignoring the sidelong glances

of the Prussians, and filled a plate so full that a sausage nearly rolled off the top. Dominic pulled out a seat next to him, which I could hardly refuse. I sat in it with as much dignity as a person can when she has just served herself enough food to fill several grown men.

"You look very well," I said.

"You don't," said Dominic with a frown. I glanced up at him in surprise, and his expression fell into embarrassment. "Oh—I didn't mean— You look quite well, I mean to say— You always look—"

He broke off, gripping his coffee, and stared into it for a moment to recover himself. "I mean you look rather warm, and . . ."

"And a bit mad?" I supplied.

"No," said Dominic, flushing.

This one is just full of social graces, isn't he? said my mother.

My heart thudded wildly at the sound of her voice. Even here, surrounded by people, I couldn't escape it.

"I feel a bit mad," I admitted, and took an enormous bite of apple turnover and almost choked as I swallowed it in haste. "I would never eat this much in my right mind, especially in front of a man."

I tried to smile at him, but he looked back at me with such alarm that I couldn't make my mouth hold the shape.

"I'm all right, Dominic," I lied to him.

"I don't believe you," he said.

I thought about telling him what I had seen in the corner. Dominic hadn't mentioned seeing anything like that. Though he had heard his father's voice. I nearly asked him about it, but I remembered the raw terror in his voice when he spoke of it. *Hell,* he had said. *It was like hell.*

"Thea," he began.

I swallowed hard and held up my hand. "You won't convince me, Dominic," I said. "Please do not ruin a lovely breakfast attempting the impossible. Who knows how many more meals we will get to take together?"

Dominic looked stricken, and it was my turn to regret my choice of words.

"Oh, I didn't mean anything grim," I said hastily. "Perhaps they didn't tell you? I've arranged with them to take you to Prussia when this is over, and give you what you need to study medicine."

Dominic met my eyes for half a moment, his brows drawn into a deep frown. Then he stared back into his coffee. "I asked you not to do that," he said. "I don't want anything that costs you your mind."

My hunger had left me abruptly, but I shoveled a sausage into my mouth anyway. I chewed, swallowed, and tasted nothing. When I allowed myself to look at Dominic again, he was still frowning miserably into his coffee.

"I am not doing this for you," I said. "But since I am going to do it, why shouldn't I make a way out for you, if I can? It costs me nothing. Nothing extra."

Dominic shook his head. He got up without looking at me and went to the sideboard. Once there, he stared at the platters of food as though he'd forgotten what he came for.

I continued to eat with determination. When Valentin came in a few moments later, I had already finished my second pastry. Dominic returned and picked at his food in grim silence. Valentin sat across from us and watched us for a moment before speaking. "You wanted to know about the man at the gate," he said to me.

"Oh. Yes." I glanced at Dominic. I had forgotten to mention to him that my father had been here, and now it was too late. I silently willed him to stay calm and quiet.

"He wished to speak to the master of the house," said Valentin. His eyes were narrowed on me, watching for my reaction. "He said his name was Vellacott."

Beside me, Dominic stiffened.

"Did he say why he wished to speak to the master of the house?" I asked calmly.

"Indeed, yes," said Valentin. "He said he was looking for a young girl he believed to be in danger. He said her name was Theosebeia Hope."

"And did he say what business of his it might be if Theosebeia Hope is in danger?" I asked.

Valentin tilted his head, then shook it. "He did not."

"And what did the guard tell him?"

"Nothing at all," said Valentin. "My men know not to speak out of turn. Karl told Vellacott all he was authorized to tell, which was that he must leave or be shot."

"Did he mention anyone else? Perhaps . . . the police?"

"The police? No."

I thought as quickly as I could, though that was much slower than I liked. My mind struggled to reach the point, like I was drunk, though I'd drunk nothing but coffee. I banished my panic and forced my thoughts into focus. My father had asked only after me. He hadn't mentioned Dominic, or Ludovico Bentivoglio. What did that mean? What did it mean that he had said that I was in danger, and not that we were fugitives from the law?

It could mean anything, I decided. It could be that he thought he would gain more help if he seemed to be looking for a vulnerable girl rather than a killer and his accomplice. Or, he might be looking for me and not Dominic. In that case, it was most likely that he wanted me for the same reason the Germans did. He knew what I knew, and what I could do. He had failed to decode my mother's notes, and came searching for my help. I already knew he wanted the Philosopher's Stone as much as Ludwig did. It should be no surprise that he wanted to catch me out and bring me back.

I found the idea of being forced to make the Stone for my father no more appealing than making it for Ludwig. Quite a bit less, in fact. I could not allow him to find me.

"You know this Vellacott?" Valentin asked.

I glanced at Dominic. He had set down his fork, placed his elbows on the table, and dropped his head into his hands.

"Yes," I said simply. "He is an alchemist. He must have some suspicion that we are here, but I hope you will not allow it to be confirmed."

"What does he want with you?"

"The same thing your Burggraf does, I should think," I said. "In any case, it won't be anything good."

"You don't know that," said Dominic.

I turned to him, my eyes widened in what would have been an effective silencing manner if Dominic had not still had his head buried in his hands.

"I know enough," I said.

Dominic straightened slowly, as though making a decision. He'd looked well enough earlier, but from the expression of anguish on his face I suddenly wondered if he ought to still be chained to the radiator.

"He's not a bad man, Thea," he said. "You saw him at his worst."

"What better time is there to know a man than at his worst?" I exclaimed, heat rising in my cheeks. "I am glad he showed his true character at once. I shudder to think of all the time and effort I might have wasted in trying to know and help him!"

"This has gone on long enough," said Dominic. "You should never have come with me to London. He's here for you. You should go with him."

While I struggled to find words sufficient to contain my contempt for this idea, Valentin broke in. "Why should she go with him?" he asked Dominic. "Who is he to her?"

"Dominic!" I warned. But his voice rose over mine.

"Mr. Vellacott is her father."

I choked on my fury. Words were momentarily lost in rage. My hands balled into fists, and I had to press them to the table to keep from striking Dominic.

"Ah," said Valentin with an infuriatingly calm nod.

"Let her go," said Dominic. "Call him back and send her with him. You have no right to keep her here when her father has asked for her."

"Ah, but he did not claim her as his daughter," said Valentin. "Miss Hope, he called her. Not Miss Vellacott. He has not acknowledged her, I think. And therefore he has no more claim upon her than Graf Ludwig."

"Claim?" The word escaped, a low hiss through my violently clenched jaw. "What claim do any of you have on me?"

"Thea, please be calm," said Valentin.

I thought I had been calm, though it had taken more

strength than they could have imagined. Now I jumped to my feet, throwing back my chair as I did.

"Let me be quite clear. I will not go anywhere with Mr. Vellacott. To that end, I may require protection from him. And it seems—" I turned on Dominic with a glare. "Also from Dominic. I advise you to keep him well under guard, Valentin, or he may attempt to escape and tell Mr. Vellacott where I am to be found. If you value the deal that we have struck, you will do whatever is necessary to prevent that."

"If you gave him another chance—" Dominic broke off when he looked up at me.

"I don't have time to give more chances!" I cried. "I only have this one chance myself, and it's halfway gone!"

He looked almost confused, as though he wasn't precisely certain why I was angry. Then the confusion turned to alarm.

"Thea, what are you saying?" Dominic asked. "Have you—has it started?"

I couldn't stand the fear on his face. I turned away.

"It is time for me to work," I said to Valentin, who made no move to rise. "Shall I see myself out?"

"You haven't finished your breakfast," he said, glancing at my still full plate.

I picked it up—I had eaten enough that there was less danger of sausages rolling off—and marched out the door. Valentin had little choice but to follow.

14

The work went as it always did. There were long, grueling periods of waiting, watching, and coddling the substances, as one would especially temperamental infants. These were punctuated by short, sharp, and sometimes alarming bursts of activity. A fire would flare. Smoke would change color or fill with sparks. And the substance in the brazier would become something else.

It was all very familiar, and it wasn't. The work was the same, the same grinding, measuring, mixing, and tending. But instead of working out Decknamen, breaking down figures of the planets and approximating quantities, I had my mother's coded notes imprinted in my mind. There were no mysteries now. I followed a receipt I understood, whose outcome I had seen. Every step went straight toward my goal; everything was clear.

Everything except my own mind.

I knew it from the yellow blur at the edge of my thoughts, and from the way Valentin looked at me at the end of the day, when I spoke to him in garbled sentences that even I could not decode. He did not invite me to dine with Rahel again. He had begun to believe.

That night, I went to bed with the dark figure that was not there crouched beside me. This time, when I hurled a shoe through it, the figure did not vanish. When I screamed at it, only Valentin answered, from outside the door.

"What is it?" he demanded. "Why are you screaming?"

"It's nothing," I replied, staring at the dark, crouching form. "Nothing is there. It's nothing."

Valentin hesitated, apparently not reassured. Then the key turned in the lock, and he came in. He stood over me, next to the figure.

"You are shaking," he observed.

I glanced down at my bare arms and noted that he was right.

"Should you be alone?" he asked.

"I'm not." I shuddered, trying not to look in the corner.

"Miss Hope," he said. "I am asking if I should stay."

I looked up at him, not understanding at first.

"Stay?" I asked. "Where would you sleep?"

"On the floor," said Valentin, gesturing to where the unreal thing huddled.

"No!" I exclaimed, panic sharpening my voice. "Not on the floor!"

"Then . . . ?" He glanced back toward the door, and I found myself desperate that he not go.

"Here." I patted the bed beside me, between me and

the figure. Valentin looked at my hand and frowned. He started to shake his head.

"Please," I said.

I pushed myself farther to the side under the covers, leaving him as much space as I could. Reluctantly, he sat down, then lay on his back, stiff as his starched blue jacket.

I couldn't see the figure past Valentin's sturdy bulk. I exhaled slowly, releasing some of my terror.

"Thank you," I said quietly.

Valentin didn't respond.

I closed my eyes. Some sleep would help, surely. My mother hadn't gone mad all at once. She'd had some time to fight it, to keep working. I only needed a few more days.

The memory of my mother's face, mad eyes and bared teeth, forced my eyes open again. My heart raced.

"Valentin," I said.

"Yes," he said.

"I'm afraid."

He was quiet a moment. "I know," he said.

He had not relaxed into the bed one inch, whether from concern over the impropriety, or discomfort with my strange, altered state, or both. He stayed only for my sake.

"Valentin."

"Yes," he said again.

"You should find another line of employment," I said.

He exhaled sharply—a nearly soundless laugh.

"So should you, Miss Hope."

But I could not agree with that, not even now. I closed my eyes and tried to sleep once more.

I succeeded. When I woke, dawn was breaking and Valentin was gone.

The dark figure wasn't, but it didn't move. It was so still, it almost seemed to be sleeping. Or perhaps it was simply waiting.

Still, I felt a little better this morning. Steadier. I went back to work.

The thing followed me into the library and settled itself in the far corner, opposite the German who'd been assigned to watch me work. I did my best not to look at either of them.

After a few hours, it was time to seal the blackened mass into the glass ovum. It was a delicate procedure, and I found to my dismay that my hands were shaking.

My hands never shook. Alchemy was a science of head and hand. Unlike my mother's, unlike Will's, my hands had always been as steady as my mind.

I went to the bronzed mirror by the door and peered at my reflection. I touched my face gently, alarmed at the cold trembling of my fingers. My eyes were bloodshot. My face was paler than usual, except for my cheeks and brow, which were a livid pink. I pressed the back of my hand to my forehead and drew it back at once. My face was very hot. In the mirror, the thing in the corner pulsed.

I stepped back. My vision blurred, and when it came back into focus, I didn't recognize the girl in front of me.

It was me, I knew that. Each feature was the same. The same curly dark hair, messily pulled back, the same high forehead and narrow patrician nose. Those were my square shoulders, my tall, spare figure. I told myself so, but another part of me was not convinced. It rejected the face, first of all. The face was wrong. I had seen it another place, on another person, where it had belonged. I didn't like that person. I shouldn't have his face. No, this face did not belong to me. I touched it again. I traced the cheekbone up, then down and under the jaw. The skin was hot, damp, and false. My fingers hooked under it, under the jawbone. There was a space there. I could get it off. My fingernails were short, as an alchemist's must be, but they were sharp enough to cut the skin, to dig in, to peel away the false face—

Valentin opened the door, and the sharp cry he made arrested me. He seized my hand and jerked it from my face.

"Gott im Himmel! Was für Teufelei is dies?"

The raw horror in his voice called me to myself.

Devilry, he said. *What devilry is this?*

My eyes went back to the mirror. Blood was smeared across my jaw and dripping down my neck. I looked at my hands, held fast in Valentin's. One was bloody, the other clean.

"Oh," I said. My vision blurred again, this time with tears. "It hurts."

"Why did you do it, then?" Valentin cried. He took both my hands in one of his and used the other to turn up my chin and examine the wound. His face twisted with revulsion.

"The boy didn't try to do this," he said. "You did not tell me it might make you hurt yourself."

It. The madness. I nodded, ineffectually, as my chin was trapped in Valentin's hand. It was my face, of course it was. The madness had made me disown it. I would have to be more careful not to listen to it.

"I didn't recognize my face," I explained to Valentin calmly, I thought. "I thought it was a lie. I thought I could get it off."

Valentin swore violently in German. "If I let you go, will you try it again?"

I had to think about this for a moment. Then I shook my head.

He dropped my hands, muttering another, milder curse as he did, and called down the hallway for bandages.

I stared into the mirror another moment, picking out each feature in turn.

That's yours, I told myself. *And that. Not his. Not your father's. Yours.*

When Valentin came in again, my face had settled back into place. The feeling that it wasn't mine had gone, leaving only lightheadedness and a sense of distance, of seeing everything from far away.

"I was going to call you in," I said as Valentin lowered me onto the armchair. "It is time to seal the ovum, but my hands were shaking."

Valentin had pressed something white and clean against my lower jaw.

"Es ist eine verdammt schreckliche Wunde," he said. I wondered if he knew any English swear words, or if it was his disgust that tipped him back into German. He must have known he wasn't hiding his meaning from me.

"You didn't see him," I said, my mind leaping. "Karl did. Karl could tell you—we have the same face."

"What?" snapped Valentin. "You and Karl do not have the same face."

"No." I laughed, earning a terrified glare from Valentin. "My father and me. Mr. Vellacott. You'll know him at once, if he comes around again. We have the same face."

"That is no reason to try to tear yours off!"

It hit me then that I had tried to do that. That I did not know how far I might have gone if Valentin hadn't stopped me. My breath caught. My mind crashed back into my body, and the wound on my jaw throbbed. I felt the phantom of my own fingernails, scraping away my own skin. My breath came back in shallow gasps. Something dark moved on the edge of my vision. I turned my head sharply away from it, but not before I saw. It wasn't in the corner anymore. It was closer.

"You mustn't leave me alone," I said, staring up at Valentin. "I don't know how much longer I will be myself. You will have to be ready."

He nodded. Another Prussian came in bearing a bottle and more bandages. He uncorked the bottle, and I recognized the sickly, chemical smell from Will's patched-up hand. Valentin pulled back the cloth from my jaw and the Prussian soaked another cloth from the bottle and began to dab at my face. It stung enough to bring tears back to my eyes. I kept my mouth clamped shut. Valentin stepped back from me, but not far. He was torn, I thought, between wanting to get away from me and knowing he must keep me under close guard. He rocked back on his heels and clasped his hands behind himself.

"Let us say your father does want you," said Valentin. "Let us say he wishes to acknowledge you as his daughter. He could bring you into society, help you make a marriage. There are other possibilities for you."

"None that save Will and my mother," I said. "And none that win you your prize, either."

Valentin rocked back again, his face a frowning mask. "Perhaps I agree with your friend Dominic," he said. "Perhaps I do not want a prize at this price."

I was tempted to feel grateful for his sentiment. I wouldn't have thought this man would care enough about me to balk at this price. He had tortured Will, after all, and threatened to do worse to him and Dominic as well if I did not comply. Though I had trusted him enough last night to want him between me and the thing, even if it meant sharing a bed. I kept my stinging jaw turned resolutely away from the side of the room where it lurked. I looked down at my gory hand, clumps of skin and blood stuck under my fingernails. The gorge rose in my throat, and I squeezed my eyes shut as if that could block out the memory of what I had done to myself. It wasn't pity he felt, I thought, but horror. Disgust. I was becoming a nightmare creature, one he did not want to tend.

"It is fortunate for both of you that this is my decision," I said. "Not yours."

The other Prussian had finished cleaning the wound and taping the bandage down. He stepped back.

"Now then." I stood, marshaling all that were left of my spirits. "We must seal the ovum before the substance oxidizes any further. Will you be so good as to hold the glass steady? I am afraid I cannot trust my own hands at present."

Valentin made no further protests. Tight-lipped and stiff, he helped me transfer the substance and melt the narrow mouth of the glass egg shut. I half buried the ovum in ash, then sat back on my heels, pressing my palms into the floor to still their trembling. I allowed myself to feel a small measure of relief. The more precise part was over. The rest I could probably do with only half of my mind. I hoped I would have at least that much.

"A sealed vessel under heat," said Valentin after a few moments. "Will it not explode?"

"That is certainly a danger," I said. "The heat must be kept regular, and gentle. And even so . . ."

The possibility frightened me. Exploding vessels were a constant threat in alchemy. I had set aside enough of the White Elixir to make another attempt should this one fail, but I feared my mind would not last long enough to complete it.

"How long now?" asked Valentin.

"Six days," I said. My mother's notes had been exact.

"Six days," he repeated. Valentin's tone was flat, but his doubts were easy to read. I shared them. Six days was a long time.

"And after the six days, there is more to do?"

"One last step," I said.

"Your friends do not know how to do what you have done." Valentin concealed a question in the statement.

"No one does but my mother," I said. "Unless my father deciphered her code. He stole her notes from me."

Well, I told myself, *in fairness, that was Bentivoglio.*

Bentivoglio stole them, and gave them to your father, who did not return them, said my mother. *He didn't throw you into the wall, but only because he did not have to. And then he threw you out.*

You threw me out, too, I reminded her.

Yes, she said. *And now you know why.*

I squeezed my eyes shut and slapped my forehead until I remembered what I had been thinking about before.

"But he didn't," I said. "Didn't decipher the code. If he had, he wouldn't have come looking for me. He needs me to make the Stone, same as you, same as your Ludwig, same as Will. I am so very needed."

Valentin stepped toward me. He had been hovering a few feet away, and apparently decided that was not close enough.

"You are right," I said. My vision was beginning to blur yellow again, but I felt no urge to commit violence. "You are too far. I could hurl myself into the fire, or worse, hurl the ovum out of it."

I stared at the ovum and the black, burned-looking substance within. It was a pitiful thing, ugly and dead. Strange to think that all my hope now lay in it, in that charred mess coming back to a kind of life.

"Did your mother try to hurt herself, when she went mad?" asked Valentin. He stood over me now. I considered this.

"You know," I said. "She didn't."

"Move back from the fire, please, Miss Hope," said Valentin.

I nodded. He held his hand out for me to take. I stared at it, blinking back the blurred edges of my sight. It was a large, strong hand. I remembered feeling it on mine in the carriage, the hard callouses and dry cracks in the skin around his fingers. It was the hand that had pulled out Will's nails, a hand that had killed, no doubt. I put my own hand in it, and hated the sight of it there, trembling and weak and needy. My fingers tightened on his.

The thing was next to him. I had to look at it now; I couldn't look away, though I wanted to.

It wasn't a man, or a woman, or a beast. It looked into me and saw straight down to the bottom. My mother had looked at me that way and thought she saw all. She'd been wrong. She had never seen all that this thing saw. No one had. I shuddered and cringed away. I wanted to weep and beg for mercy. But there was no mercy in that thing.

"Miss Hope?" I heard Valentin say as if from far away. "Thea?"

The thing was opening, turning down. Becoming a chasm, pulling me toward it. Once I fell in, I could never climb out. Despair seized me. *Like hell,* Dominic had said. Worse than death.

"I should have written it down!" I cried. How had I not written it down?

Valentin was asking questions. He understood as well that I was going, that I might not come back. There was one last step, and no one knew it. I opened my mouth to tell him, but the words caught, became nonsense. All I could feel was panic, all I could think was terror. I tried again and realized I did not remember. I didn't know anything. I screamed.

I fell into the dark thing, into blackness and horror, and forgot everything but falling.

15

I was gone for an age. There was no time where I went, nothing but darkness, terror, confusion. The feeling of being consumed. Eaten, like a meal. Death was better. If I had been capable, I would have admitted it. Dominic was right. Nothing, no one was worth this price.

There was sound. For the first age, it was only a howling, like wolves or wind, unrecognizable. Then I started to hear differences. Voices, though I did not remember their names. I hated them and longed for them at the same time. I gathered myself, attending to them. It was another age before I understood the voices belonged to people, and a third age before I understood they were screaming in the same agony I felt. I was not alone here, but it was no comfort. I almost recognized them, sometimes, but there was not enough of any of us left to know one another.

232 ~ SAMANTHA COHOE

Then, there were other voices from farther away. Not screams, but words with meaning. I heard with little understanding.

"She did this to herself," a woman said. "If you cannot save her, then it is no one's fault but yours, and hers."

"She is a child!" The man was angry. "A child, and you forced her to destroy herself!"

"She believed you would have done the same, you know," said the woman. "That was what she told Valentin."

Valentin. The name made me feel . . . something. A tangle of emotions, fear and anger and comfort twisted into a hard, hot knot. That knot reminded me that I was a thing, a unity that felt. But it distracted me from the voices. I lost them, and continued to fall.

And then—

A mind on mine. A will, examining me. Probing. A test. A predator sniffing around its prey. I knew it. It was the dark figure, the thing. Either it would eat me, or—

It would let me go.

The agony changed, like teeth withdrawing from a bite wound. I was released.

I began to know what was around me. The screams became distinct. I knew the voices. Mother. My mother. And another—Dominic.

No.

Then, abruptly, their voices were gone, replaced by weeping. Weeping as wild as the winds. I seized it. I held it. I pulled myself out.

"Must you chain her this way?" cried the weeping man. "Look at her wrists! Have you no pity?"

"Those chains are all that kept her alive," said another man, one who was not weeping. "She does not feel them."

But I did feel them, as soon as he said that. I felt a horrible burning, slicing feeling. Wrists. I had wrists.

"She is more peaceful now," said the weeping man. "Weaker. She couldn't do much harm. Please."

There was a silence. Without the voices, I felt myself slipping. If only I could see them, then it wouldn't matter if they ceased to speak. But how? How did one see?

The pain on my wrists changed. It flared, and my eyes flew open.

Too much. The light burned my pupils. They closed again, but the weeping man cried out, and I held on to the violence of the sound.

"She opened her eyes!"

"That means nothing," said the other. "Her eyes were open the whole of the first week. It does not mean she is seeing anything."

She . . . her . . . she. Yes. That was me. A she. A woman.

I opened my eyes again, this time blinking until I could bear the light.

Two men leaned over me. I knew them, but could not place them. There was a tall, thick one and a tall, weeping one. I hated them both. I jerked forward.

"I told you!" shouted the thick one. He pulled on the chain at my wrist and fastened it hard again. I looked about me and found I was spread across a bed, my wrists chained to opposite posts. My hatred deepened. Anyone could do anything to me while I was held like this.

"Thea!" cried the slender man. He wasn't weeping any

longer. "Are you there? Thea?" Excitement filled his voice. "I see her!"

I stared. Oh yes, I knew this man. He was more familiar than he should be.

"Father," I said.

He cried out. The other, thick man made a sound of shock as well. I stared up at him.

"V—" It was a hard word. I tried again. "Valentin."

His mouth dropped open. He looked very foolish.

"Release me," I said. I pulled against my chains and winced. My wrists were rubbed raw.

"Thea, my child!" Vellacott started to weep again, tears leaking out of his red-rimmed eyes. "My child."

Irritation twisted inside me. I shook my head. I tried to form a denial, but the words caught in my thick, dry mouth.

"Water?" I whispered.

Valentin was the quickest. The water coursed into my mouth, sloshing down my throat like a river. I choked on it.

"Es tut mir Leid," muttered Valentin. "I'm sorry, sorry."

I remembered now, enough that I needed to know.

"The Stone?" I asked. My father's face fell. I looked to Valentin, who shifted on his feet.

"I tried to do as you said, after you went—" He stumbled and did not say where I went. I was glad. He did not know. "But the glass burst."

"Burst." My heart sank, almost back into the deep. But I held it. I kept my eyes open. I fixed them on my father.

"Why is he here?" I asked Valentin.

"He came back," said Valentin. "Looking for you. And

we thought, perhaps . . . we thought he could help. You had said he took your papers. Your mother's papers."

I remembered that. I glared at my father. "He did."

My father had the decency to lower his eyes in shame.

"Your friend broke some of the code," said Valentin. "But it changed, halfway through. We couldn't decipher the rest."

"So . . . so . . ." My broken mind struggled to function. I hated its slowness. But when I finally understood, I hated that even more.

"My friend? Will?"

"The other one," said Valentin.

"Dominic," said my father quietly.

The way he said the name sent a chill straight through me. I half remembered a scream in Dominic's voice. I shook my head against the thought.

"Dominic? Where is he?" I demanded.

The men exchanged a guilty look.

"No," I moaned. "You monsters. You shouldn't have let him."

"He wanted to do it, Thea," said my father. "He wanted to do it to save you. He said he owed it to you. And now that you're awake again, you can finish what he started, and save him in turn."

Fury gripped me, and I snarled at him. A bestial, mad sound. My father's eyes widened in terror, and he started back as I threw myself forward and was caught by the chains.

"Let me go!" I screamed.

"I can't, Thea," said Valentin. "I can't. Not yet. Look at you."

"And Dominic?" I cried. "Do you have him chained to a bed as well? What have you done to us?"

"Nothing!" Valentin exclaimed. "You begged me to restrain you. If I hadn't, you would have murdered yourself!"

I remembered this as well now. I remembered tearing at my own skin, screaming that I could not escape my own body. I shuddered. Horror beckoned to me. I hadn't really escaped, not yet. I was only holding on to the ledge of my sanity by a few slipping fingers.

"The Stone," I whispered. It was my only hope. "Is it . . ."

"It's in the ovum," said Valentin. "Just as it was when you left. Dominic broke the code, repeated the process. I was able to help him a little. I had watched your steps carefully."

"How many days has it been sealed in the ovum?"

"Six tomorrow," said my father.

Tomorrow. All I had to do was cling to the edge of sanity until tomorrow, and complete the process. One last step . . .

"Thea," said my father. "Meg's code changed. We haven't been able to discern the end. We don't know what to do tomorrow."

I laughed, but the sound came out wrong. I could see from the looks on my father's and Valentin's faces. Yes, Mother's code changed on the last step. She had reverted to one of ours, one that we had made together. It was based on the letters of my name. I stopped laughing for a moment to wonder why. Perhaps she wanted me to finish, if she was not able to. A small, warm feeling stirred in me, which I quickly squashed. More likely, she had already begun to go mad, and had reverted to an earlier code without meaning to.

"Thea," said my father again. He was working to something, I could tell by the cowardly twitch of his mouth. I glared at it and wondered, did mine do that, when I was about to ask for something I shouldn't? "Thea, we must know the end of the process. If you go again, before it is time . . ."

"I won't." Panic gripped me at the thought. He wouldn't say it like that, not if he knew.

"But if you do," he persisted. "Then we would miss our chance to save you and Dominic."

"And Will," I said. "Where is Will?"

I looked around the room, as though he might be hidden in one of the dark corners. It occurred to me that this room was unfamiliar. Valentin had kept me out of his Ada's room for my descent into hell.

"He is as he was," said Valentin. "Perhaps a little worse. I moved him to a warmer room, as you wished."

"Thea—" began my father again.

"Enough begging," I snapped. "I'll tell Will. Not you."

My father and Valentin exchanged another glance. I wondered when they had become so cozy. When had they aligned themselves against me? But Valentin nodded and went out.

Vellacott and I were alone in the room, and suddenly I wasn't quite mad enough not to feel the awkwardness of his discomfort. He looked at his hands, then at me, then back at his hands.

"Thea," he said. *Again.*

"*Thea,*" I mimicked in an unkindly nasal imitation of his voice. "Much more of that and you'll make me hate the sound of my own name."

My father looked stricken for half a moment, then laughed. I watched him with curiosity. His face changed when he laughed, even when it was a wry laugh like this one, without much happiness in it. He was warmer. More sincere. Harder to hate. When he stopped, he smiled sadly and fondly at me, and something twisted deep in my belly.

"If I ever doubted you were Meg's daughter, five minutes' conversation with you would be all the convincing I needed."

I had nothing to say to that. A wave of exhaustion crashed over me. I was dizzy with it.

"Why are you here?" I whispered.

"I came for you, Thea," my father said. "I should have listened to you."

I heard his words, but not the meaning of them, not at first. I was slipping.

No.

I held on to his voice, the pleasant timbre, the possible sincerity.

"I behaved terribly," he was saying. "I know I don't deserve your forgiveness. All I can hope is that I can somehow make amends to you. You were right. You were right about Bentivoglio, and you were right to protect Dominic as you did. I feel such shame when I think of my actions then, even my thoughts."

I hit my head against the headboard behind me, and the sharp pain cleared my mind.

"Thea?" My father half rose from his chair at the foot

of my bed. He came closer, along the side. "Stay, Thea," he said. There was such desperation in his voice. Did he really want the Stone so much? He leaned over me, pressed a hand to my forehead.

"I'm here," I said.

The door opened, and in a moment Will was at my side, pushing my father away.

"Oh God, Bee," said Will. There were tears in his deep, shadowed eyes. "I'm sorry, I'm so sorry. I should never have asked this of you."

"Leave us alone," I said to my father and Valentin, standing at the foot of my bed. When they didn't move, I threw myself forward, despite the pain that shot through my wrists. "Get out!"

They obeyed, and Will sat beside me. His hands were on my face, pushing back my damp hair. I closed my eyes for a moment, letting his touch draw out the tension.

"When it burns red," I said, reciting my mother's last line. "Apply three minims of stibnite. When it fuses, the Stone will be complete."

I opened my eyes, and saw Will staring into them. He nodded.

"I can do that much," he said very quietly.

"Don't trust them." I was so tired. I wanted sleep, but didn't know if I would ever wake.

"I'll fix this, Bee," said Will. "Trust me."

16

Valentin returned. He came to my side, peered closely at me. I knew, of course, what he looked for, and tried to show it to him. He touched my forehead.

"Please let me help Will," I said. "Please take me to the workroom. You need me there."

He stared at me a long moment, and then nodded. He produced a key and unshackled me. I slipped my wrist out as the manacle released, moaning. I pulled myself up and rolled my shoulder. Relief flooded me. Valentin rounded the bed and unchained my other wrist. I wrapped my arms around myself, then held my wrists up in front of me.

"How long was it?" I asked.

"Sixteen days," said Valentin. "I am sorry."

I pushed myself to the edge of the bed and gripped the side. I dropped my head as a spell of dizziness overtook me.

I shook it away and pushed myself to my feet. I grabbed Valentin's arm when I almost fell, and felt him flinch away. A small, private smile twisted my mouth. I had become a thing that frightened a man twice my size. I did not want to think how dreadful I must look, after sixteen days of chained madness. The smell was appalling, even to me.

I had a bath. Valentin summoned Rahel's companion, Berit. She helped me into and out of it with a look of deep distaste for my dreadful state. I did not mind. I felt the same distaste, and an even deeper relief once I had bathed and dressed.

I inspected my wrists. They were hideous. Scabbed over in patches, red and even bleeding in others. One of them oozed yellow pus. The pain was acute. I hadn't felt it this strongly when I awoke. I decided to take this as an encouraging sign. The blur was still there. The confusion at the edge of my thoughts still pulsed, fingering its way to the center. But I was calmer. The bath helped.

Valentin returned with bandages and an ointment that I could not imagine was strong enough for the job it was expected to do. He sat beside me and held my hand in his with a gentleness that surprised me. He spread the ointment into the wounds and wrapped them. There was something different about him. He looked sad.

"I did warn you," I said.

"You did," he agreed.

"I warned my father, too, but he didn't listen any better than you did," I said. "Why is he here? Do you know?"

"He is here for you," said Valentin. "He wants to help you and take you home."

I shook my head. "I don't believe that."

Valentin raised his eyebrows, but without his customary cold incredulity. "Why not?"

"He doesn't care about me," I said.

Valentin secured the bandage on my wrist and released my hand. He sat back and regarded me. "I do not know your father well," he said. "But from what I have seen of him in these last weeks, I think you may be mistaken about that."

He helped me to my feet. It was slow going, down a hallway and then the stairway. Screams traveled down them. I looked up at Valentin, a painful question on my face. He nodded.

"Yes," he said. "Dominic."

We made our way up the stairs, Dominic's screams tormenting me at each step. My heart pounded and my vision blurred, but I forced myself on, clinging to Valentin's thick arm. I would be there when the Stone was made. It was mine, my work. I would be there to be certain they used it as they had promised to.

Dominic's screams stopped, and in the sudden quiet I heard raised voices from the library. Valentin hesitated before the door, glancing at me. He knocked before I could make out what the voices were saying. They fell silent.

"Komm herein," said a woman with a low voice. Rahel. I straightened my spine to the best of my ability as we entered, pushing past a German who held the door open. I wished I could walk without clinging to Valentin's arm.

"Ah, Miss Hope," said Rahel. She stood in the corner of the room farthest from the fire, her hand on the ledge of the open window and a chair behind her. An oil portrait of a man whose dour expression rather mirrored her own hung over her on the wall to her right. My father stood opposite her, shoulders squared against her.

Will coughed. He was kneeling by the fire, which sent up thick yellow smoke. My throat tightened at the smell.

"Come in," said Rahel again in German. "Welcome. You are in time to help us settle a dispute."

My father crossed toward me, hands outstretched. I did not take them, but he held them out anyway, turning his palms up in dramatic appeal.

"Let me finish it, my dear," he said. I winced at the endearment, which sounded false on his lips. He pointed at Will. "He'll break it! His hand is barely healed and he coughs every second moment! If he was ever a competent adept, he most certainly is not now!"

"Do it, then," I said. "I cannot stop you."

Vellacott glared at Will. "He will not tell me the last step. He said you wouldn't wish him to. But now that you are here, now that you are awake, you can tell me."

A smile curled my lips. I shook my head.

"Thea, for heaven's sake!" my father cried in exasperation. "What good are your secrets now? What does it matter who finishes it?"

They were fair questions. And yet it did matter. The Stone was mine. I would finish it, even if I couldn't keep it. Even if no one but those of us in this room ever saw, at least we would know who had made the Philosopher's Stone. I would know.

"If Will can't do it—" I looked at Will, down at his trembling, blackened fingers, then into his despairing eyes. "I will."

"No, Thea," said my father. "It is too dangerous for you. You've only just begun to heal. We don't know what causes it—the smoke alone—" He stared at the fire, realization dawning. "You shouldn't be here!"

Vellacott reached for my arm. I jerked away, nearly losing my balance. Valentin pushed my father back with one hand.

"Karl," said Valentin to the German by the door. "Nimm ihn raus." *Take him out.*

Vellacott's eyes widened in alarm as Karl advanced on him. "No. No. This is too dangerous!" Karl seized my father's arm and dragged him easily to the door. "Thea, this boy is not worth—"

Karl slammed the door shut, mercifully cutting short my father's pleas. It came as no surprise to me that my father was also on the list of those who did not feel Will was worth my sacrifice. I turned to meet his eyes and found him looking uneasily at the woman in the corner.

Rahel had resumed her seat. Her hands were folded neatly on her lap. She had fixed Will with a cold glare that put me in mind of a cobra mesmerizing its prey. The muscles of Valentin's arm tensed against mine. Somehow the subtraction of my father and his protests had left the room more full, thick with unspoken but nonetheless obvious hatred. I thought of the reasons Rahel had to wish Will harm. Something she had said at dinner that first night came back to me with an ominous clarity.

Some debts cannot be paid by anyone but the debtor.

I took a step forward, pulling Valentin with me.

"Why are you here?" I asked Rahel in German.

"Why am I here?" She turned her head toward me. Her

expression did not change. "Why am I here, in my own father's house?"

I met her cold gaze. "Yes."

"*My dear,*" she said in English, mimicking my father's false tone. "I am only here to witness the making of history. The fulfillment of every alchemist's hopes."

"You care nothing for alchemy," I said.

"That was when I thought it was charlatanry." She cocked an eyebrow. "Now it seems it might be real."

I searched her eyes, wishing I could believe that was all she had in mind and wondering what I could do if it was something else. Rahel saw my hesitation and sighed.

"You have made a bargain for something dear to me," she said. "I am here to be certain you have delivered nothing less than was promised."

"Something dear to you," I repeated. "Do you mean—" We both looked at Will.

"You mean his life?" I finished.

"Say rather, his death," Rahel said. "Valentin says I must give up his death."

She gazed at Will, her cobra look growing more pronounced.

"For the Philosopher's Stone itself? It may be a fair trade. But believe me, *my dear* Miss Hope, I will accept nothing less."

She leaned back slightly in her chair and folded her hands on her knees. "You had better get to work."

Will stayed at my side, helping when he could. He held me steady when I shook. He put his hands on my face and called me back when I started to slip. Rahel watched us, coiled in the corner. Valentin stayed closer to hand, standing just far enough that he could still reach me in two or three quick steps. Will and I ground the stibnite. We knelt by the fire, and I carefully opened the glass egg. I brought the hot poker to its side and heated it through. Yellow smoke filled my mind, but I blinked it away again and again. Gently, so gently, I sprinkled the stibnite into the warmed ovum. I slumped back into Will's arms and watched in an agony of expectation while the tiny grains sank into the now again white substance.

Nothing happened. I closed my eyes, buried my head in Will's chest. Darkness clawed at me. I had held it off as long as I could. His heart stuttering in my ear would be the last thing my sane mind comprehended. And then.

It is time.

"Bee." Will's voice was low, then sharp and loud. "Bee, look!"

I came back. I opened my eyes to see the red sparks in the mustard smoke of the fire. The substance in the ovum had ignited. It burned through, the gold of fire, and then a dark, pure ruby red. Just as it had done when my mother attacked me.

"Hold me," I whispered. "Don't let me hurt it."

But to my relief, I didn't want to hurt it. I had an urge to seize it, to hold it close, but not to harm it. I loved it. I thought, with horror, of how my mother had thrown her own against the wall, shattering it. Murdering it. I would as soon murder my own child.

But after all, she had tried to do that as well.

The color deepened, and yet at the same time grew more luminous. I gazed at it, longing to touch it, but somehow certain that I had to wait.

"It's beautiful," I breathed.

A light flashed out of it, so bright it blinded. Will cried out, and so did Rahel and Valentin, as though in pain. But I felt no pain, only warmth, and something else. Something wonderful that wanted to come into me.

"Is it finished?"

Will rose, pulling me with him. I didn't want to. I rose but kept my eyes on my Stone.

"Is it finished?" Rahel demanded.

It wasn't. It should have been, but I could feel its incompletion in my body and on my breath. It was pulling me toward it, as the madness had done, but with a relentless light instead of darkness. It wanted me, to give me something, and to take something in return. And it knew, as certainly as I knew all this, that I must not tell Rahel. This was private, something between the Stone, and myself, and no one else.

"Yes," I lied. A sweat had broken out on my brow. I wanted to kneel before it and touch it, but I clung to Will and kept my hand locked by my side. "Yes, it's finished."

"Good," said Rahel. "Karl! Martin!"

"No," said Will. The fear in his voice pulled me back to his side, in the present. "You promised. Valentin, you swore!"

Dimly, I understood. I forced myself to turn away from the Stone. Will's arms were around me, holding me in front of him. The other Germans entered the room. There were knives in their hands. Will's hand tightened on my arm.

"Valentin," said Rahel. "You may take the Stone now."

He took a step toward us. Panic flared in me. I had known this moment would arrive. Once the Stone was made, my leverage was gone. I had only Valentin's word to rely on now.

"Not yet," I said. "You said I could cure him, and Dominic."

"Cure yourself," said Rahel. "Valentin will want to know that it works, after all."

Help me, I said to the Stone. It wanted to. I felt its longing for me, just like I longed for it.

"Will first," I said. I summoned all my strength and turned my attention to Valentin. He was hesitant, I saw that. He didn't think any better of Will than Rahel did, but unlike her he didn't seem quite happy to go back on his word. "You promised. I did everything you wanted. Let me heal Will first."

Valentin glanced at Rahel.

"Certainly not," she said. "I am not some Roman tyrant, to strengthen a man the better to torture him. He will die quickly, and with little pain."

Despair welled in me. I had made the Stone. Against the odds and at such a cost. To me, to Dominic, to my mother. It was a victory that rivaled any in history, and yet my triumph was to become a defeat so terrible, so total that I would not recover. To lose Will *and* the Stone?

I would not.

I twisted out of Will's arms and dove for the fire. Before any of them could stop me, I smashed the top of the ovum and shook the Stone out onto my hand. My fingers screamed from burns where they had touched the ovum, but the Stone itself was warm and just a little soft. There were no instructions for this, but I knew exactly what to do. I pressed it to my skin, pushing down the neck of my dress so that the Stone was just over my breast. The Stone throbbed in time with my own heartbeat. I felt it reaching in, reaching for what it needed to make itself whole. Warmth and strength came with it, spreading through me in curling tendrils. This was the best feeling I had ever felt. Better than falling asleep in a warm, soft bed after a long day of work while rain pattered on the shutters, better than the pleasant blur of champagne and the scent of apple blossoms and Will's mouth on mine. I wanted to close my eyes, to savor and sink into the sensation. But the others scurried about, weapons and voices raised. I forced myself to attend, in time to see Martin bearing down on Will while he backed into the wall.

I was strong, I felt that. Not as strong as I would be soon, and even then not strong enough to take on all three of the Germans. Karl was steps away from me, knife out, not expecting resistance. I smiled.

I seized his wrist with my free hand and squeezed. He cried out and released the knife. I let him go and caught the weapon before it hit the floor. He was surprisingly slow to react. I lashed out, slashing at his throat. He dropped, clutching his neck. There was blood, but not enough to make me think he would die. I dropped the Stone into my bodice where it continued to pulse, safe against my skin.

Rahel stood in the corner, glaring at me but unafraid. "Valentin!" she cried. "Befasse Dich mit ihr!"

He lunged for me, but I was quicker than he was. I charged on Rahel, flipped her around, my arm across her chest, and put my knife to her neck.

"HALT!" I screamed. Martin swung his knife at Will. I screamed again in wordless horror, but Will dodged the blow. He threw himself to the side, lost his balance, and sprawled on the floor in front of the fire.

"HALT ODER SIE STIRBT!"

Stop or she dies. Martin stopped. If my howl of rage hadn't convinced him, then Rahel's strangled groan must have. I stood a head taller than her. From the corner of my eye, I saw a thin trickle of red on her neck. The knife I held was very sharp.

"Thea," said Valentin, holding his hands out as though approaching a wild horse. "Be careful, Thea. I know you do not want to hurt her."

"You're right." My breath came quickly, but I kept my voice steady. "But if any of you touch Will, I'll do it anyway."

There was a moment of tense silence, broken by Will, coughing from the floor. Karl, the big, slow man whose knife I held, whose throat I had slashed, was frantically and wordlessly wrapping cloth from his shirt around his neck. A small part of me was relieved to see that I hadn't cut deep enough to sever his windpipe or hit an artery. Rahel squirmed under my arm, and I sank my knife just a little deeper into her skin. She went suddenly and completely still, but this time she made no sound.

"Don't," gasped Valentin. "Be careful! You're close to the vein!"

I knew that. I had to be, to keep her frightened and still. I fought to keep my hand steady. I was as afraid of what I might have to do as Valentin was.

"You leave. You and the other men with you." He hesitated. "Now!" I screamed.

"Yes, yes, we're going," he said. "Karl, Martin—lass uns gehen."

The men obeyed without hesitation. Valentin backed toward the door, then paused for a moment at the threshold.

"What will you do?" he asked me.

"What I earned," I spat. "Get out."

With a last, worried look at Rahel, he backed out the door and shut it behind him.

"Lock it," I said to Will. He pulled himself to his feet, coughing into his arm, and did as I said. Then he pulled over a chair and tilted it under the doorknob. When that was done, I lowered the knife and pushed Rahel toward the armchair in the corner. She staggered, then sank into it, pulling out a handkerchief and pressing it to her neck.

I put a hand over my heart, where the Stone still throbbed. It wasn't finished. It had paused during the fighting, somehow knowing I could not attend. But now that my pulse was slowing, fingers of warmth started to spread through me again.

"What's the plan, Bee?" said Will. "We can't hold them back forever."

"It's almost finished," I said, my voice coming out a whisper. "Then I cure you, cure Dominic, and we leave."

Will nodded slowly. He coughed into his arm again, and brought it away bloody.

"Sounds good to me," he said. "Though I don't see how the last part is going to work. We're dead the minute you let her go."

"*You're* dead," Rahel snapped at Will. "I have no quarrel with *her*."

"A quarrel with Will is a quarrel with me," I said.

"Then you are much stupider than you look. Why would an intelligent young woman want to take all the quarrels of a worthless rogue? Why claim so many enemies you need not have? For him?"

Rahel spat toward Will. He was standing warily, far enough away that it did not reach him.

The Stone had paused again, and I felt the warmth begin to retract.

"Be quiet," I said to Rahel. I needed my mind clear for this to work, I could tell. And Rahel's venom toward Will distracted me. It started a buzz of worry in the back of my mind that I couldn't easily push aside.

"I thought you must not have known what he did, but Valentin told me that you do, that you choose him anyway." She winced slightly and pressed the handkerchief harder against her neck. "Even when you read the letters. How you could forgive such treachery, I do not know."

"Letters?" I asked, in spite of myself. My pulse began to speed up. "What are you talking about? What letters?"

"We don't have time for this, Bee," said Will.

"The letters between them. My poor little fool of a sister and your precious Will," said Rahel. "All his lies, his broken promises. I left them in the letter box in Ada's room and instructed Valentin to keep you there. But . . . don't tell me!" She peered at me, her mouth half open. "You did not read them! But you must have seen the letter box! I left it there in the vanity!"

Of course I had seen it, and some part of me had recognized it for the trap it was.

"I am not in the habit of invading the private correspondence of others," I said.

But I couldn't stop myself now. I looked at Will, and I couldn't pretend he didn't look frightened.

"Bee." There was an edge of desperation in his voice.

"She is a liar. I don't know what she thinks she has. She must have written the letters, forged my handwriting—"

Rahel leaned toward me, her full, parted lips curving into a malicious smile.

"You don't know," she said. "You don't know he seduced her?"

"I know you believe that." I meant to sound defiant, but I didn't fool any of us.

"Ah, let me guess his story. He scorned her advances, and she lied to us all? Turned my father against him?" My expression betrayed me, and she laughed. "Tell me, then, how did he explain the baby?"

"Baby?" asked Will, with an attempt at scorn. "What baby?"

"Yours, you spineless creature." Rahel's joyless smile disappeared, and her face burned with rage again.

Will's pale face paled even more, but he turned to me. He reached for my hand, and when I pulled it back he met my eyes and held them instead. "She's lying, Bee. If Ada is with child, it isn't mine. It can't be. I swear it."

Rahel laughed scornfully. "And you believe that?"

I wanted to. Oh, how I wanted to. I searched his beautiful eyes and saw the same man I had always seen, the one who loved me, the one who *knew* me. The only one I could trust.

There is only one way to keep a man from betraying your trust, said my mother's voice. *Don't give it to him.*

I tore my eyes from Will's. "I want to see the letters," I said to Rahel.

"Clever girl," she said.

"Bee!" cried Will. I steeled myself against the hurt in his voice. If he had told the truth, he would forgive me for wanting proof. But if he had lied to me, I might not be able to forgive myself.

"Get up," I said to Rahel. She obeyed. I went to the door.

"Valentin," I called. "I know you're there."

There was a short silence. Then, Valentin's voice. "Yes?"

"You and your men, go outside to the gate. I must be able to see each of you from the window in five minutes, or I'll start cutting off the Fräulein's fingers."

Quick, hard bootsteps echoed down the hall, and at a glance from me Will went to the window to look.

"I see Valentin," he said. "The two who were up here. And more . . . three more."

I tried to make a mental tally of the men I knew Valentin had here. I was certain I had never seen more than six together, including Valentin. I couldn't be certain there were not more, but this would have to do.

I took Rahel by the arm and held my knife to her throat again, then nodded at Will.

"They could have left someone," he said. "They could run back in the moment we leave this room."

"I know." I couldn't meet his eyes. "I'm sorry. I have to know."

"You do know," he said. "You know me."

"I think I do. I have to be sure."

His shoulders sank, and without looking at his face I could picture the pain there. He moved the chair and opened the door.

We went down the hall and stairway as quickly as we

could. No one jumped out at us. We heard no pounding of soldiers' feet as we went. Once inside Ada's room, I shoved Rahel toward the bed and Will and I pushed the wardrobe in front of the door with great effort. There was no lock from the inside, so the heaviest furniture would have to do.

"They could lock us in," Will observed.

"With Rahel?" I shook my head. "I doubt it."

Still, the idea made me feel sick. I'd hated this room before, and now that my mind swam with nauseous images of Will and Ada embracing, I wanted to tear it apart, make kindling of the furniture. Rahel sat primly on the edge of her sister's bed, and from the sour, sucked-in look on her face I suspected she was fighting the same mental pictures. She tilted her head at me and nodded to the vanity. I went toward it. Dread slowed my movements, turning my feet to lead.

"Bee, please." The sadness in his voice wrung my heart. "Can't you simply trust me?"

I opened the vanity, took the box out and pulled it toward me with both hands, and stared at it. I hesitated a moment. I tried to measure my fear and dread against my hope—hope that whatever Rahel had cooked up would not convince me, that I would find a way to prove it a lie. The Stone's pulsing ebbed low against my breast, waiting, I knew, until I had room for it in my heart.

I opened the box and saw the first letter on the top. It had been folded backward so that the writing faced out instead of in. No doubt this was Rahel's work, and no doubt she had left the letter she considered most damning on top. I hadn't expected that. I had expected one final step, that of picking up the letter and opening it. One last chance to change my mind, to decide not to know. Too late now. I read, my vision blurring with tears.

> *My dear Ada,*
>
> *I think of nothing but you. You said, when you left me alone in bed, that you were afraid I might forget you, now that I have had what I wanted from you. I do not remember what I said, but I know it was not enough, because I could never deny that falsehood enough. Sweet Ada, how can you think one night is all I want from you? How could one taste of your love be enough for me, when you are everything? You are my world now, a world as vast as the universe, but which contains only you and I. It is just the opposite of what you feared. I can never have enough of you.*

There was more, but I tore my eyes away.

"Bee—it isn't—"

"Don't," I said quietly. I wiped away my tears. "I know your hand, Will, even in German. How could I not, after all the hours I spent poring over your letters? You write such beautiful letters."

I crushed the paper in my hand. I carefully closed the lid of the box.

"You don't want to read the rest?" Rahel asked. "There are plenty more, all of them just as lovely."

"Bee," he said. A cold blankness carpeted my mind, and I forced myself to look at his face. I was almost curious what he might say.

"It didn't mean anything to me."

"You're a liar, then. Clearly you made her believe that it did."

"Yes," he said. "I lied to her. What else could I do? She threw herself at me, she was mad for me. I thought if I didn't do as she wanted she would tell lies about me—"

"Oh, stop," I said. My curiosity was gone, overwhelmed by disgust. "Please stop. Is this what you think of me? This is what you think I want to hear? I would rather discover that you really did love her than believe you were such a craven, lying—"

My voice caught. All I could feel was fury, and yet I seemed to be on the verge of sobbing.

"Call back my men, Miss Hope," said Rahel from the bed. "They will let you heal yourself and your apprentice friend. And I will make it so this worm can never ruin another innocent girl."

I shook my head slowly, but even as I did, I heard Valentin's voice from the door.

"Thea," he said. "Let us in, please. We won't hurt you. There's someone at the gate. I think—I think it might be—"

"Who?" demanded Rahel.

"It's Vellacott. He brought the police."

Rahel swore in German.

More boot-falls. I took a step toward the window and saw the gate swinging wide. The police ran through, into the house.

Will stepped toward me, then folded into a fit of coughing. It was a powerful one, shaking his whole body. He staggered, his arm out. On an instinct, I took his arm and he fell into me. His head and hands were on my shoulder and chest before I came to myself and pushed him back. He staggered toward the window. I reached for him, but shock had dulled my reflexes. He slipped out of my arms, clutching something in his hand. The window was open. He threw himself out of it.

"Nein!" screamed Rahel. "Valentin!"

I ran to the window. Will was climbing down the trellis underneath more quickly than I would have thought he could. His feet knew the places that held. Of course they did. He had climbed up and down that way before. He dropped to the bottom.

Rahel pushed me out of her way and screamed from the window. I watched Will stagger to the gate and mount a horse tethered there. I was frozen in place. Broken. My chest was caved in, a cold sucking wound in the place where my heart had been.

No—the cold, sucking wound was in the place where the Stone had been. Will had taken the Stone.

The door splintered, caving over the wardrobe that no one had moved out of the way. Valentin climbed through and pulled Rahel away from the window, away from me.

I started to sway and reached out to hold the window frame. I stared at the gate Will had vanished through, wondering where he could have gone. It seemed a long time before two of Valentin's men ran into view, starting toward the gate, after Will. But they were stopped by two policemen. The Prussians shouted at them, pointing after Will, but it seemed the police did not speak German. They took the Prussians firmly by the arms and escorted them back into the house.

Will was getting away. I felt the Stone's distance from

me growing, and as it grew so did a strange panic inside me. I wanted to jump out the window after him, but I could not move my limbs. Everything in me screamed for the Stone, like a mother might for a kidnapped child.

"Thea!"

My name rang up the stairs and through the hall. Someone was looking for me. I found I didn't much care who. Still, I managed to pull my wits together and look around myself. The room was empty. Rahel and Valentin had left, perhaps to set after Will. I had to do the same. I put one foot in front of the other—a simple action that required a herculean effort—and immediately lost my balance. I staggered toward the bed and grabbed its post.

"Thea!" It was my father's voice, closer now. In another moment he appeared in the doorway.

"Thea!" He ran to me and put his hand on my arm. "Are you hurt? Are you—?"

Mad? Was I? I closed my eyes and tried to take stock of my body and mind. I was full of cold and panic, but not because the madness pulled at me. I couldn't feel that chasm, the danger of falling. All I felt was the Stone—or rather the absence of it. And that feeling was stronger every moment. I opened my eyes. My vision blurred, but not with the yellow mist from before, only with tears. And at this moment, crying was the sanest thing for me to do.

A sob escaped me.

"Oh, my poor child," said my father. The sympathy in his voice broke what was left of my control. I let him pull me into his arms, where I sobbed into his chest.

17

We left London. We left the house, the Germans, the mess Will had left behind. We spoke to the police before we went, but they did not hold us.

We left Dominic.

That had been the worst of it all. I watched as Valentin negotiated with the police for Dominic. They argued. Money changed hands. *Graf Ludwig will want to study him,* Valentin said as we watched Dominic writhing against the full-body restraints, screaming past the bit they had put in his mouth to keep him from biting off his own tongue. I had been where he was and felt what he felt. If there was a hell, there could not be worse torments there than those he now suffered. And he had done it for me, expecting nothing in return.

I could not thank him, where he had gone. I could not beg his forgiveness. I could do nothing for him at all.

Will got away. He was no longer in London, I could

feel it by now. The Stone was not as close to me as that. And so when my father said we should go home, I didn't say what I felt—that I had no home. I went back with him.

Now I was in Oxford, sitting in the dim parlor of my father's rooms, nursing a long-cold cup of weak tea. I was like a beef cow that had been clubbed on the head to stun it before slaughter, except the slaughter itself had been left unfinished. I would not die, but without the Stone I was only half alive. And it was Will—my first friend, my only love, my ally against the world—my Will who had taken it from me.

I set down my tea cup so hard the saucer underneath cracked in two. The thought of Will had been the only thing that could wake me from my stunned bovine state in the last few days. But I did not like the way it woke me. My rage frightened me. It was too strong to control, and under it was too great a pain. If I started to allow myself to feel it, I knew at once that I couldn't bear it. Perhaps I chose these cowlike feelings.

I put the cup aside and picked up the pieces of broken china. I felt the slightest pang of guilt; my father didn't have many good dishes. At least I could clean up the mess.

Unlike the one you left behind in London.

I'd heard my mother's voice often since we returned to Oxford, enough that I had begun to wonder if she really was speaking to me from the hell of her madness. Always, she urged me on, insisting I must find a way to get the Stone back. As if I didn't already know that. As if there were a way.

It wasn't my fault. I did all I could.

It was all you could do to let him snatch the Stone from you? To watch while he ran? When did you become this helpless, useless—

I threw the china into the bin, making a loud enough crash to drive the voice, but not the thought, from my head.

I went to the window and stared out at the busy street. It was well into springtime now, but you wouldn't know it from the dreary sky or the cold, wet streets of Oxford. I allowed myself to think for just a moment of going back to France, where spring at least came with sunshine and blossoms.

Apple blossoms. Which smelled of Will.

I shook the thought of him from my head. I wouldn't go back to Normandy, then. I'd go to Paris, to join the revolutionaries—

Just as Will and I had talked of doing.

But I knew I couldn't leave, even if I had anywhere to go that wasn't poisoned. Not while Will was still in England with the Stone.

Find it. Find it! What are you waiting for?

I did not argue with her. I wanted nothing but to obey. My pulse sped up, and my breath came fast and shallow. How could I stand here, doing nothing, while the Stone was lost to me? It needed me. When I let myself, I felt it calling me. And I did not know how to answer its call. I did not know how to find Will. I did not know what he might be doing to the Stone.

Something twisted inside me, and I gasped.

A shock followed, thrilling down every limb, every nerve. A wave of fury, revulsion, and pain. I gripped the sill and closed my eyes. I couldn't breathe.

There was something strange about the pain. I felt it, but as though it were someone else's. Someone else who was dying.

No. Someone else whom I wanted to kill.

I saw him, somehow. Will lay on the ground, gasping, clutching his nearly stopped heart. The Stone was beside him, pulsing with our rage. It spoke.

Not him. Never him.

The vision faded. The pain went with it, but not the rage.

Will had tried to finish the Stone. He had tried to fuse it to himself.

My Stone.

My heart thundered dangerously, blood crashing in my ears. My knuckles tightened on the sill, but I imagined them as fists, smashing into Will again and again.

We rejected him. The Stone didn't want him any more than I did. It wanted me. Under my fury, a grim satisfaction welled.

The Stone had nearly killed Will for trying to make it his. It wouldn't have Will. It didn't want him. It wanted me.

I started to breathe again. And then I started to think.

The Stone was mine. It had chosen me, and it needed me to become complete. Will could do nothing with it. He knew that now. That meant he would come for me. All I had to do was wait.

I sat back down at the table and my mind went blank. When my father came up from the kitchen with another tea tray, I came back to myself, unsure how long I had been gone. I tried to ignore Vellacott's worried glances. He asked if I was well, and I nodded without conviction. I was not, and would not be until I had the Stone again.

"Sugar?" asked my father, then shook his head. "Oh, I forgot, you don't take sugar. I'll remember next time—"

"No," I said quietly. "I like sugar. It was Mother who didn't."

"Ah." My father set down the cup he had held out to me, carefully added a lump of sugar, and made a long production of stirring it. When he finally handed it back to me, his eyes glinted with moisture. I sipped my tea and hoped he would manage not to cry. In the two weeks since I had returned to Oxford with him, he had seemed on the verge of some emotional display more than once. I did not think I could bear anything like that without breaking down myself.

"Thea," he began, then stopped and smiled slightly. "Or perhaps I should call you Theosebeia, since it would make me less likely to repeat it quite as often? It might lessen the danger of making you hate your own name."

I didn't understand him at first, then realized he was referring to my rather harsh words at the Graf's house in London. I frowned and tried to make out whether he was attempting a joke or a reprimand.

"Theosebeia." This time he sounded distant, as though he weren't saying my name at all, but invoking a long-past memory. He shook his head. "I still remember how she laughed at me when I said it would be a fine name for a child."

He smiled past me, and I had a sudden feeling that if I looked over my shoulder my mother might be there.

"*You* said it would be a fine name?"

"You might well look incredulous!" he said with a small laugh. "I couldn't believe it, either, when you told me your name. Evidently she didn't want me to have the slightest hand in your upbringing, and yet she chose a name I had loved and she had scorned. I thought on it constantly, when you fled Oxford. It seemed as though it meant something."

"Meant something? What?"

"I couldn't puzzle it out." He looked at me with a hopeful air, as though I might know.

But I couldn't puzzle it out, either. My mother had never said anything about my father that indicated any lingering tender feelings, as he evidently hoped. I considered whether she might have been hiding them from me, but found it unlikely. My mother's affections didn't linger once she had moved past them. They simply expired.

"She must have liked the name more than she let on. Or else—" Anger bubbled up in me for a moment. "Perhaps she simply didn't bother to think of a better one."

"Ah." Vellacott raised his eyebrows. "But it is a very fine name for an alchemist, you must admit that."

"It's a fine name for an alchemist's pupil, I suppose," I said. "As far as I know, Theosebeia never did much alchemy of her own. In any event, I am not an alchemist any longer."

I regretted the words as soon as I said them. I clamped my mouth shut to keep any more such pronouncements from coming out. The low-burning despair in me flared up, as though I had cursed myself. Not an alchemist? Only if I failed to get the Stone back. And I could not fail.

But my father saw none of that. He nodded, agreeing with the curse I had placed on myself.

"I am glad you see it that way, my dear," he said. "It is much too dangerous for you, that much is clear, despite your immense abilities, and indeed your unparalleled accomplishments—"

He broke off with a look of pain, possibly thinking of how he had failed to benefit in any way from those unparalleled accomplishments. For all he had tried to call it off at the end, he had been as eager as the rest of them to use my alchemical abilities. Indeed, in the beginning he had shown as little concern for the cost to me as any of them. I remembered Bentivoglio's assault on me, his theft of my mother's papers. My father had kept those papers. I looked at him again, remembering. He still hadn't returned them.

"I've been thinking." He looked down at his teacup where his fingers drummed a quick, nervous beat. "That is to say, I've made inquiries, for a house in town. Somewhere more suitable than this for you and me to live together. As father and daughter, I mean."

He glanced up at me quickly, to see if I had taken his meaning. He did not seem to see what he hoped for.

"It would certainly hurt my standing with the masters," he continued, still tapping his cup and talking rather more rapidly than was his usual manner. "But I do not think they will remove me from my fellowship. It is hard to say, of course. I do not have many examples of such things happening in the past, and how they were dealt with, but I feel confident I can convince them that it is the best course of action. Sadly, I fear I must give up my dream of a department of alchemy, with all that has happened. I could not subject undergraduates to that kind of danger, in any case—"

I did not know how long he might go on in this vein, and decided to stop him. My mother had never been patient with nervous babble. *For God's sake, say what you mean or keep quiet.*

So, he wanted to acknowledge me. That was something, perhaps, if I could trust it. But it was not enough.

"I shouldn't like to be responsible for jeopardizing your standing with the masters," I said. He opened his mouth to reply, and I hurried on. "In any case, I have not found Oxford much to my taste."

"But . . . Thea . . ." A pained expression twisted my father's handsome features. "You cannot go back to France. Where else is there for you now?"

Against my will, I saw myself as he must see me. Without alchemy, what was I? Friendless, motherless, exiled and with no way to provide for myself. I had nothing and no one but him. No wonder, then, that he offered to take me in. He did not want to acknowledge me, but he felt compelled. No father with any conscience at all could turn away such a needy child as he believed me to be—indeed, as I would be, if I did not find the Stone.

I pushed the thought aside. Will was coming for me. He knew he could not use the Stone without me. And once I had the Stone, I would not need my father.

"I will think on it," I said.

He didn't ask what there was for me to think on, but the question showed on his face.

"I am grateful for your kindness." And I knew I should be, though all I could feel was shame to be such an object of pity to a man I barely knew.

18

A letter came one week later, addressed to me, with no return address. I took it from my father, ignoring the unspoken question on his face. I knew the hand, of course, but he didn't. I took it with unsteady hands and shut myself quickly in my room.

I sat down gently on the edge of the bed, my head down and my arms wrapped around my body like a wounded child. I had lain in this bed impatiently awaiting this letter for days, but now that it had arrived I needed more time. I opened it with trembling hands.

Dear Bee, it said.

It was one page only, in the same beautiful hand that had written to Ada. I swallowed my nausea and read on.

I know. I have no right to call you that, not now. I have no right to beg your forgiveness.

I have no right to ask for anything from you.

And yet I must. I must beg for your forgiveness, because without it my life will never mean anything. I can't leave England knowing you are still here, and hate me.

I lied to you. I had a foolish affair, and I lied to you about it. I should have told you the truth at once. My fear of losing you made me stupid and cowardly. I wish I could make you see how little it meant, and how much you mean and will always mean to me. What woman could ever compare with you? There is no one like you in the whole world. Who has your mind, your talent, your courage? No one. No one in the world. Nothing in the world is worth anything without you, not even the Stone.

Come with me, Bee. We can wield it together. You made it, and you paid the price for it. You should benefit. We will go to France first, to heal your mother. And then—wherever you choose. I will go anywhere in the world if it means I can be with you.

One more chance, Bee. If I fail you again, I'll hand you the knife to kill me.

*I love you. And if you do not love me now, I
will make you love me again.*

*I have booked us passage on a ship leaving
from Portsmouth on April twenty-sixth.
Come, and meet me on the dock at sunup.
I will wait as long as I can. If I must go
without you, know that I will live in hope of
finding you again one day.*

*And if you cannot forgive me, tell the
Germans. If you cannot forgive me, I may
as well let them have their revenge..*

*Still, your loving
Will*

I didn't cry. My hands shook, so I put down the letter
and sank them into the bed. My vision started to blur, so I
closed my eyes and drew a breath. I couldn't let myself feel
what I felt. The madness was still too close. I put it away.
I made myself think.

So. He thought I did not know that the Stone had rejected him and would do nothing without me. He thought
he could fool me with another letter, even after I'd seen
how little, how much less than nothing his letters meant. I
bit down on my lip and tasted blood, but my vision cleared.

He told you where he would be. He is trusting you with his life.

It was my mother's voice, but it was the very last obser-
vation I would have expected her to make.

Yes, I reasoned. *But only because he must. If I do not come, the Stone will not cure him. He knows this is his only chance, whatever the risks.*

Do you think you will find one better? she asked. *I never did.*

I pressed my hands to my ears.

"I'm not you," I said aloud.

I had to focus. I had to think. I shook my mother from my head.

I wasn't going anywhere with Will, of course I wasn't. But he had the Stone. I had to go to him, at least long enough to take it. And then . . . and then . . .

And then you'll believe him. There was scorn in her voice, but insistence as well. *Why not? Once you have the Stone, he will be faithful. He would not dare be otherwise.*

What good is that? I don't want forced fidelity.

My darling. Cold laughter. *There is no other kind.*

I slapped myself. It stopped her laughter, for the moment, but still her words echoed in my head.

You never forgave, I thought. *You never forgave any of them even a part of what Will has done.*

And suddenly you wish to emulate me?

"I wish to make this decision without *you* in my head!" I said, and screamed to silence her.

The scream brought me to myself. That, and my father's voice crying out from the parlor. The doorknob rattled, and I remembered that I had locked it.

"Thea, may I come in?"

His desperate tone belied his calm words.

I stood. I went to the door and hesitated, my hand on the knob. I said nothing.

"Thea, please let me in," said my father. "I can help you."

I almost believed it. After all, he was willing to

acknowledge me. I leaned my head on the door and thought for a moment of what it would be to become Theosebeia Vellacott, the fellow's daughter. Not an alchemist. Not an illegitimate, fatherless girl. Perhaps my father would introduce me to the wives and daughters of the other Oxford scholars. Perhaps they, in turn, would introduce me to their sons and brothers. And then . . .

But there my mind went blank. I could picture nothing further than a dull tea with a pale, faceless young man, and the humiliating knowledge that my only task in life now was to conceal my true self long enough to trick him into marrying me.

And even that was a fantasy. My father might truly wish to provide me with everything in his power, but what was that, really? He couldn't hide me from Graf Ludwig, who would surely bring me back if his hunt for Will failed. Or from the other hopeful alchemists who would eventually hear what I had done. All it would take was another rich lord without scruples to decide he'd like me to do it again, and I would be locked back in another bedroom, madness beckoning.

And all that, only if I could force myself not to go after the Stone. Which, of course, I could not.

"I'd like to help," he said in a quieter voice.

And this time, somehow, I believed him.

He wanted to help me. I considered this for a moment and was surprised to find a small seed of warmth trying to take root amid the thorny fears and furies.

I opened the door. His face betrayed alarm at the sight of me.

"Are you well?" he asked anxiously. "You look—Thea, you are not in danger of becoming . . . ill . . . again, are you?"

"I do not think so," I said without confidence.

"Is there something you need?" asked my father. "Have you eaten? Or, perhaps tea?"

I could face the thought of neither, and shook my head.

"You said . . ." I stared down at the floor. It took me longer than it should have to force out the words. "You said you would like to help."

"Yes." My father reached out his hand as if to pat my shoulder, but lowered it before it reached me. A sad laugh escaped him like a sigh. "I would. But I'm not sure how to do it. Perhaps you could tell me?"

I nodded. "Come in."

I sat on the edge of my bed. My father hovered hesitantly for a moment before sitting beside me. I gathered my thoughts. It took long enough that my father felt compelled to speak.

"I can't help but think I've made a terrible mess of things, Thea." My father knit his long, pale fingers together in his lap and stared at them. "I know you are tired of hearing me make excuses for myself. But I can't stop thinking of what I did."

I looked at him sharply. My mind was so focused on my present dilemma that my first thought was some new betrayal. Had he intercepted Will's letter perhaps, or told Valentin where Will wanted to meet me?

"If I hadn't turned on Dominic and driven you away, none of this would have happened," he went on. "Neither of you would have been dragged into Will's troubles. I hate to think of what you suffered because of me. But you at least recovered. Dominic—"

I winced. The thought of Dominic sent real pain through my body and a twist of panic through my mind.

"I can only hope he will recover, somehow," said Vellacott. "Like you did."

I shook my head.

"You—you think not?" My father's face fell.

"The Stone let me go," I said. "It chose me. I don't know why, but it did. That is why I recovered."

My father stared at me.

"It . . . chose you?"

I had not put it into words yet, even in my own mind. But I knew it all the same.

"It was in my mother's papers. In her notes. Alchemistam ultimam lapis elegit. Get them. I'll show you."

My father rose hastily and left the room. He returned with my papers and a shamefaced look.

"I should have thought to return them to you sooner—"

"It doesn't matter now." I flipped through the papers until I found the one with the warning. I pointed to the scribble in the margins. "There."

My father bent over it with a frown. "The Stone chooses the last alchemist," he translated. "And woe to whom it does not accept. What does it mean, the last alchemist?"

"I'm not sure . . . It's to do with making the Stone, obviously. Maybe the Stone can only be made once, so whoever makes it is the last alchemist. As for the Stone choosing, I thought it meant you had to be worthy, like Brother Basil said. Virtuous," I said. "But it isn't that, not that at all. It simply . . . chose. It wanted me, and not Dominic or Bentivoglio or my mother. So it let me go."

"What do you mean, it let you go?" He turned to me, his forehead creased. "Are you saying that the Stone somehow . . . held your mind?"

"Yes. It is what causes the madness. The Stone took my mind, and Dominic's. And Mother's. I saw them. It . . ." I recalled the laid-bare feeling of madness, the sense of being consumed. I shuddered. "It feeds on them."

"But how can that be? It didn't exist yet, when you went mad. It wasn't finished."

"Not finished. But somehow it was already there, in some form. I felt it. I—I saw it." I thought of the dark figure and shuddered. "I know."

We fell silent. I did not want to think of the sinister implications of what I was saying. I felt my mind trying to slide past them.

"Will tried to fuse with the Stone," I told him. "It rejected him. It wants me to complete it."

I took Will's letter from my bedside table and handed it to him. I stood before him while he read it. When he finished, he looked up at me.

"Thea," said my father. There was wariness in his eyes and warning in his voice.

"I'm going to meet him, Father," I said. "I'm going to get the Stone and use it to cure Dominic and Mother."

"Thea, think of what you've just told me," said Vellacott. "The Stone is dangerous. You say it is feeding on their minds—what will it do to you, if you complete it? We don't understand it. We don't know how it works or what it will do."

"I know it needs me to work," I said. "And I know it heals any ailment. Every text says that."

"But, Thea, the risks—"

"I know them," I said, and suppressed another shudder. "Dominic knew them, too, when he took them to save me. He said—"

I didn't want to say what he said, after he had recovered from the first threat of madness. I forced it out.

"He said it was like being among the damned in hell. And it is," I said. "It is. I can't leave them there."

My father's head drooped. He took a long, shallow breath. He shook his head.

There was no way to explain to him how much I needed the Stone. How everything in me screamed for it. It was something I needed for myself, but he did not see that. I tried another angle.

"You said you feel responsible for what happened to Dominic," I said as gently as I could manage. "Then think how I must feel. When the situation was reversed, he chose to face the same risk for me."

"I know," said Vellacott. "I was there. I didn't stop him."

"Then you will not stop me," I said.

He looked up at me again with an anguish I had not expected. I took a step back. It was too much. I could not accept responsibility for that much misery from him. I went to the window and let him gather himself.

"If you still wish to help, I would be grateful if you would go to London and find Valentin," I said. "Tell him to meet us across the channel in Caen with Dominic if he still wants the Stone."

"You will go to your mother first?" Vellacott asked.

I nodded.

"Valentin will take the Stone from you," said my father. "Will you let him have it, when you have healed them?"

I did not answer at first. I closed my eyes and let myself feel the low throb of longing that flared up into fierce desire at the thought of giving up the Stone.

Give it up? No. Never.

But first things must be dealt with first.

"Tell Valentin I will," I said.

19

I arrived in Portsmouth late, the night before I was to meet Will on the docks. The salt air hung so heavy that I tasted it when I licked my cracked lips. I walked down the dock and stared at the ships in the enormous port, my eyes glassy from the sharp sea wind. The church bells tolled the late hour, and a ship in the harbor fired its guns in agreement.

Will was here, somewhere. And the Stone.

The Stone. I had felt it calling to me, stronger and stronger as I drew nearer to the port. It was a throb inside me that never stopped, a soundless keening that set my mind and heart racing. Since Will had taken the Stone from me, I had never stopped feeling the lack of it. Now, though, I felt nothing else. It knew I was here, and it wanted to find me as much as I wanted to find it. I had to have it. I would do anything, *anything* to have it.

A quiet voice inside myself, struggling to speak through the Stone's pull, tried to remind me of what the Stone had done to me in the past, to my mother, to Dominic. Was it good to long so much for something with the power and the will to do so much harm?

Power to do harm is still power, said my mother's voice. *That power in your hands becomes the power to do good. To do anything.*

Her voice was so much louder than the quiet one inside myself. So much easier to listen to. I pushed my doubts aside. The thing now was to get the Stone, to heal my mother and Dominic. The rest would come afterward.

I took a room at the cheapest inn in Portsmouth Point, the cheapest part of town, reasoning that I would be likely to find Will somewhere he could afford. I stood at the door of the inn and hesitated to enter it. The water lapped quietly against the jetty beneath me, and the air was thick with mist and the brackish smell of the harbor. It was very quiet and very still. From where I stood on the point, I could see the docks crowded with ships, the town behind them, and the white-pocked hills beyond the town. The Stone was here, somewhere. I felt it.

I went inside and booked a room. I avoided the cloudy mirror on the wall, but I still saw my ill appearance reflected in the concerned frown of the innkeeper. I clutched my shawl tight and found myself worrying about how this cold damp affected Will. I tried to dismiss the thought, but to my dismay the anxiety remained. It was only habit, I reassured myself. I did not truly care if he was cold, no matter what it did to his lungs.

I climbed the creaky wooden stairs slowly. It was a necessity—my breath came shorter with each step—and it was also a good way to listen. Sure enough, his cough tore through the walls, and even from the stairway and down the hall, I knew it was him. He was on the third floor, one above mine. I gripped the rail and waited in vain for my heartbeat to slow. He coughed again. It was worse than it had been in London. I had not thought it could get worse, but it had. He couldn't have long.

I made my way slowly down the hall to his room. I waited outside his door until the coughing subsided. I waited a long time. He must have heard me.

"It's not locked," he said from inside. His voice was little more than a gasp.

I opened it. The room was snug and dark from the unpainted walls of wood. Faint light filtered in through one small window; just enough for me to see how dreadful Will looked. More corpse than man. He made an effort to sit up when I came in, but failed. What had been left of the flesh on his body had wasted away, and the dark circles under his eyes seemed to have spread to his whole sunken face. His lips were red with blood. He clutched a mass of red-stained handkerchiefs in his hands. He looked up at me with flat, hopeless eyes when I came in. I tried to hate him. I tried to call up his betrayal, his lies, his selfishness. None of that could take hold. He had been so beautiful, and so alive. All I could feel was sadness that now he was not.

"Bee," he said, so very quietly. "Thank you for coming."

"I didn't come for you." I tried to hide my pity. I doubted I succeeded.

"I know." He gasped, coughing into his handkerchiefs. "You came for the Stone."

I looked around the room, then closed my eyes for a

moment to listen for it. Will spoke, confirming what I already knew.

"It isn't here."

My mind filled with panicked questions, but I forced them down. He hadn't lost it. He would have hidden it somewhere, until he could be sure I would do what he wanted.

"Then I cannot heal you," I said.

His eyes lit with a trace of pathetic hope. "You can make it work, then? Are you certain? It nearly killed me when I tried."

I nodded. The Stone would work for me. I was certain of almost nothing but that.

"Then you will, but not until we're away," said Will with a little more force. "When you're on a ship with me to France, and we've left England and the Germans behind for good."

"So it is already on the boat?" My pulse quickened. A reckless plan, if it was. Too many things could go wrong. "That was foolish, Will. We don't leave until tomorrow, and you look like you might not last the night."

He made a ghastly wheezing sound. For the half moment before it became a cough, it was almost like laughter.

"Very true," he gasped. "I might not last the night. But you should try to see to it that I do. The boat sails with the early tide. If I don't get on board, the Stone will be thrown into the sea."

My anger rekindled. I pressed my clenched fists into my thighs. A new reason to hate his illness occurred to me. If he were well, I could hit him in his selfish face. But nature had taken my revenge for me.

"Even now," I said in a low voice. "Even now you think of nothing and no one but yourself. If you let the Stone be thrown into the sea my mother will never be well. And I—I will have nothing. You know that, and you do not care."

"You're wrong about that," he said. "I do care. I've always cared about you. Just not quite as much as I care about myself."

There was a spindly chair in the corner. I felt an urgent need to sit down. I pulled it over and sank into it.

"I think—" I met his sunken eyes. "I think that is the only honest love speech you've ever made."

He coughed again, and I closed my eyes against the way his wasted body shook with it.

"What other honest love speech is there?" he asked when it had subsided. "You want the truth, Bee? You already know it. I was willing to watch you suffer and perhaps lose your mind if it could save my life. I hated to do it. It caused me more pain than anything else in the world could, except my own death." He coughed again, and when he stopped his death hung in the air between us, feeling very near.

"I love you, Bee. I truly do, but love has a limit. Men say they'd die for their beloved, but that's nonsense." Will's eyes were wide and deep. Looking at them was like staring into an endless void. "Easy to say when you don't have to do it. I know death now, Bee. I've had to face it, truly face it. And I choose not to go, if I can help it. I'm only human."

"I'm human, too." I looked at my hands, balled in my

lap. "But I was willing to face something worse than death for you."

"There's nothing worse than death," said Will.

"You are wrong about that," I said.

"Perhaps," said Will. "But you expected a cure. And in the end you got one."

But Dominic didn't.

I rose and went to the window. It had started to rain. I tried to count the ships in the port, and the ones in the harbor. I could probably rule out the proud, many-sailed British warships. He would have made some deal with one of the humbler merchant vessels. But even so, there were too many.

"You won't find it without me, Bee," said Will, reading my thoughts. "You still need me, for a little while longer at least. Then you can have everything you want, except revenge." He made a ghastly wheeze of a laugh. "I'm afraid I can't let you have that."

"I'm not looking for revenge," I said.

"No?" He frowned, then coughed. "I don't like that at all, Bee. What kind of lover would forgive me for what I've done without making me pay first?"

I looked at him in surprise and realized he was being quite sincere.

"Forgive you?" I asked. "You expect me to forgive you?"

"Not at first," he said. "First you'll need to punish me. I understand that. I deserve it. But then you'll see what I see, Bee. We're meant for each other. No one will ever understand you as I do. No one else could ever make you happy."

"Perhaps not." That much, at least, I believed. No person could fill the hole his betrayal had left behind. But the Stone would. I knew it would.

"Bee—" Another cough took him. I watched his body convulse with it. When it had finished with him, he looked up at me, alarm all over his face. "Why are you so calm, Bee? You should be angrier with me."

"What would be the point of that?" I asked. But he was right. It was strange, the blank feeling that came over me when I looked at him, when he coughed like a man not long for this world. "I'll keep you alive through the night, and in the morning we'll sail together. You will give me the Stone. I will heal you. And we will go our separate ways."

"No." Will pushed himself onto his elbow. "I won't lose you. You love me, Bee, I know you do underneath—"

This time, somehow, the cough was worse. Deeper and fuller than the others. Will clutched the bloody handkerchief to his mouth, but brought up too much blood for it to contain. It spilled down his arm. I looked away until it was over.

"You have to tell me where it is," I said when it finally stopped. "You do not have time for this, Will. Do you want to go on suffering this way? Tell me where it is, and I will come back. I'll heal you tonight."

He looked up at me, his eyes dark pits of terror. He knew it was the only way. He would agree.

"Swear," he whispered, blood dripping down his chin.

"I swear it," I said at once. "I swear, I will bring it here first. I don't want you to die like this, Will, whatever you've done. I would not wish it on my worst enemy."

"You have a worse enemy . . . than me?" he whispered, then coughed again.

"I never wanted you as an enemy," I said. "You know I loved you."

He stared at me, struggling for breath. Then he closed his eyes. "I love you still," he whispered.

"Then trust me," I said. "You know you can."

"No." He shook his head. "I need proof."

"What proof?" I asked.

"Proof that you love me." He opened his eyes again, and now I could see something else in them, something dark behind the fear. "Marry me."

I almost laughed, though nothing could be less amusing.

"Be serious, Will," I said. "You are dying. Now is not the time—"

"Now is the only time I will ever have." He reached for my hand. It was a desperate movement that seemed to require his whole body. I wanted to cringe away, but I held myself still. His hand clamped on mine, slick with blood. "There is a minister at the church down the street. I told him to come in the morning, but he will come tonight if you ask him. Tell him I'm dying, and this is my last wish."

He was coughing again, but instead of pulling his hand away his grip tightened. He seemed stronger, suddenly. It dawned on me, slowly and horribly, that he meant this. He had planned it all along. He was going to insist.

"You don't even believe in marriage," I said faintly. We had argued about it, once, though not seriously.

"But you do," he said. A sickly smile twisted his mouth. "If you say the words, I will know you mean it."

I stared at him. Disgust curdled my stomach. I could

almost see, from his mind, how it made a grotesque kind of sense. This creature, this thing that had once been Will, wanted to bind me to him with whatever power could come to hand. And nothing was more binding than the bonds of marriage. The Stone would be mine, but what was mine would be his.

"Don't do this, Will," I said. "If you care about me at all, you will not do this to me."

"I knew it." He fell back, loosened his grip. "You mean to betray me. If I tell you where it is, you'll leave me here to die."

He turned away. I stood. I backed out of the room. And when I had shut the door behind me, I ran.

20

I wasn't going to marry Will. The very thought of it made me want to scream. I ran down the stairs, out of the inn, into the cold salty night.

I wasn't going to marry him, but I found myself looking up into the night sky for a church spire and following it to the church steps. A cold, horrible solution occurred to me. I could marry him, take the Stone, then let him die. Become a widow. I did not want to marry him, or let him die, but wasn't it better to do both than lose the Stone, or live with Will as my husband?

What else was there? If I refused him, the Stone would die. Oh, I could look for it, of course. But I had little hope that I would find it. I tried to ignore it calling to me. Would the calling stop, one day? When it lay at the bottom of the sea, perhaps? I didn't know which was worse: the thought of living with this longing unfulfilled for the rest of my life, or the fear of what would be left behind when it went away.

A breath became a sob, and I choked on it. If I let myself cry now, I would find it hard to stop. I had to think, but my mind swam.

Is this all it takes to deter you?

My mother's voice again. The only voice in the world I wanted to hear even less than Will's.

I would have done anything to make the Stone mine. Anything. This? This is nothing, and you quail. The Stone should have chosen me instead.

I shook my head. Nothing? Would it be nothing to take Will's hand and swear to love and obey him? To bind myself to him for the rest of my life, or at least his? Even if I let him die immediately after, it would be a horror. Bile rose in my throat. Once I had dreamed of marrying Will, and now he had turned it into a nightmare.

I stood and started away from the church. There had to be another way. I walked down to the docks, staring at each ship. The Stone pulsed in me, but no stronger before any particular vessel. It was only a few hours before dawn. When it came, I could run down the dock and call out to each ship's captain, trying to convince them to give me what Will had hidden. It would be impossible to reach them all before they sailed, but perhaps I would be lucky. Perhaps I'd find the right captain, and somehow he would be persuadable.

Despair lurched in my belly. It was too small a chance of success. Too great a chance I would lose the Stone. Lose everything. I had to do what Will insisted. I turned it over in my mind and forced down my revulsion. It was small comfort that I did not have to be married to him for long. Despite everything, I did not want to see him dead.

I turned from the docks in time to see a tall, blond figure in a blue military-style coat walking away. I squinted after him for a moment. My heart stuttered with instinctive fear. Valentin.

We were supposed to meet in Caen, not here, though it was no great surprise that he had chosen this port to sail from. I calmed myself. Then I followed.

I thought I stayed far enough behind to remain unseen, but on the steps of a tavern, Valentin turned. He looked directly at me, skulking in the shadows across the street.

"Thea," he said.

My first, foolish thought was to run. I reminded myself of what I had to gain. I stepped into the light of the gas streetlamp.

"Is my father with you?" I called across the street.

"Yes," said Valentin. "Is Percy with you?"

I did not answer at first. I knew what I needed from Valentin, but the old impulse to protect Will had not yet died.

"Do not worry, Thea," said Valentin. "I am here to do as you asked. Your father made a convincing case. I have brought Dominic, and we will all go to France with the Stone to heal your mother. When that is done, you will give me Percy, and the Stone. Just as you said, yes?"

It was late. The street was still and dark. No one was out but Valentin and me, and yet the shadows seemed full of witnesses.

"Yes," I agreed. A lie. "But I need your help."

Valentin went very still. "What kind of help?"

"He has put the Stone on one of the boats, but he will

not tell me which one unless I . . . unless I do something I am not prepared to do. He requires . . ." I hesitated. Will deserved it. This was the only way. Yet still the word left a nauseous taste in my mouth. "Persuasion."

Even in the dim light I saw the grim satisfaction spread across Valentin's face.

"Tell me where he is," he said.

I swallowed hard. Will had broken quickly the last time Valentin had used his methods of persuasion on him. It would be the same this time. The threat alone might be enough. But . . .

"He is close to death," I said. "You will have to be careful. It would not take much to kill him."

Valentin crossed the street and stood before me, examining my downturned face. He held out his hand. I looked at it for a long moment. This was a hand that had held me against my will. I would be a fool to trust it.

I took it anyway.

We went into the tavern, and the heat of a roaring fire poured over me. That alone was enough to mark this place as a superior sort of establishment to the one on the dock. Four other Germans sat around the table nearest the fire. Between them, looking miserable and travel-worn, was my father. His eyes met mine and widened in alarm. I shook my head, hoping to reassure him.

"Miss Hope requires our assistance," Valentin said. He looked at me expectantly.

"He is at the Gray Gull," I said. "The inn on the point."

Valentin nodded to the burliest of his men, and two of them rose at once and left.

I moved to sit at the table, but Valentin took my arm.

"There is something you should see," he said. "Herr Vellacott, as well."

It was not an invitation, but a command. The two remaining Germans escorted my father up the stairs ahead of us. We stopped in the hallway before the room. Even through the door, I heard the muted sounds of madness, bound and gagged. Thrashing. Hoarse, muffled screams. I had made these sounds, not so long ago.

Dread pooled in my stomach like poison, leaching into my limbs and turning them to lead. For a moment there was nothing I wanted more than for the door to stay shut. I did not want to see the horror that had befallen Dominic, and my mother, and once myself.

"Please," I began. "I don't wish to see him."

"I know. But I think I must remind you why you made the bargain with us that you did." Valentin looked at me, then opened the door and pushed me through. "And why you must not break it."

Dominic was bound hand and foot, and a leather strap was tied between his teeth. His mouth was open, and his jaw and throat worked at screams that came out rough and nearly soundless. He must have screamed his voice hoarse. His face was scratched red and raw, and his eyes were as hot as comets falling to earth. The smell was overpowering.

I approached Dominic slowly. He saw me, in a way. Enough to want to tear me apart. If he could have gotten free right then, he would have done just what my mother did. This was what had become of my only true friend.

Will had done this. He had run away with the Stone and left Dominic to this madness.

"Yes," agreed Valentin. "It is bad. You know better than I, don't you, Thea? You did the right thing, to ask for my help. I know you would not have asked if he had left you another choice."

"Oh, he left another choice," I said.

"What choice?" asked Valentin.

At once, I regretted bringing it up. I did not want to say it. It was too vile, even for Will. I did not want to see the look on Valentin's face when I told him. When I looked up, it was my father's eyes I met. He stood behind me in the doorway. I would tell him. To my surprise, I found I wanted to.

"He's found a priest. He wants me to marry him in the morning. Then he'll tell me where the Stone is."

My father's eyes flashed with anger, then he closed them. When he opened them again, the anger had changed into something softer.

"Oh, Thea," he said quietly. "I'm sorry."

Valentin swore in German. "That beast," he muttered in disgust. "Nothing is too low for him. Nothing."

He paced the room. Fury radiated off him. I looked at my father, trying to discern what feeling it was I saw on his face. Valentin's fury I understood. To him, it was yet another demonstration of Will's depraved character, and I was another girl, like his Ada, whom Will was bent on destroying. But my father wasn't looking at me and seeing someone else. He looked sad. Sad for me.

My mother had never looked at me like that, at least not that I could recall.

My mother had told me I should marry Will, and called me weak for hesitating. My mother—

Is that what you want? To be coddled like some infant? I thought what you wanted was the Stone. Your father would make you a child. I want to make you the last alchemist.

Liar, I shot back at her. *You wanted to be the last alchemist.*

"So . . ." said Valentin. He stopped pacing and wheeled on me. "Good. He will not have his way." He glanced at Martin. The abuser. The torturer.

The smell of the disinfectant they had used on Will's fingers after they mangled them returned to me. The glint of fury in Valentin's eyes filled me with fear. I had asked him to be careful, but there was nothing careful about the way his hands curled into fists.

"It will be enough to threaten him. To frighten him. You haven't seen him, Valentin. He's much worse. Torture might not work." Valentin snorted, and I continued in desperation. "Not because he is brave—just because his body might not last long enough under torture for it to do any good."

"I am willing to risk that," growled Valentin.

"But I am not!" I cried. "Please, Valentin! I can't lose the Stone. I can't."

"What is the alternative?" Valentin demanded. "If the threat of violence alone is not enough, what would you have us do? Do you propose to become Mrs. William Percy?"

I looked away.

"You are still protecting him," said Valentin in disgust. "Why? For such an intelligent girl, you are quite a fool."

"Don't speak to her that way," snapped my father. Valentin snapped back, but the argument they fell into was drowned out by my mother's voice in my head.

The German is right. What do you care if Will is tortured? What do you care if he dies, so long as he gives up the Stone first?

I care, I replied. *Anyway, I thought you wanted me to marry him.*

The voice in my mind filled with exasperation. That was not unusual for my mother, but there was suddenly something else there, something unfamiliar.

Marry him, torture him, kill him. What does it matter? Do what you must so that we can be together.

I stood straighter. A prickle crawled up my spine, like some many-legged insect under my skin.

We?

I wanted to be wrong. I had accepted my mother's voice in my head. It was some kind of lingering effect of the madness, I thought, or perhaps she really had somehow found a way to speak to me. But this—

Who are you?

You know, Theosebeia.

And I did.

I looked down at Dominic again. The dark signs of warning my mind had tried to glide over caught it, and held. The Stone was using my mother's voice. My mother, whose mind it had stolen and feasted on. The Stone had a will, and intelligence. It devoured minds. It had done this to Dominic. It had done this to me. It could do it again.

What would it mean, to join myself to a thing like this?

It will mean that you are the last alchemist. The only adept to achieve their heart's desire. The final maker of the Philosopher's Stone. The only one to ever be truly mine.

"Thea!" My father's hand was on my shoulder, pulling me from the Stone's enticements. "He is here."

A German was in the doorway, talking to Valentin.

"Here, I think, Otto," said Valentin, in response to a question I hadn't caught. "No need to soil another perfectly good room."

Otto called down the hallway, and moments later a big German with a scarf knotted tight around his neck came in carrying Will in his arms like an infant. Martin pulled a chair forward, a small, horrible smile twisting his mouth. The big German—Karl, the one whose neck I had slashed—set Will down in the chair. Will nearly fell out of it, collapsing into helpless coughing. Martin bound his hands behind him, then left the room. Now Will could not even cover his mouth while he coughed. Blood and spit dripped down. He slumped forward, looking at no one. He looked barely alive. I knelt beside him.

"Will, please," I said. "Just tell them. Don't make them hurt you."

He opened his eyes, and the ghost of a smile flickered on his bloodstained lips.

"When I said you should punish me," he whispered. "This wasn't what I had in mind."

Guilt writhed like snakes in me. "I don't want this, either, Will," I said. "Please."

Martin returned with a leather satchel. He opened it, revealing a wide selection of knifelike implements.

My father made a guttural noise of horror and disgust.

"Valentin, is this really necessary?" he asked.

"Not at all," said Valentin. "The moment he tells us where the Stone is, we stop."

Martin selected a slender silver instrument with what looked like a sharp scoop at the end. I stared at it, eyes wide, and pictures of what it might be meant for formed in my mind, one shuddering horror after another.

"Ah yes," said Valentin. "We won't start with the fingernails. That took so long last time. Martin is very patient, but I am not."

Martin took Will by the chin with one hand and tilted his head back. The other hand held the scoop.

"Let's see how attached you are to your eye," he said in German.

He laughed. It was some kind of joke, apparently. He brought the instrument to Will's face. I jumped to my feet and pushed him back. Martin stepped back and glared at me.

"Karl!" he snapped.

Karl took me by the arm and pulled me back. I struggled in vain. Martin took Will's face in his hand again. In the abstract, the thought of Will facing torture in this state had been enough to make me ill. But here in front of me, it was unbearable.

"No!" I screamed. "Valentin, stop him!"

But Valentin's face was set.

"Will! Tell him!" Will squirmed. His shallow breath came in frantic gasps. Martin brought the scoop to his eye. "I'll heal you, I swear it. Will, please, please—"

Will coughed, spraying blood on Martin, who stepped back, grimacing with distaste.

"I'll tell," he wheezed. "No torture necessary. I'll tell."

I stopped struggling. I stared at him, hope warring fear in my chest.

"The truth," said Valentin. "Or Martin will take you apart piece by piece."

Will nodded, almost imperceptibly. "The *Sweet Margaret*. Captained by John Blake. It's anchored offshore now. Won't reach the dock until tomorrow."

Valentin looked at Otto. "Go to the port master," he said. "Find out if there is such a ship scheduled to dock."

Otto nodded and left. I pulled against Karl's grip, and he let me go. Will was coughing again. I went to untie his hands. My own were shaking. My heart thudded low in my chest, weighed down by despair.

This was a foolish idea. Now they will kill him.

"No, Thea," said Valentin. "He will wait right there."

Valentin turned to Karl and started issuing instructions. I knelt beside Will and looked into his eyes. He closed them, and a shudder passed through his frail frame.

The *Sweet Margaret* was the name we had given the splintery rowboat we puttered around the Comte's pond in. It wasn't a real ship. Will had lied. Otto would find out soon enough and come tell Valentin.

Fix this. However you must. If he dies, you lose me.

I stood. I backed away from Will, toward my father. I gathered my thoughts. I had to get Will out of here before Valentin discovered he had lied and tore him apart. Will wouldn't survive whatever came next, and he knew that I knew it. He had left his fate to me, forcing my hand yet again. Something brushed my shoulder, and I started.

"All will be well, Thea," said my father.

It was a kind, useless thought. Nothing would be well, unless I somehow made it so. I looked toward Dominic, thrashing in vain against his bonds. Across the room, Valentin leaned back against the wall, beside the door. His eyes were narrowed on Will. I could almost see the tortures he had planned in his furious glare. Martin and the other German stood near Valentin. It was good to have an ally in my father, but it would have been even better to have one of Valentin's sort—broad, muscular, military. While the four Germans were arrayed around the door, escape was not possible.

You need a distraction. He would make a fine one.

I turned my attention back to Dominic and shook my head sharply. I couldn't use Dominic. He had begged me to make sure he didn't hurt anyone else.

Lose me and he will remain as he is forever.

I made the decision hardly knowing that I did. Will began to cough. The Germans turned their faces away from his uncovered mouth. The fit was loud, and lasting. I whispered in my father's ear, certain the Germans wouldn't hear me.

"I need you to distract them. Argue with them. Draw their attention away from Dominic."

My father's eyes widened in question, then in dismay. He started to shake his head.

"Please, Father," I whispered. "I must."

He looked at me for a long moment, then nodded.

Will stopped coughing, and my father took a step toward him.

"That's enough of this." He sounded stern, almost outraged. "It's barbarous to treat a dying man this way. He told you what you wanted to know. Untie his hands! Give him water!"

My father walked to Will's left side and placed a hand on his shaking shoulder. Dominic was in the right corner of the room. I moved as quietly as I could while my father continued to shout.

"Are you men or beasts?" he demanded. "Look at him!"

I moved quickly. I undid the straps at Dominic's feet. They were threaded through the board he'd been placed on. It would take a moment's thrashing for him to pull the straps through their holes and free his legs. I moved to his hands, and Valentin saw what I was doing.

"Are you mad?" he cried, and ran toward me. My father threw himself into Valentin's path. In the few seconds it took for Valentin to toss him aside, I had untied Dominic's hands. Dominic hurled himself forward, onto Valentin. The strap still between his teeth muffled his screams, but not the impact of his body against Valentin's, and then of both their bodies on the ground. I ran past their scrambling forms and seized Will by his bound arms. I pulled him to his feet.

Martin lunged for us, but my father had seized a chair and swung, connecting with his head. Martin wheeled on my father, away from Will and me. I threw open the door and pushed Will out, then hesitated on the threshold. I looked back into the chaos in my wake.

Martin had easily wrested the chair from my father and thrown him against the wall, where he crumpled. Martin turned back toward me, a feral growl on his lips. But an even more feral noise behind him stole his attention. Dominic had risen to his feet. His arms were spread. His hands were bloody. Valentin scrambled backward, violent red scratches drawn down his face. The other German lay facedown in the corner, unmoving.

"Martin!"

Valentin screamed for help as Dominic hurled himself back on top of him. Martin ran to his captain's aid. My father braced himself against the wall and pushed himself to his feet. He staggered toward me. Took my arm. Pulled me through the door out of the room.

Don't hurt Dominic.

I didn't know who I was pleading with. The Stone? Could it protect him, somehow? And if it could, would it?

"Don't hurt him!" I called to Valentin.

My foolish, useless words were cut off when my father slammed the door behind us.

Don't hurt him? What choice had I left them but to hurt him? They would try not to. Just as I had tried not to hurt my mother. As Dominic had tried not to hurt Bentivoglio.

Will was already hurrying down the stairs, clinging to the walls, then the bannister.

We ran after him, my father and I. We left Dominic. Again.

It hurt to do it, like wrenching out some part of myself and leaving it behind. And then, almost at once and very abruptly, it didn't. The pain was blocked, and all I felt was hunger.

We reached Will. I threw his arm over my shoulder. On the other side, my father did the same. Together we rushed him down the stairs and out of the inn, into the treacherous night.

21

I did not know how long we had until Valentin dealt with Dominic and came after us. We kept moving, as quickly as we could force Will's collapsing body to go. We turned down one side street, then another, but keeping a general direction toward the dock.

"Which ship, Will?" I hissed into his ear.

He coughed and shook his head.

"Don't be stupid, Will," I said. "We have to go. Your only hope is getting on that ship with me and the Stone."

"I know," he gasped, when the coughing slowed. "But the ship won't leave until sunup."

"It's nearly sunup now," said my father. He pointed eastward, and sure enough there was a faint lightening of the blanket of night where the coastline met the water.

Will stopped moving his legs and folded his face into

one of his shoulders, coughing. It was amazing, how he had managed to make even as blunt a truth as his body's final collapse into death a tool that served his own ends. He didn't want to answer me, and I could hardly make him until he was done. He looked at me, wary and assessing.

"You still don't believe I'll heal you?" It was infuriating. To be this close to having the Stone and have something as feeble and broken as Will still standing in the way. For a blinding moment I could not see anything so very terrible about Martin's case of implements. I should have let him carve out Will's eye, if he could have pulled the location of the Stone with it.

"The *Ariadne*," he said. From the cowed look in his eyes, I wondered if he had discerned the direction of my thoughts. "It's a merchant ship, just stopping in Normandy on its way east. It's docked on the far north side of the port."

"If you're lying again, Will, so help me—"

"No," he gasped. "What choice do I have now but to trust you, Bee? I am putting my life in your hands."

"Then you are lucky Thea is more worthy of trust than you," spat my father.

We ran, dragging Will between us as best we could. My desire for the Stone grew, like a hum building in my mind until I could hear nothing else. I was almost there. Just a few more moments, and the Stone would belong to me.

Or would I belong to the Stone?

The thought came from far away. It was a nagging voice I did not want to hear. Easy enough to ignore. Easy enough to turn my mind away from the warning, dire though it was.

Too easy. And anyway, it was too late now. What choice did I have? I had to heal Dominic, heal my mother, even heal Will. I had promised him, hadn't I? The rest of it—the power, the future it would give me, the legend I would become—that was why I longed for it, perhaps, but not why I chose it. Not the only reason.

The *Ariadne* was a merchant brig. I made out its many masts in the faintly growing pre-morning light. Sailors climbed in the rigging, unfurling the sails. A few figures moved on the dock beside it.

"The captain's name?" I asked Will.

"James Pyne," he said.

I pulled Will forward, but my father didn't fall into step beside me.

"Wait, Thea," said Vellacott. "Are you . . . are you sure you want to do this?"

"Of course I am sure," I snapped.

"I'm not," said my father. "I'm afraid for you."

My father's voice was like the nagging one in the back of my mind—irritating. I pushed it back.

"It's too late for that now."

This time when I pulled, my father came. We hurried down the dock, where a few uniformless sailors worked on the rigging. On deck I saw a man in a blue coat and crimson waistcoat. The lapels he wore marked him as some kind of officer.

"That's him," muttered Will.

"Captain Pyne," I called to the officer. "May we come aboard?"

The officer looked at me, then at Will.

"Your health hasn't improved since we spoke last, Mr. Percy," he called down. "Are you quite certain you still wish to make the voyage?"

Will broke into coughing again, so I spoke for him.

"He is certain," I said. "He left an item in your keeping. Is it on board?"

"It is, miss," he said, then glanced at my father. "Though Mr. Percy only booked passage for two."

"We'll pay whatever is necessary," I said. "But we need to come aboard right away."

"I can have the gangplank lowered in a moment—"

But there was no knowing how long that would take. I looked about anxiously. In the distance I saw several blurred figures running. It could be them.

"Please— We must be quick—"

"There's a ladder," said my father. He pointed to a rope ladder hanging a few yards away.

We were at the rope ladder before the captain could protest. I went first, throwing off Will's clinging arm. The captain offered me his hand at the top. I took it and looked backward. The running figures were closer now. They might have seen us. Will was struggling up the ladder, my father behind him.

"There are some men after us, Captain," I said. "I hope you will not allow them aboard."

He reached down to seize Will by the arm and haul him up. "Of course not, miss," said the captain.

I squinted at the figures. There were two of them, the right sizes for Martin and Valentin. One was limping.

"They have weapons," I said.

"So do we." The captain patted his sidearm. "No one boards my ship without permission. Your berth is there—the first cabin past the quarter deck. Make yourself comfortable, and do not fear. We sail at sunup."

The captain helped my father over the rail and pulled up the rope ladder.

"And . . . the item?" I asked.

"In your cabin," he said.

I crossed the main deck to a higher one, past which was the door to which the captain had pointed. Will staggered after me. I entered the cabin before he caught up and shut the door behind me.

The cabin was snug but clean. The gleaming, paneled walls were bolstered by beams almost low enough to hit my head when I walked upright under them. There was no furniture but a neatly made bed built into the wall, under the porthole window. On the bed lay a handkerchief, folded over a small burden.

I did not need to uncover it to be certain of what lay there. I felt its call. My hands and legs trembled with the effort of not running to it and pressing it to me. I took a step toward it. Then I stopped.

The door creaked open, and Will stumbled into the cabin. He leaned with one arm just above his head, bracing his sagging body against the ceiling beam. He stared from the handkerchief on the bed to me, still standing two paces away.

What are you waiting for? For a strange moment, I didn't know if it was Will's voice I heard or the Stone's.

"I don't know what will happen," I said, finally giving voice to the fear I had pushed aside. "When I join with it."

"Yes you do, Bee," said Will. "You know you will complete the work of every alchemist since this mad, magic chase began all those years ago. You will have more power than anyone in history. You will—" He coughed and gasped. "You will have everything we dreamed of."

My arm lifted, unbidden, but I didn't step forward.

"Bee," Will said. His voice was a ragged ruin of its former self, but it wasn't only the hacking coughs strangling it now. Desperation choked him. "I would have done anything for this—to be you. For it to choose me. Why— *why*—"

He broke off into coughing again, so hard he couldn't stand upright. He dropped to his knees. I looked from him to the covered Stone.

"You sound like her," I said.

He looked up at me, his face a grim mask of death. A viscous, bloody bubble clung to the edge of his lip. His eyes met mine. He knew who I meant.

"It chose you over her," he whispered. "Over me. It chose you over every other alchemist who ever came near it."

I walked to the bed and drew back the handkerchief. The Stone was different than when I had last held it. It was a dark red now, the light in it smoldering rather than blazing. My finger brushed its surface, and hot joy sparked from my hand to my heart.

It chose me. It was mine. All I had to do was take it. No need to bind myself to Will, no need to offer it to Valentin afterward. If it could really, truly be mine . . .

I hadn't allowed myself to hope that far. And yet what other hope did I have? I had hoped that perhaps Father could make a place for me, but he couldn't. I had hoped Will and I could make one together, but we wouldn't. Mother was right. There was no place in the world for me. But with the Stone, I could change that. I would not need to change myself to suit the world. I would change the world to suit me.

I took it.

I held it out in my palm. A thrill traveled up my arm and through my body, waking every part as it went. My spine lengthened, my vision sharpened. The Stone's power was threading through me, claiming everything as it went. It traveled into my chest, up my spine to the base of my skull. The Stone's movement through me was bliss. I didn't want it to stop. I didn't want anything else. I could have let it drag me down into the sea of pleasure it offered. I could have drowned there. I lifted my hand to bring it to my chest. The cabin pitched, and I held my hand out to brace myself. We had set sail. I lifted the Stone again.

My father's cry called me back almost to myself.

"Don't, Thea— Drop the Stone! Your mother wouldn't want you to take this risk for her sake!"

He had thrown open the door. He walked toward me, holding out his hands in supplication. He was looking at me as he had in Dominic's prison-room, as though he felt for me. It was pity, yes, but not the kind I could not bear, which seemed a mere half-step from contempt. He looked at me as if he truly wanted something better for me than this. And once more, I believed he did.

Perhaps he was even right about my mother. Perhaps if she were truly here, she would look at me that way as well. A wave of longing rushed through me, pushing back the Stone's advance. Longing, not for the Stone, but for my mother.

Your mother would have sacrificed you a thousand times to have what is in your grasp.

The Stone pushed its way into my mind again, but this time I resisted.

You don't know what she would have done, I told it. *You don't know her.*

I knew her well before the end.

I lowered my hand. Fear pulled at me. I didn't want to think about what it meant, but I did want to drop the Stone.

Power surged through me, flowing downward. Will had thrown himself at my feet and wrapped his arms around my legs. The Stone was reaching through me, working on him. Light spilled through my fingers onto Will.

His coughs quickened, then turned into gasps. The hollow, rattling sound of his breath deepened into deep, full gulps of air. It was healing him. *We* were healing him. The power was like an extension of myself, knitting Will's broken places, cleansing his organs of illness. I hadn't chosen this. I didn't have the power for it. And yet I was doing it.

The Stone was not fused with me. I still felt the distance I had set between us—but somehow it was using me, pouring through me. I knew why. It wanted to show me what we could do, together.

Will fell back. He let go of my feet. Slowly, he rose. He stepped back from me and brought his hands to his chest.

The Stone hadn't cleaned him. He was still covered in his own dying blood. But even so he was beautiful again.

His stained shirt hung open, showing his once again perfectly formed chest and shoulders. He patted himself down, a slow smile forming on his full, glowing face. I stared, too. I couldn't stop. It wasn't simply that he was beautiful, muscular and glowing, like a Greek statue come to life in a cramped ship's berth. It was that I had made him that way, when moments ago he had been nearly a corpse, and not a pretty one. Many dismissed the mythical claims about the Philosopher's Stone. They said those powers couldn't be bestowed by anything in nature. And they were right. This was magic. Magic that could be mine. For a moment, my guard fell, and the Stone threaded its way further into me.

Will looked up at me, and warmth filled his shining blue eyes.

"Bee," he said. "You truly are a goddess."

I took a shaky breath and tried to speak. I couldn't. My father, who had sunk back into the paneled walls on the cabin, stepped forward. His eyes were wide. His mouth was open. He looked as awestruck as Will, but as though he had seen a monster rather than a miracle.

"Thea . . ." My father took another step toward me. "Is it still you?"

It took me a moment to understand the question. I didn't answer. I wasn't quite sure.

"Are you blind?" Will asked. "She is more herself than she has ever been!"

Will turned to me. "Bee, you see it now, don't you?" he asked. "You can have everything you want, everything you've ever wanted. Think of the power, the prestige . . . You'll be the greatest alchemist of all time. And I will be . . . whatever you want me to be. Your servant, your lover—whatever you want!"

And he would be, too. Faithful, or at least obedient. Just as my mother had said. Or was it the Stone that had said it? My memory blurred.

"Everything I want," I murmured.

"Not everything, Thea," said my father. "I thought that, too, once. That's the man I was when you met me. I cared for nothing but alchemy. You saw what it made me. How I treated you. It wasn't until you were gone that I saw everything I had been blind to when all I could see was the Stone."

"You blame the Stone for that?" I asked.

"No!" he cried. "I blame myself, as you will blame yourself if you allow the Stone to change you!"

But it did not sound so terrible, to be changed. After all, what was I without it? Without alchemy? Just a clever girl with nowhere to apply her talents. Beyond that I did not know. And at this moment, I did not care to learn.

"It isn't just for me." I said it only because I needed some response, but it reminded me of what I had almost forgotten.

Will was partly right. I did want the power and fame the Stone offered me. Perhaps I wanted them most of all.

But they were not all I wanted. It took an effort to recall this.

We will heal them, I said to the Stone. *My mother and Dominic.*

I had to know for certain. I felt the Stone hesitate.

You tempt me with power. With Will. Why do you not tempt me with that? We can heal them, can't we?

The Stone did not respond at first. We were too close, now, for it to lie to me. *He was sick. They are not sick.*

"Yes, they are," I insisted, aloud. "Their minds are sick."

They are not sick. They are mine.

"So let them go," I said.

I felt its absolute refusal. I pushed back against it, but it was unbending. It would not yield. The effort exhausted me. My mind pulled back. Dominic and my mother seemed so far away. I remembered that I cared what became of them, but not why. Did it matter, what became of lesser people?

Lesser people? That wasn't what I thought of them. It did matter. I tried to tell myself so, but my thoughts tangled. I was upset. Best not to think about it. Set them aside, grieve after I made the decision.

The decision . . .

What decision?

"Thea?" My father was before me, holding me by both shoulders. He looked up into my eyes. He was searching for something. His eyes darkened. He hadn't found it.

My father jerked away and stared up, like he saw something.

The sound of musket fire rang out from the deck.

Will shrank back and huddled against the wall of the cabin. His face crumpled from confidence to horror in half a moment.

"They came," he cried. "They followed."

My father opened the door and climbed up to the deck. I followed him. Just outside, he threw out his arm to hold me back.

A privateer ship had come up beside the *Ariadne*. Small

pools of smoke hung in the air over each ship. Another shot fired, and another small pool appeared. I could just make out the dark blue uniforms of the Germans. The *Ariadne*'s crew had taken shelter here and there on the deck. The captain was not very far from us, crouched behind a bulkhead and reloading his sidearm. He saw us.

"Get back in the cabin!" he shouted. "They're trying to come aboard!"

A shot burned past me, so close I could feel its heat. Behind me, Will screamed. I turned to see him falling backward through the doorway, blood blossoming on his newly perfect shoulder. He'd been hit.

I looked over to the privateer. It was a smaller vessel, but full of well-armed sailors, judging from the clouds of gun smoke. Through the smoke, three grappling hooks flew across the water and caught in the rigging of the *Ariadne*. Three men holding the attached ropes climbed onto the guardrails of the privateer. Martin swung first, but a musket shot grazed his arm. He fell into the water between the ships with a scream.

My father pulled me down to my knees and turned so his body was between mine and the direction of the musket fire. "Give it to them, Thea," said my father. "Give Valentin the Stone. Let *him* heal Dominic if it can be done."

I shook my head.

That small denial was all the assent the Stone needed. It moved. The crawling fingers of its power thrust forward.

Blinding light filled my mind, my sight. My hand, holding the Stone, glowed red. I dropped to my knees, my arms thrown wide.

We were fusing. The bliss that had been promised

before was gone. All I felt was a total powerlessness. The light cut through the fog in my mind like the crack of a gunshot through the rumble of the sea. I saw it all.

I saw what it meant to join with the Stone, now that it was too late.

It was a transfer of ownership of myself. My mind was pushed aside, watching from far away. I tried to move my eyes to my father, tried to force my lips to beg for his help. I failed.

In my desperate mind, I screamed for the Stone to release me. It did not answer. It did not even attend. It did not need to convince me now. It had what it wanted from me.

I was a prisoner in my own body.

Something happened then. My eyes moved, of the Stone's volition, to my father. He had something in his hand. He had taken it from me. He was running toward the ship's rail, to where Valentin was about to make another attempt to board the ship. My eyes went down to my hand, where a moment ago the physical Stone had been clutched. It was empty now.

My body rose. Its movements were awkward and slow, but the Stone would learn to control it better soon, no doubt.

My father had reached the ship's rail and held out the Stone to Valentin. He thought he could help me this way, by giving the Stone away. He did not know it was too late. We were joined.

Still, my body ran after him. The Stone made my hand seize my father's arm, but he tore free, staggering away. He cried out again to Valentin, whose second grappling hook caught the rigging once more. He swung. A musket shot missed him, but a quick-thinking sailor in the *Ariadne*'s rigging cut the rope. Valentin fell into the water.

My father cried out as Valentin went down. Then he stared out at the privateer, perhaps assessing the distance. My body lurched toward him at the Stone's command. He met my eyes, then staggered back, staring in horror. I wondered what he saw. It certainly wasn't me.

He drew back his arm to throw the Stone.

My body hurled itself at him, but it was too late. Vellacott hurled the Stone toward the privateer and watched as it fell short, into the water.

My body climbed the rail and, before my horrified father could stop it, hurled itself into the water after the Stone.

I felt the cold and, as the pull of my arms dragged me down, the emptiness of my lungs.

I saw it, a flash of red sinking faster than I was. My arms pulled harder. My body gained on it, then caught it in its hand. My body clutched the Stone tightly.

But even if it had been lost, I would not have been free. The Stone had not wanted to lose a part of itself, but it was not terrified. Losing the physical Stone in the channel would have been like losing an arm or a leg for it. It would still have lived in me. Even destroying the physical Stone wouldn't change that.

I felt my lungs burning, my senses blackening. My body had swum deep. The Stone turned it and made it swim up. I felt the Stone's haste, and something else.

Fear.

It was afraid my body had been underwater too long. It was afraid I would drown.

Destroying the physical Stone would not free me from its grip. No.

But freeing me would destroy it.

And there was only one way for me to be free.

I summoned every bit of power I had left over my body. It wasn't much, but the Stone was focusing its strength on propelling me upward with my arms and legs.

I forced my mouth open.

Terror had gripped me when the Stone took me. But this was another terror. The terror of death. The fear of what came next, especially if it was nothing. To live like this would be a torment, but a part of me would have chosen it over nothing at all.

But. To be a slave to a wicked thing was its own death. To be the vessel it used to do its evil will. I had brought it into the world. All the havoc it had wreaked along the way—what it had done to my mother and Dominic, and whatever it might do next—all of it was my responsibility.

Dominic would destroy it.

The thought came into my mind unbidden, but at once it hardened my resolve.

I would kill it. And perhaps that might undo its works. Might even free my mother and Dominic.

This was the only way we might all be free.

I forced my lungs open. I breathed in water. I sucked it down, filling my mouth, my throat, my airways. I felt my body shutting down, but from a distance. There was little pain. That was a mercy.

I thought of Dominic. He had said he didn't fear death, because he'd confessed.

God forgive me, I thought, just in case.

My flooded lungs stopped working. Then, not much later, my heart.

The last thing I felt was the terror and fury of the Stone.

I died knowing it died, too.

22

A rhythmic pulse.

The beat of a heart.

Mine.

A mouth on my mouth. Then, a rush of water and the flow of air.

They had brought me back.

I cast about in a blind panic for the Stone's presence in my mind. I did not feel it.

I was coughing. Then I was sitting upright. Someone had pulled me. But not from within me, from outside.

I looked up, my eyes following my mind's command, and saw Valentin hovering over me and behind him my father. We were on the deck of a ship, but it was not the *Ariadne*.

"Is it you, Thea?" my father asked. "Are you yourself?"

I looked down at my clenched fist. I opened it slowly,

finger by finger, savoring each one's instant obedience. Inside was a fistful of wet black ash.

"Is that . . . ?" Valentin asked.

I traced a finger through the ash. I did not quite know what I was feeling for. Some spark of life, perhaps. Some sign of what it had once been. There was none.

I had drowned myself to destroy this thing. Naturally I was relieved to find that I had succeeded.

And yet.

I had also spent my life trying to create it. Before Will, and then after him, every hope for my future had come from the prospect of its success. Until, like Will, it betrayed me.

The heartbreak was familiar, but no less painful for it.

"What happened, Thea?" my father asked.

I didn't want to tell him.

Valentin stood, his eyes on the black mess in my hand. I was not the only one whose hopes were dashed by the Stone's destruction.

"It's clear enough, isn't it?" Valentin asked. "She destroyed it somehow. What I wish to know is why?"

Valentin stepped back from me. He stared across the water at the swiftly departing *Ariadne.* His still face twitched. That and a hot gleam in his eyes were the only signs of his anger.

"I saw him," he said. "Will. You healed him. Is that it? You healed him, so you were finished with the Stone? What about Dominic? What about your mad mother?"

"Dominic," I said. Fear quickened my pulse. "Did you hurt him?"

"Very little, though it was no thanks to you that we did

not kill him." Valentin's voice was rising. His eyes flitted from me to the *Ariadne*. A muscle worked in his jaw. It was killing him to watch Will get away, even with a bullet in his shoulder. "And all for nothing. I should go belowdecks and kill him now. He would be better off."

"Dominic is here?" I asked. "He is on board?"

I climbed laboriously to my feet without waiting for Valentin's answer. I tried to run, but my legs failed me. My vision blurred. I would have fallen if not for my father's arm around me.

"A few moments ago your heart wasn't beating," my father said. "You need rest."

I shook my head, though my body screamed its agreement. "I need to see Dominic," I said. "You do not understand. He might . . . he might be . . ."

But I couldn't say it. The hope was too fragile to be spoken out loud. Mercifully, my father did not press. He made some silent plea with his eyes to Valentin, who was just interested enough to lead us down the companionway stairs to a cabin much smaller and fouler smelling than mine on the *Ariadne*. The cabin had no window. The only light was what filtered faintly in behind and above us. I squinted as my eyes adjusted.

Dominic lay on the ground in the corner, completely still. My father and I crossed the cabin in two shaky steps and knelt beside him. He was bound hand and foot, and the strap was still in his mouth. He might have still been mad, but unconscious. Or he might have been dead. It occurred to me then, for the first time, that killing the Stone might have killed him, too. And if it had killed him, then it had also killed my mother.

Then *I* had killed my mother.

I hesitated long enough that my father felt for the pulse for me.

"He's alive," he said. "I think he's sleeping."

Dominic opened his eyes.

Even in the dim light, there was no mistaking the difference. Before, they had been burning coals, wells of fury and hatred toward every object. Now, they were just Dominic's. Warm brown, bloodshot, intelligent. And at the moment, very confused.

My father untied the strap in Dominic's mouth first of all, then set about freeing his hands.

"How . . . ?" came Valentin's voice from behind me.

I sat back on my heels and stared at Dominic. Relief battled the empty ache in my heart. He was free. My mother was free. My great achievement amounted to this—that I had managed to undo the devastation I had inadvertently caused.

"You did it." Dominic's voice was hoarse and as raw as an open wound. "You made the Stone. You saved me with it."

"I made the Stone." The memory of longing I had felt for it was like a phantom pain in a lost limb. "And then I destroyed it. I saved you *from* it."

My father finished untying Dominic's feet and looked up at me.

"It was taking you," he said. "I saw it. I looked in your eyes and you weren't there."

Valentin heaved a deep sigh of frustration and stalked to the door. Martin stepped into the doorway, blocking his way.

"We should tell the captain to turn around, go north," Martin said in German.

"The ship carrying William Percy is going to Caen," said Valentin. "So we go to Caen."

Martin cast an unfriendly eye on me. "The Graf will want her more than he wants Percy. She made the Stone once, she could do it again."

I met Valentin's eyes as he turned them on me and shook my head.

"I can't do it again, Valentin. I destroyed the Stone itself, the true Stone, not just its corporeal form. It had a kind of shadow existence apart from its body." I cast about in my mind, trying to make enough sense of what I had experienced when I was one with the Stone to put it into words. "When it fused with me, it was vulnerable. It was afraid I might drown. I thought . . . if I died, it would die, truly die, forever. It can't be made anymore. It doesn't exist anymore."

"You did not die," said Valentin.

"Near enough," said my father.

"Das ist lächerlich," Martin told Valentin. "She is a liar. The Graf will want you to take her to him. You know this."

Valentin's face did not show the conflict I knew must be in his mind. It would be bad enough to go back to his master without the Stone. But to have let the last alchemist go as well, when she had been within his power?

The last alchemist. A sour laugh curdled in my throat at the thought. I was doubly the last alchemist now. I had been chosen to make the Stone, to be taken by it. That was what the Stone had meant by the name. And then I had destroyed it forever. I had made myself the last alchemist in a different way—by preventing anyone from coming after me.

"We go to Caen," Valentin repeated.

"I will keep her aboard, then," said Martin. "You find Percy, and return. Then we all go north."

Fear tightened my chest. I closed my eyes. This was exactly what Valentin ought to do. It was the only way to fulfill his orders. It was the only way to win his prize. And once I was there, would the Graf accept my explanation? What would he do to me when I could not give him what he wanted?

Valentin said nothing.

"Sir," said Martin. "We will all suffer if you let her go."

I looked up once more and found Valentin's eyes on mine. He nodded once. I breathed a deep sigh of relief. He was going to let me go.

"I will tell the Graf you disagreed with my decision, Martin," said Valentin. "In fact I have no doubt you will tell him yourself. Perhaps he will give you my place when I have gone."

"Gone?" asked Martin. "What about Ada?"

Valentin's carefully contained rage slipped free. He seized Martin by the neck of his jacket and shoved him against the wall.

"If you wish to remain aboard this ship until we reach land, you will keep her name out of your vicious mouth."

Before Martin could do more than gasp with shock, Valentin threw him out the door and followed, shutting it behind him.

I turned back to Dominic and my father. Despite the dramatic scene that had just unfolded before them, they were both staring at me as though they had seen nothing more interesting than my face. After a moment, I looked down. They were too shocked, it seemed, to remember it was rude to stare.

Dominic cleared his throat, a painful sound.

"You need water," I said. "Food, too, I don't doubt. I'll see if I can find anything."

I stood, but my head spun, and I staggered. My father took my arm and helped me sit again.

"I'll get it, Thea," said my father. "You rest, please."

He left, and Dominic cleared his throat again, then winced.

"We're not in London anymore, I take it." His voice was a rough whisper, but despite the circumstances, there was humor in it.

"No," I said with a small smile. "We're going to France."

"I gathered that much," said Dominic. "And . . . how long has it been?"

I swallowed. I didn't want to tell him how long it had taken me, how long I had failed him and left him in torment. "A few weeks. I am sorry it took me so long."

"So long," he echoed. "Yes, it felt so long. Years. Ages."

I knew what the look on his face meant. I knew that terror.

"It's over," I said. "You're free."

"We both are," said Dominic.

I couldn't argue. I had been a prisoner first in my mind and then in my body. I wasn't any longer, and yet I did not feel free. All I felt was the ache of loss, and the gray bleakness of the future. But perhaps it was common for freed prisoners to feel this way.

"Thank you, Thea," said Dominic. "You've been a good friend to me."

"Not as good as you were to me," I replied, and meant it.

He shook his head and smiled. It was a comfort to sit next to a good and selfless man who was entirely convinced that I was just like him, so I let him go on smiling and believing in me.

Someday I might have to tell him everything I did wrong. But not now. Less than an hour ago I had been dead and Dominic even worse. We deserved this moment, when loyalties were pure and rewarded, and debts were paid. We had saved each other, and we were friends.

23

We disembarked in Caen. I said goodbye to Valentin. I thanked him.

Perhaps it was strange to thank him. He'd been my captor. He had forced me to risk my mind, intending to steal the product of my labor. He had tortured Will.

All that must have been on his mind when he stared at me in surprise.

"You are welcome," he said, then frowned as though he had said the wrong thing.

"Why—" I was almost afraid to ask, lest he change his mind. "Why are you letting me go?"

I didn't ask about the price he would pay for it, but we both knew what it was. The pain of loss was already etched in the lines of his face. Valentin shifted his weight and looked over his shoulder, back toward the sea.

"Even if you are wrong that the Stone is truly dead," he

said after a moment. "Even if you could make it again . . . I could not make you do it. Once was too many times. And I am . . ."

He broke off again, still staring at the sea. He sighed. "I am sorry," he said. "For ever having done it at all."

"Oh," I said. "And . . . and I'm sorry, too. About Ada."

He nodded his acceptance, as I nodded mine.

"I wasn't fair to her, in my mind," I said. "She'll never know it. But I still feel I should apologize to someone for it. To you, I suppose."

The ghost of a smile flitted across Valentin's face. "She would like you," he said. "The two of you aren't as different as you think."

I smiled back at him and didn't argue. I found, to my surprise, that I believed him.

We left each other that way. Both quieted from the shock of finding friendly feelings under the skin of enemies.

My father hired a carriage to Honfleur, and I described the Comte's estate to Dominic. The apple orchards, the pond, the neat little cottages where the farmers lived. I talked too fast. He noticed my fingers drumming against the carriage bench before I did.

"She'll be fine, Thea," said Dominic.

He had so mistaken the cause of my anxiety that I didn't understand him at first.

I glanced at my father, whose long fingers were beating a similar staccato. He stared out the window. His face was tight, but his eyes gleamed with eagerness. I did not like to see that. She was sure to disappoint him.

"Father," I began carefully, "you understand that the Comte isn't merely my mother's patron?"

"Yes, yes," he murmured. He gave a little jerk of his head, as though shaking off the thought. "But she burns through them quickly, does she not? She could be done with this Comte already."

That was entirely true, but my father should have seen it was no help to him. He was one of *them*, and she had been done with him seventeen years ago.

"Father—" I began slowly, but he cut me off.

"Oh, I know, Thea, I know," he said. "I know I'll be lucky if I get so much as a smile from her. You forget, I knew her."

"And that was before she spent two months in madness," I said. "I doubt it improved her disposition."

It was a glorious day. The sky was the truest blue, and a light breeze stirred the trees just enough to waft the scent of their blossoms toward us. We turned off the road and up the drive to the chateau. Poplars arched gracefully over our path, and the green roadside was blanketed in flowering astrantia and foxgloves. The chateau was small, as chateaux went, but its facade was a lovely, many-windowed vision of white stone and elegant Norman spires.

I stepped out of the carriage and looked at the beautiful house I had once thought of as home. Summer in Normandy was as splendid as ever. This was the kind of scene that seemed designed to invoke pleasant nostalgia. But all my fond memories here were of Will and alchemy. The scent of the wildflowers turned my stomach.

328 ~ SAMANTHA COHOE

"It's a castle." Dominic's eyes were wide with wonder. "I didn't know you lived in a castle."

"It's only a country house," said my father. "And not a very large one."

I knocked on the doors. There was no answer. I knocked again.

The Comte didn't keep many servants, but there should have been someone to come to the door.

"Do you think they left?" asked my father.

"Perhaps," I said. "Perhaps they had to go . . ."

"There have been reports in the newspapers of French nobles leaving—"

The door opened, and the Comte himself stood before us.

I stared. I had never seen him so informally dressed before, even in the dead of night when we both ran in our dressing gowns to my mother's sickbed. His hair was unpowdered, uncurled, and pulled back with a simple leather thong. He wore a gray shirt so plain and workmanlike that I could hardly believe it belonged to him.

"Thea!" he exclaimed. He threw his arms around me and began talking rapidly in French.

"Mon dieu, Thea, how did you know? How could you know she was awake when it was only last week—" He pulled back and broke off, staring at my father and Dominic, then back at me. "But you cannot be here! What are you doing here, Thea! It is not safe! But come in, come in."

We all entered, and the Comte led us past the grand parlor and through the dining room into the kitchen. Every room we passed was half emptied or more, and the furniture that remained was covered in white sheets. Even the kitchen appeared depleted, with the absence of the

cook and kitchen maid and the baskets of produce and ba-
guettes they brought in every morning.

There was a wooden table in the center of the kitchen,
and Adrien motioned us to sit.

"She is well—quite well, Thea," Adrien said as he bus-
tled about. He put a kettle on the stove and cut some round
peasant bread. "I was just making her some breakfast. She
said she was hungry. Hungry, Thea! Can you imagine!"

He offered us bread and butter from a blue porcelain
crock. We all helped ourselves.

"You must be Thea's father . . . Professor Vellacott, yes?"
Adrien asked my father. "It is good to meet you. But—
truly, you will have to see your mother and leave at once.
I myself will be going as soon as Marguerite is strong
enough to travel."

"You're leaving?" I asked. "But where are you going?"

"To Austria. It is all arranged. I have cousins there, you
know, and some capital." Adrien handed Dominic a piece
of bread, then stared like he hadn't noticed him before.
"Who is this? A servant?"

I was grateful Dominic did not speak French. "No, no,"
I said. "He is a friend. His name is Dominic. A good and
worthy man. But . . . he cannot go back to England. There
was a misunderstanding, and . . ."

I looked between Adrien and Dominic for a moment.
There was skepticism on the Comte's face. Now was not the
best time to spring my plan on him, perhaps, but from the
haste with which the Comte moved and spoke, time seemed
to be in short supply.

"I hoped he could stay with you, Adrien, but if you're
going, then I hope he can go with you."

The Comte's face clouded, but I pressed on.

"He wants to be a doctor," I said. "I hoped you could sponsor his studies, as a favor to me. Please, Adrien."

The Comte turned a frank, assessing stare on Dominic.

"Tu ne parles pas Français," he said to him. "Sprichst du Deutsch?"

Dominic shook his head.

"He can learn," I said quickly. "He's very intelligent."

"He is," my father said. "He was my apprentice in Oxford. He would make a good doctor. If you can take him, make the introductions for him, then I will pay his way."

I looked at my father in surprise, and then wondered at myself. It should no longer surprise me when my father did the decent thing. I had seen it enough times now to expect nothing less. I smiled at him, and he smiled back with a trace of sadness.

"If you wish it, Thea, then I cannot say no," said the Comte. "But what about you, ma chérie? I hope you will come with us as well."

"Oh," I said. Strange as it seems, I had not given a moment's thought to where I would go after I saw my mother. I felt as though my future had gone blank when I destroyed the Stone, and now I was simply going about tying up the loose ends before disappearing with it. My father and the Comte both looked at me in mute appeal. My father looked away first, lowering his eyes. There was faint hope in them, tinged with fear of disappointment. Seeing it, I realized for the first time: my father truly hoped I would go back to Oxford with him. He feared that I would not.

"Thank you for the invitation," I said. "But I should like to speak to my mother first."

"Of course, of course!" said the Comte. He poured the nearly boiling water into a teapot and placed it on the breakfast tray he had assembled. "Let us go."

Adrien went in before me. He set the tray on my mother's lap and murmured to her for a while. I hung back, gazing around the room to keep from looking at her. It was unchanged. Nothing had been packed or removed. Bottles of cosmetics of her own making crowded her vanity, as if she had only just used them. My mother sat by the marble hearth in a high-backed chinoiserie chair, staring into the fire. She did not turn her head when Adrien went out, and I approached.

I stood beside her for several minutes before she looked up and stared at me in silence.

The weeks of her madness had taken a toll on her beauty, though I imagined it might be temporary. Her hair was combed back and hidden under a cap. Her rosy cheeks were sunken and sallow and her eyes were as bloodshot as Dominic's.

After several moments of silence, I stepped back and sat in the chair beside her.

She poured herself a cup of tea, took a drink, and set it down again. "It was you, wasn't it?" she asked quietly.

I knew what she meant, but I did not answer.

"You destroyed the Stone." She took another sip of tea and stared back into the fire.

"How did you know?" I asked her.

"I knew when I woke that it was gone," she said. "I could feel it."

I considered this, and discovered I could feel it, too. Here, in this room, the contrast was particularly striking. There had been an energy here before, a drive that was gone. I had thought it only in my own mind, but my mother had known. Something had gone out of the world with the Stone.

"Alchemy is dead," said my mother. "And you, my daughter, killed it."

She gripped her cup more tightly. I watched her fingers, whitening on the porcelain, instead of her face.

"I had to," I said. "I would have been its slave. And you would have stayed in your madness forever. It would never have released you. This was the only way for you to be free."

She made a tortured, dry sound that after a moment I recognized as an utterly mirthless laugh.

"Free? Is that what I am now? And what am I free to do, Thea? To languish? To be forgotten? To become like every other helpless woman in this dreadful world of men?"

Her words cut through the layers of shock and denial to the core of my own fears. I didn't want it to be true, that there was nothing for us now. But I felt it, too.

"You will never be like anyone else, Mother," I said. "Alchemy or no."

"If I am not an alchemist, I am nothing," she said with the finality of a curse.

It grated on me like sand on an open wound. I had said the same thing, but I hated it now. It was all I could do to keep sitting.

"You are Marguerite Hope," I said. "You are a brilliant scientist. A scholar."

She didn't respond, as though what I said was too inconsequential even to be worth denying.

"You are my mother."

The words hung in the air like the unanswered question they were. She seemed to consider them.

"The mother of the last alchemist," she muttered after a moment, and from the bitter tone in her voice I knew she found the title as ironic as I did now. "All that work, all that training. I succeeded, in a way. I made you great. And for what?"

I couldn't answer her. I couldn't look at her.

"I was a good mother for an alchemist," she said. "But there are no alchemists now. You saw to that. I do not know how to be an ordinary mother to an ordinary girl."

I wiped my eyes carefully. She wasn't looking at me. With any luck, she would not notice. I cleared my throat.

"You could learn," I said. "You are very intelligent."

She took another drink of tea, then a small bite of her bread. A cool calm descended on me. I remembered it. It was the detachment I had learned to feel when I wanted something from her that she certainly would not give.

"Does your father want to take you back to Oxford?" she asked.

"I think so."

"Do you want to go?"

"I do not know."

She looked at me again, but I did not meet her eyes.

"He isn't like me," my mother said. "He does not need alchemy to give him a place in this world."

I nodded. He had his fellowship.

"Does he care for you, Thea, do you think?" my mother asked.

I looked at her then. I might have thought it an insult, my mother asking if my father cared for me. But I saw in her eyes that it wasn't. She wanted to know.

"He does."

"I thought he would," she said. "I was afraid of it, for the longest time. It was why I never told him about you."

The fire was burning down in the hearth. I went to it and put a log into the embers and watched it catch fire.

"Adrien and I are going to Austria," said my mother. "But you should go with your father. When we are settled, perhaps you can visit us."

I nodded. My throat was too thick for speech. I rose, kissed her cheek, and left.

My father waited for me in the hallway. He stepped forward as I stepped out.

"I know you probably wish to go with your mother to Austria," he began at once. "I know the Comte has more money and more connections even abroad than I could offer you. But—I realized I had not said it—I do hope you will come back with me to Oxford, Thea. I would so like to be your father." He winced, then shook his head. "That isn't quite what I meant to say—"

A hideous noise escaped from my throat. It was a sob, but it might have been vomit from the mortifying sound. I clapped my hands over my mouth and turned aside, shaking, desperately blinking back tears and swallowing down weeping. My father put a hand on my shoulder and said something I could not hear over the noise of my efforts not to fall apart. When I could, I looked at him.

"Thank you, Father," I said, wiping my eyes. "I'd like to go with you."

A smile lit his face like daybreak. I nearly burst into tears again at the sight of his happiness. It was more than I had expected him to feel at the prospect of so much time to spend with me.

"Good, good!" he said. He took my arm, and we walked back toward the kitchen. "I was thinking I could give you private chymistry lessons, if you like. It's not as thrilling as alchemy, of course, but you have such a gift for it, and there is much good work to be done in the field. Or perhaps philology? I know several scholars who would be happy to work with someone of your talents. Alchemy isn't the only field where you could make a contribution, Thea."

"Make a contribution," I said. I liked the sound of that. It was the sort of thing dependable people with good hearts and clear minds did. The sort of thing Dominic would do.

"Oh, I know it doesn't sound very exciting—not compared to, well . . ."

"No, I'd like that," I said.

We walked back toward the kitchen, but very slowly. My father kept glancing at me, as if trying to guess my thoughts from the look on my face. I nearly asked him what he had gathered, so unsure was I of what was occurring in my own heart. It felt pitifully weak, like a newly hatched bird, featherless and blind. So much of what my heart had long loved had been uprooted. The only things left were young and tender. They were fresh green sprouts in newly turned earth, where before there had been weeds.

I could salt the earth, as Mother did. Refuse to tend new loves when the old had failed.

But I would not. They would grow. I would see to it.

"I don't know how to be a daughter, you know," I said to my father. "But I would like to learn."

"We will learn together," he said.

And I believed him.

Dominic wasn't in the kitchen. I went to look for him outside and found him sitting in the sunshine by the stream, sinking his fingers into the grass, his eyes closed.

"It's such relief," he said. "Like coming back from hell."

I sat beside him. I turned my face to the sun and closed my eyes as well.

It was a relief, when I let myself feel it. The torments were over. The task was done. Nothing hung over me now, except the rest of my life.

"Your father says the Comte will take me to Austria. Sponsor my medical training."

"Yes," I said. "You will have to learn German."

"Will you come with us?" he asked.

"No."

He looked at me then. "You're going with your father."

"I am taking your advice. You kept telling me to give him a chance."

Dominic smiled. "I suppose that's true."

The stream was fast moving and deep with summer rain, yet clear enough that we could see straight to the bottom. Fish swept past. One jumped through the surface and fell back again with a small splash. The sunlight caught the rippling surface and gleamed like jewels.

It was such a beautiful day.

"I shall write to you," I said. "And I shall visit."

"Good," said Dominic. "Thank you. I hope—"

He broke off, then turned his face toward the sun again. I knew what he hoped. It was what I hoped for him. The sunlight, the babble of the stream, the summer air was full of what we hoped for each other.

"I know," I said. I thought of my father and the house he would find for us to live in as a family. I thought of the work I would do, and the work Dominic would do across the sea. There had to be a place in the world for someone like Dominic. It was a test of the world, more than a test of him. "So do I."

Dominic nodded, then stood.

"Take care of my mother, if you can," he said. "I'll do what I can for yours."

I laughed a little at this as I rose to my feet, and so did he.

"I think I have the better end of that bargain," I said.

"She can't be all bad." He shrugged and turned to me. "She raised you."

And today, with the sun on my face and a new chance at hope in my heart, I could let myself believe even that.

ACKNOWLEDGMENTS

When you're a practical person whose insubordinate heart gives you a highly impractical dream, it takes a lot of people believing in you to make it happen. I am incredibly lucky to have those people in my life and it's because of them that *A Golden Fury* exists. Here are my heartfelt thanks to you all, in no particular order:

To Caleb, thank you for not only supporting me, but also for always assuring me that you wouldn't have if you weren't sure my writing was really good. You weren't nearly so enthusiastic when I wanted to get into sewing, for instance. To Leslie Weinzettel, my first friend and also my first "reader," thank you for listening to my dumb Tolkien-rip-off stories so avidly when we were kids. Good thing my writing and your taste have improved since then! To Dad, for all the very early writing advice, some of which I don't ignore! And for the beta reads and encouragement. To Micaela, for liking this book enough to read it more than once, and Matt and Mom, who will read it one day, perhaps. Love you guys.

To my phenomenal agent, Bridget Smith, and the team

at JABberwocky Literary Agency. You knew what this book needed and, once you pointed it out, I did, too. You said this would be a great debut, and look! You were right. I never stop being thankful to have you on my team.

To my wonderful, talented, dedicated editor, Jennie Conway. I'm so honored that you loved my book enough to make it your first young adult title. Together we've made it something I'm incredibly proud of. There's no editor I'd rather have shepherding my books.

To Coral Jenrette, thank you for the many, MANY insightful critiques, for always being ready to console me after every setback and celebrate with me at every success. To Derek Reiner, thank you for your refreshingly bleak outlook on publishing, your alchemical expertise, and your ever-encouraging feedback. Sorry about the migraines you have suffered on behalf of my manuscripts. I hope they were worth it. To my Critters: Kellye Crocker, Oz Spies, Lisa Hernbloom, Derek, and Coral. You make my writing and my life so much better. To Catherine Egan, my first critique partner. The first time I really believed I was a good writer was when you loved *Heirs*. I wish we still had hours and hours to stand around talking about books and *Buffy* while our babies tired each other out.

To DJ DeSmyter, Meghan Harrington, Melanie Sanders, Chrisinda Lynch, and the entire team at Wednesday Books. You are so, so good at what you do, and I'm incredibly grateful to benefit from it. To Kerri Resnick, design wizard, for my BEAUTIFUL cover. I wanted so badly to love it, and thanks to you, I do.

To Shannon Doleski, Prerna Pickett, and Jenny Elder Moke. Thank God my impractical dream came true, because it meant I got to meet you pervs. You've made my whole debut year. To #TeamB, thanks for all the moral support and advice. You are my kind of people, to a woman.

To Lawrence M. Principe, thanks for writing *The Secrets of Alchemy*! I'm sure you didn't expect your excellent history of science book to provide most of the alchemical research for a YA fantasy novel, but life is weird like that.

To Pater Edmund Waldstein, O. Cist., for checking my German and consulting on Prussian titles and names. My apologies if you find this book is unacceptably pro-revolution.

To my pals at SloHi Coffee, especially Stephanie Watters. Thanks for your patience when I parked myself at your bar to write for hours, for not rolling your eyes at all my dramatic sighing, and for the free "samples." To Book-Bar Denver and Keith's Coffee Bar, also great places to escape your kids and write a novel.

Speaking of kids, huge thank-you to Isaac, Davey, and Una for being the lights of my life and the apples of my eye. You didn't really help with the book, though.

Thank you to the brilliant authors who have read and recommended *A Golden Fury* before its release: Rosamund Hodge, Emily Duncan, Hannah Capin, Tracy Townsend, Marie Brennan, Gita Trelease, Catherine Egan, Lisa Maxwell, and Ellen Goodlett. Thank you, thank you.

And finally, thank you to God, cui est gloria in saecula saeculorum.

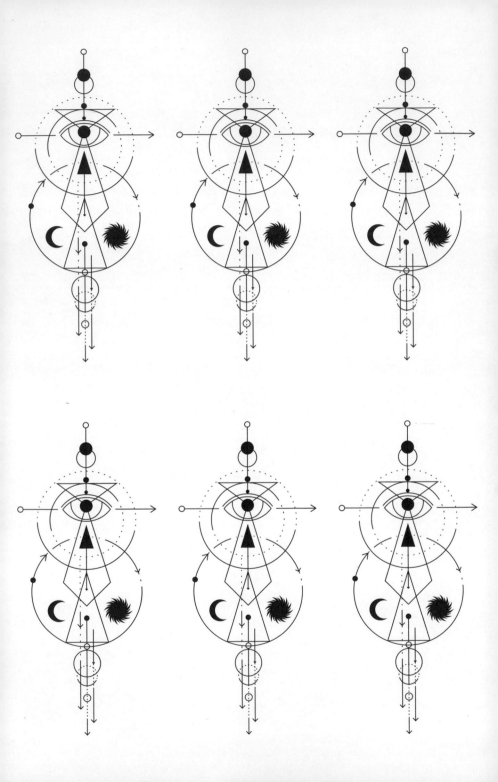